TESSA CAST A SIDELONG LOOK AT HIM. ONCE SHE REALIZED HE WAS LARKING, SHE LAUGHED.

Penwyck pointed to an exhibit of staff weapons—a lance, a spur, pick, and halberd. "Dressed in my suit of armor, I could fend off enemy attackers with these ferocious weapons, and thus insure the safety of our fortress."

Tessa laughed again. "And would that make you my knight in shining armor?" she asked coyly.

Penwyck's eyes locked with hers. A moment before her vivid blue gaze fluttered away, he replied softly, "I expect it would."

She moved a few steps away from him. "You have already rescued me once," she said firmly. "Forgive me for not thanking you properly, sir. I was . . . quite relieved to see you last night."

Penwyck stepped closer to her. In this charged moment of silence, the earl felt that same near-overwhelming urge to gather the lovely Miss Darby into his arms and . . .

Books by Marilyn Clay

MISS ELIZA'S GENTLEMAN CALLER
THE UNSUITABLE SUITOR
FELICITY'S FOLLY
BRIGHTON BEAUTY
BEWITCHING LORD WINTERTON

Published by Zebra Books

MISS DARBY'S DEBUT

Marilyn Clay

Zebra Books
Kensington Publishing Corp.
http://www.zebrabooks.com

ZEBRA BOOKS are published by

Kensington Publishing Corp.
850 Third Avenue
New York, NY 10022

First Printing: October, 1999
10 9 8 7 6 5 4 3 2 1

Printed in the United States of America

One

May, 1816

Tessa Darby's gloved hand gripped the railing of the huge clipper ship as its mighty hull sliced through the blue-green water. Eager for a look at what lay ahead, Tessa anxiously scanned the fog-shrouded harbor. Suddenly a shaft of bright sunlight broke through the mist and Tessa got her first glimpse of London, England. *Home!* She was home at last. Lifting her chin, she inhaled a deep breath of salt-tinged air.

"Are you quite certain you will be all right, dear?" asked Mrs. Benton-Caldwell, Tessa's traveling companion from America. "I confess I am having second thoughts about leaving you all alone once we've docked."

"I shall be quite all right!" Tessa replied excitedly, her vivid blue eyes straining to see all that was fast becoming visible to her of the vast city of London.

A half-hour later, she and Mrs. Benton-Caldwell were swept along with hundreds of other passengers, all animatedly talking and laughing at once as they surged down the rickety wooden gangplank toward the press of humanity crowded onto the busy quay.

"I do wish I had the time to see you settled in here," Mrs. Benton-Caldwell fretted.

"But you would miss the stage to Margate, ma'am. I shall be quite all right, really. Your family has long awaited your return home." Not half so long as Tessa had waited to return to England, she added to herself.

Though she was a grown-up young lady of nineteen now, Tessa had been a mere babe in arms when her mother, a young widow, had left the bosom of her family to follow her handsome new husband, the powerful Senator John Hamilton Darby, to his home in America—a sprawling estate situated on the outskirts of Philadelphia.

Once in America, Tessa had soon been presented with a baby brother, David. At the tender age of ten, she'd been told the truth of her own heritage. Senator John Hamilton Darby was not her *real* father. Her real father had been an Englishman, a dashing young military officer who'd served valiantly in King George's Light Dragoons. Unfortunately, the young man had lost his life in battle before he'd ever laid eyes on his infant daughter.

The truth had stunned Tessa. Though it was abundantly clear to her that since her baby brother had come along her stepfather had lavished all his love and devotion upon him, Senator Darby was still the only father Tessa had ever known. From that point on, however, the subtle gap that already existed between stepfather and stepdaughter widened.

Over the years, Tessa's mother's sympathy for her little girl grew, and she often confided to Tessa how very much she resembled her handsome papa, the dashing young captain who'd stolen her heart away the night of her come-out ball in London.

"You have your father's handsome auburn hair, sweetheart," her mother would whisper in her ear, her tone a trifle wistful. "And his brilliant blue eyes. Pay no heed to your stepfather's rebuffs. You are *your* father's daughter and he was a wonderful man. Captain Benning gave his life for England."

Tessa pushed down the painful emotions from the past that welled up within her as she and Mrs. Benton-Caldwell reached the end of the gangplank and at last stepped onto solid ground. She would not give in to sentiment now. Today was the most important day of her life and she would let nothing spoil it.

Squaring her shoulders with fresh resolve, she shifted the

heavy valise she carried from one hand to the other. The mass of people scurrying thither and yon on the dock seemed to stretch as far inland as she could see. Suddenly a wave of fear gripped Tessa. How was she to make her way through this teeming throng and reach Portman Square—located *somewhere* in this vast city of London—before nightfall?

Tessa's elderly companion seemed every bit as anxious as she.

"My, one wonders how anyone finds their way about here!"

The women had taken only a few tentative steps forward when a rough-looking fellow, somewhat shabbily dressed, elbowed his way out of the crowd and boldly addressed Mrs. Benton-Caldwell.

"You and your daughter be needing a ride into the City, ma'am?" The fellow politely tipped his hat at the older woman, but his toothless grin was aimed straight at Tessa.

"Oh!" Mrs. Benton-Caldwell exclaimed, her tone a mixture of both alarm and relief. "Why, yes, my d-daugh . . . that is, Miss Darby would be needing a . . . you *do* have a public conveyance, do you not, young man?"

"It be awaiting at the curb, ma'am," the fellow replied proudly. He jabbed a thumb over his left shoulder, then brushed past the older woman and bent to snatch the heavy valise from Tessa's gloved hand. "This way, if ye please, miss."

"Oh, my! I hadn't expected to part company so quickly!" Mrs. Benton-Caldwell cried. She wrapped her free arm about Tessa's slim shoulders. "Good-bye, dear! It was a splendid idea of your father's that we travel together. I mean to write him the minute I reach Margate and tell him what a dear girl you are!"

Tessa blinked away the tears that sprang unbidden to her eyes as she returned the woman's warm embrace. Having Mrs. Benton-Caldwell to look after her these past weeks had been a special treat.

"We shall see one another again soon!" the older woman stated firmly. Her gloved hand swiped at the moisture that swam in her faded brown eyes. "Mr. Benton-Caldwell insists that I not stay above a quarter year, you know," she added with a laugh.

Tessa's lower lip trembled as she managed a brave smile. "Indeed." But she knew she'd never see her friend again. Despite her stepfather's stern warnings to her, she had no plans to return to America. Not ever.

After Tessa's valise had been secured to the back of the rather shabby-looking hansom cab, she climbed into the small vehicle and settled herself against the worn leather squabs. Although the din from the bustling shipyard still deafened her, her view of the teeming quay and the huge ship moored beyond it were now blocked by the cab's tall black hood, which extended high above her head.

When a sudden jerk set the small coach in motion, a fresh stab of apprehension—and excitement—shot through Tessa.

Her wonderful new life was upon her!

Since the age of ten, she had dreamed of making this trip to England, although in her dreams her mother had been with her. But their plans had been dashed when, less than a year ago, a sudden illness had carried her mother aloft. Tessa had grieved till she feared she might wither away herself. From the ashes of her pain, a new dream had taken shape. She would come to England alone. To do so would enormously please her mother.

The idea did not please her stepfather.

"You've no home in England to return to," he'd callously reminded Tessa. "Although you persist in calling yourself English, young lady, you are an American. You carry my name. You are my daughter. I intend you to marry Senator Hancock's boy, and there'll be an end to it."

"I will *not* marry George Hancock!" Tessa had cried. Her blue eyes snapped with fury. "I find nothing in him to admire. I do not agree with his politics and I . . . I do not love him!"

Senator Darby snorted with derision. "What do you know of politics? For all that, what do you know of love? You will do as I say, girl! I will brook no stubborn resistance from you on this head."

As her stepfather stormed from the room, Tessa's younger

brother, David, cast a sympathetic eye upon his tight-lipped sister. Tessa loved David dearly, but the soft-spoken young man was no match for their powerful father. Though just barely eighteen years of age, a promising career as a statesman had already been mapped out for David by the influential John Darby. In the whole of David's life, he had never once defied their father.

Not so Tessa.

As a very little girl, she had tried hard to earn her father's approval. About the time she realized that all her efforts to please him were in vain, she had also learned the truth of her lineage. From that moment forward, she balked at anything the strong-willed man told her to do. He was not her father and she knew he did not love her.

The child's willfulness did not go unnoticed or unpunished. As a direct result of Tessa's insubordination, the esteemed United States senator took to banishing his stepdaughter to her room for weeks at a time. Great stacks of books were sent up, with hastily scribbled notes instructing her to read one after another and write lengthy themes and essays on subjects of his choosing.

"The girl will learn to respect me!" he'd bellow. "I'll teach her to know her place if it's the last thing I do!"

Tessa obstinately refused to obey the man until one day she discovered she *liked* reading, and in a flash of brilliance, realized that if she were ever to be free of the hated man's tyranny, an educated mind was the most effective tool she could have.

Although she refused to think of herself as an American, she discovered the right-thinking principles that had led the colonists to revolt against the British crown back in 1776 constituted the key to her own freedom. Men—and women—*were* entitled to life, liberty, and the pursuit of happiness. The subjugation of the human spirit was wrong. Women were every bit as bright and intelligent as men, and they had a right to think for themselves and to conduct their lives as they saw fit.

Tessa's stepfather himself had placed Thomas Paine's manifesto on *The Rights of the Common Man* in her hands. Tessa had devoured it. Paine was an *Englishman!* His words had inspired her stepfather's countrymen to fight for their freedom, and they also inspired Tessa to fight for hers. How ironic, she thought, that Senator John Darby had devoted his life to freedom and democracy even as he kept his own daughter a prisoner in her own home.

Thomas Paine's dream of liberty spawned a dream within Tessa. Her own father, her *real* father, had given his life for England. Tessa was determined now to follow in his footsteps.

Throughout England, defenseless women and children were being forced to work long hours in abominable conditions in the new industrial townships and villages. Pregnant women were being made to give birth whilst bent double as they worked in the mines. Children were dying from starvation and overwork. These poor women and children needed help! They needed a voice, someone to speak on their behalf against such inhumane treatment.

Armed with a tattered copy of Paine's *Common Sense* and *The Rights of the Common Man* and a dozen or more themes and essays Tessa herself had penned on the subject, she determined to find a way to help them.

But persuading her stepfather to allow her to leave America and travel to England alone had been another matter altogether. To Tessa's immense chagrin, the ploy that finally worked with the heartless senator was the one trick Tessa had vowed never to employ. Despite the fact her mother had tried to impress upon her the importance of a woman remaining gentle and contrite in dealing with a man, using feminine wiles to get what she wanted was something Tessa Darby had sworn never to do, but she was desperate.

Holding her auburn head at a coquettish tilt, her words dripping with enough treacle to gag a grizzly, she'd informed her stepfather one night at dinner, "I shall be a far superior wife to George Hancock once I have learned how to go on in London society, Father. You know Mama's dearest wish was for me to have a London Season."

Tessa knew she'd made headway when Senator Darby set his knife and fork down and actually paused to consider what she'd said.

At length, he nodded. "Sending a daughter to London for the Season will elevate my consequence, as well. Americans are still in awe of anything English, although I fail to understand why."

Remembering to keep her voice soft and gentle, Tessa proceeded to further convince the brutish man. "You met Mama in London. She was a great favourite here."

Again, the large man nodded. His one redeeming quality was that he had always loved her mother dearly. Noting the faint softening of the hard lines around his mouth, Tessa nearly gasped with joy when the senator solemnly declared, "I will make the necessary arrangements for your passage."

Across the table from her, her brother, David, gasped. "But where will you stay, Tess? You've no family left in England."

"She will stay with Alice Langley," Senator Darby replied firmly. "But only for the Season, mind you. You will return home and take up your duties as young Hancock's wife once Parliament recesses."

Tessa could hardly contain the thrill of excitement coursing through her. "Alice Langley was Mama's bosom bow in London," she reminded her brother. "Mama said Alice always wished she'd had a daughter to bring out. Alice had only sons. Three, I think."

Engrossed in conversation with her younger brother, Tessa failed to note the faint frown of disapproval that appeared on her stepfather's face as she spoke.

Two

But here she was on her way to Portman Square! She felt so happy and exhilarated she thought she might actually burst from sheer joy.

She consulted the small gold timepiece she wore pinned to the bodice of her blue serge traveling suit. Only two of the clock in the afternoon. There was plenty of time to take a turn about famed Hyde Park and still arrive at Alice's in time for tea!

"Driver!" Tessa leaned forward to gaze up at the jarvey perched on the bench behind the hood, his sturdy hands gripping the ribbons. "I have decided I should like to take a turn about Hyde Park," she called up to the man, "before you deliver me to Portman square."

"Very well, miss."

Tessa settled back again, a fresh wave of excitement coursing through her. Suddenly she was struck with another idea, this one positively brilliant. She snatched up the thick leather satchel resting on the bench beside her and drove one hand into it. Yes! They were right where she'd put them those many weeks ago when she'd packed up her belongings in readiness for her trip. What better place to launch her campaign than Hyde Park?

Tessa's excitement grew as the little carriage jounced over the cobblestones on its way across Town. Soon after it wheeled past the magnificent portals marking the entrance to Hyde Park, Tessa spotted her quarry—six or seven young ladies fashionably attired in pretty muslin frocks, beribboned bonnets, and carrying painted parasols. The girls were talking and laughing amongst themselves as they strolled along a footpath, their appearance and demeanor clearly telling Tessa they were members of London's upper crust, which meant that their fathers or uncles or brothers were very likely M.P.s.

As the lone horse drawing the hansom cab clip-clopped alongside the young ladies, one or two of them glanced up as Tessa turned again to her driver.

"Stop right here, please!"

"Here, miss?"

Tessa was already on her feet, the sheaf of literature she'd brought with her all the way from America clutched in one hand.

"Ladies! Come quickly! I've something to give you!"

Eager for adventure, the giggling girls ran toward the friendly girl hailing them from the small black carriage now drawn to a standstill in the middle of the dirt road.

"Read this, please!" Tessa urged, pressing page after page of her precious hand-printed literature into each girl's gloved palm. "Tell your fathers and brothers something *must* be done about the defenseless women and children who are being ill-treated in our country's mills and factories! Do read it, *please!"* she urged again and again.

Absorbed in her endeavours, Tessa was unaware the hansom cab was blocking traffic along the park's main thoroughfare. Nor did she notice when two fashionably dressed gentlemen riding horseback were forced to rein in their mounts to avoid colliding with her conveyance.

Seated astride a magnificent chestnut stallion, Harrison Belmour, the fifth Earl of Penwyck, regarded the tall, auburn-haired young lady passing out leaflets from the side of a hansom cab with . . . *horror!*

"Appalling lack of propriety!" Lord Penwyck sputtered to his companion, Mr. Lowell Ashburn. His blond hair and merry blue eyes were a remarkable contrast to the dark-eyed, dark-haired earl.

Although the curious sight presented by the young lady had also arrested Mr. Ashburn's interest, the good-natured expression on his face was also in direct opposition to that worn by the affronted earl.

Mr. Ashburn's lips twitched as he cast an amused glance at his incensed companion. "So . . . I take it you'll not be adding her name to your list of eligibles?"

"God's blood!" Lord Penwyck sputtered, the force of the expletive causing the large chestnut beneath him to dance sideways. "Not even if she were the only unmarried female in London!" Though he thrust his aristocratic chin up, his square jaw was all but obscured by the high points of his starched white collar. Penwyck spurred his high-spirited mount into action and horse and rider skirted briskly past the hired cab.

Riding an equally frisky bay, Mr. Ashburn soon caught up to his friend. "By the by, how many names are left on your list?"

One of Lord Penwyck's dark brows shot upward. "Following the events at Almack's last evening, I have narrowed the field to four."

"I take it Miss Tentree's antics, however . . . entertaining . . . did not impress you favourably."

"Indeed not! That a young lady should deliberately make a spectacle of herself is the outside of enough. Very young girls should *not* wear watered gowns in public." Lord Penwyck's well-shaped mouth set with disgust before he added, "The mask the young lady wore did nothing to conceal her identity."

"Indeed not." Mr. Ashburn's blue eyes twinkled merrily. "Not that anyone was looking at the chit's face when there were far more interesting things to—"

A half grin softened Penwyck's chiseled features. "I did not say I did not enjoy inspecting the young lady's wares. What I meant was I would never take such a hoyden to wife."

"So," Mr. Ashburn continued in the same vein, "that leaves Miss Lydia Carruthers, Lady Amabel—"

"Cut line, Ash!" Penwyck interjected irritably. "I have no desire to make public the fact I am on the lookout for a bride."

"Well, your mother knows you're looking, don't she? Would think the countess has a right to know."

"Mother realizes I am considering the possibility of marrying. She is not aware I have drawn up a list of candidates."

Another whoop of laughter spilled from Mr. Ashburn's lips. "Fustian! Your mother is as well-acquainted with you as I am, old man. She knows there is a list involved somewhere!"

Penwyck directed a quelling look at his highly amused companion. "You appear to be making sport of my propensity to solve problems in an orderly, methodical fashion." The fifth Earl of Penwyck again urged his mount into a gallop and exited the park well ahead of his long-time friend.

The sound of horses' hooves rang on the cobblestones as the pair of gentlemen headed toward the intersection of Park Lane and Piccadilly.

When Mr. Ashburn caught up to the earl and their cattle were leisurely cantering alongside one another, Lord Penwyck said, "Considering the horrific scandal my family has suffered these past months, it is hardly surprising I wish to select a mate wisely. The young lady who becomes my countess must be above reproach in all respects. I refuse to bring additional shame or embarrassment to my family's doorstep. Mother could not bear it," he concluded forcefully.

"I understand your position perfectly, Penwyck." Mr. Ashburn's tone was solemn with sincerity.

After a pause, Lord Penwyck added, "I daresay my plan has worked admirably well thus far. Quietly observing the actions of this season's crop of eligibles has already averted disaster several times over. Upon spying a transgression, I simply scratch the young lady's name off my list. No one's the wiser and I run no risk of dangling after some mama's darling, then crying off when I discover the young lady . . . unsuitable."

"Quite so." Ashburn nodded. "Though once you have settled upon the perfect candidate, may I caution you against revealing your calculated machinations to her? I daresay most women prefer something a bit more . . . romantical."

A dark brow cocked as Lord Penwyck quizzed his companion. Realizing the truth behind Mr. Ashburn's observation, his lips began to twitch.

Ash was quite right. Women today were besotted with the idea of love. And, not just green girls. A mere fortnight ago, Penwyck had had the devil of a time disentangling himself from his latest bit o' muslin. The pretty actress's tears had ruined above half a dozen perfectly good neckcloths before Penwyck finally convinced her that despite the enjoyment he received from his twice-weekly visits to her flat, he had no intention of purchasing a season ticket granting him the right to private performances in her boudoir for the remainder of his life.

Why, Penwyck had even heard tales of young ladies actually refusing to marry for the *right* reasons—the linking of estates, the restoring of corrupt fortunes, and the like. Were he the father of such a daughter, he'd not countenance such rubbish, nor would he countenance a refusal to obey from the woman he married. Biddability sat at the top of another of his important lists, the required qualifications for his future countess.

The gentlemen rode the remainder of the distance to their destination—Boodle's Club—in silence. Once there, they'd no sooner entered the game room—where they meant to while away the long afternoon seated before a green baize table—when Lord Penwyck, a stricken expression on his face, exclaimed, "Damme!"

"Say what?" Ashburn glanced up, then grinned when he caught sight of the esteemed earl pouring over a sheet of cream-coloured linen paper. "Forget to do something on your list, old man?"

"Forgot to *put* something on my list," Lord Penwyck replied, in a tone laced with disgust. He neatly folded the page up and returned it to an inside coat pocket. "Forgive me, Ash, but I must forgo our game today."

Long strides carried the earl's impeccably-dressed form back down the corridor, a relaxed Mr. Ashburn close on his heels.

Penwyck paused in the foyer to retrieve the hat and gloves he'd only moments ago handed to the butler.

"Completely slipped my mind that Winslow is calling at the house today to collect some important papers," the earl said as the two men exited the club and headed back down the steps to the curb. "Been searching for them this age. Finally found them in a little-used drawer of father's desk."

Ashburn nodded. "Your father would be quite proud of the way you're handling things, Penwyck. You've done an admirable job since you inherited. Truth to say, everyone is . . . well, *astonished* actually, considering the appalling circumstances you inherited."

"Thank you, Ash," Penwyck murmured. He tossed a coin to a waiting stableboy, which sent the lad scurrying to the mews after Penwyck's horse. "I admit the task did seem daunting at the outset, but I was determined not to let the dismal state of affairs get the better of me."

"Everyone knows where the blame lay," Mr. Ashburn pointed out. "Squarely at the feet of that wastrel brother of yours."

A half grin appeared on Penwyck's face. "You are the only man I'd allow to speak in such a fashion against my brother Joel. I'd have gone to the gallows for him if it came to that."

"And the coward would have let you!" Ashburn sputtered.

Penwyck's dark head shook with resignation. "What's done is done. Joel Belmour is no longer a blight on the family name. His gambling debts have all been paid, and his by-blows—at least the ones I am aware of—are well provided for. Were the true facts surrounding his death to come to light, I would deny any knowledge of it. I trust the same can be said for you, Ash."

"You have my word on it," the earl's loyal friend replied. "Although how you can abide letting the world think the scoundrel died a hero is more than I can fathom."

"Joel caused our mother more shame than any woman should be required to bear. For her sake, I have chosen to shield the true facts. For all his transgressions, she loved Joel dearly."

At that moment the stableboy reappeared, the ribbons firm in his grip as he led the earl's prized stallion toward them. Lord

Penwyck stepped to the mounting block and nimbly settled onto the large chestnut's back.

Once cushioned in the leather saddle, Penwyck glanced down at his friend. "I rather expect I shall have to cry off attending the races with you next week, Ash. Would be unforgivable of me to leave town just now, what with mother's houseguest arriving."

"Ah." Mr. Ashburn nodded. "The young lady from America."

"Mother has plans to bring her out, but, having raised only sons, she's had precious little experience in that quarter. I think she is rather relying on me to show the girl how to go on," he added warmly.

Mr. Ashburn's blue eyes twinkled again. "Perhaps the American girl will make your list of eligib—"

"Not a chance!" Lord Penwyck exploded. "Mother tells me the girl received a privileged education, but I rather expect to find a good many rough edges. The young lady was raised amongst savages in the new world, you know."

"Well, whatever her faults"—Mr. Ashburn grinned—"I daresay you are the very one to bring her up to the mark."

Quite true, Lord Penwyck thought as he urged his mount forward, and it was a task he meant to take on willingly in order to insure no further scandal besmirched the Penwyck name.

Suddenly, an image of the young lady he and Ash had observed earlier handing out leaflets in the park sprang to mind. Thank God he'd been spared the formidable task of taming that abominable spectacle!

Three

Tessa was about to lift the door knocker to number twelve Portman Square when horses' hooves ringing on the cobblestones behind her claimed her attention. Glancing over her shoulder, she watched an elegantly attired gentleman dismount from his horse, hurriedly toss the reins to a waiting footman, and stride up the walk to the very stoop where she stood.

Thinking perhaps he was one of Alice Langley's sons, a smile of greeting sprang to Tessa's lips. But it froze in place the very second the gentleman caught sight of her . . . and scowled.

"You!" he sputtered as he brushed past a stunned Tessa. "Did you not give away enough of that radical literature of yours just now in the park, young lady?"

Tessa's blue eyes widened, but before she had a chance to reply, the gentleman added, "I assure you, no one in this household is interested in anything you have to say. Now go along with you!"

He made a shooing motion with one hand, then jerked open the door to the tall, narrow town house and disappeared inside.

"Why—" Tessa stared with disbelief as the door slammed with a resounding thud behind him. She at once grasped the brass knocker and insistently rapped it several times over. Hearing the muffled sound of voices from within, she leaned forward in an effort to hear what was being said.

"In the park just now . . . some cause or other . . . get rid of her, Jenkins."

Suddenly, the door opened the veriest crack and a prim-faced man stuck out a white-gloved hand. "Here is a contribution for your cause, Miss. If you will please go along now."

"Sirrah!" Tessa cried, ignoring the five-pound note the butler was thrusting at her. "I am Miss Tessa Darby, come from America. I am here at the invitation of Alice Langle . . . I mean the *former* Alice . . . what I mean to say is Lady Penwyck is expecting me. You will please announce my presence to the countess at once."

Regarding her suspiciously, the butler pushed open the door and, with a nod, invited Tessa to step inside.

Moments later, as she followed the retainer down a carpeted corridor toward the rear of the house, Tessa kept a sharp eye out for the gentleman who'd rudely addressed her on the doorstep. Although she feared he might be one of Alice Langley's sons, she fervently hoped the man was only paying his mother a call this afternoon and did not, in fact, live here. She'd taken an instant dislike to him and did not wish to meet up with him on a daily basis throughout her lengthy stay in Town.

The butler left Tessa in what she assumed to be a withdrawing, or sitting, room. A scant second later, he returned to inform her Lady Penwyck would join her shortly and he would have her portmanteau delivered to her bedchamber.

Tessa thanked the man a bit smugly, then glanced about at her surroundings. Though not on the same scale as her stepfather's lavish country estate, the Penwyck town home was quite elegant.

Although . . . gazing a bit closer at the furniture in this room Tessa was struck by its rather helter-skelter arrangement. Chairs and sofas seemed to have been shifted about to suit whoever happened to be in the room at the time. The haphazard fashion was a decided contrast to the way her mother decorated. There, every last stick of furniture and all of Senator Darby's precious ornaments and costly paintings were displayed in carefully selected spots and never touched thereafter. Clearly that was not the case in Alice's . . . er . . . Lady Penwyck's home.

Atop the mantelpiece and scattered upon several small tables—even strewn about upon the chairs—was an incongruous assortment of bric-a-brac: ladies' magazines, smoking paraphernalia, sewing implements, assorted packages of colored thread, stacks of books, and yellowing newspapers.

How singularly odd, Tessa marveled to herself. Glancing round again, she concluded the disordered jumble seemed far more inviting than the brusque gentleman who'd only moments ago accosted her on the doorstep. Contemplating the man's rudeness made her stomach muscles clench all over again.

Her ruminations were interrupted by a feminine voice.

"My dearest Tessa! You are here at last!"

Tessa turned as a gray-haired woman—not nearly as tall as she, who at five feet, seven inches was considered tall for a young lady—bustled into the room, her long silk skirt rustling about her small frame. A welcoming smile upon her lined face, Lady Penwyck reached to fondly embrace Tessa.

"I am so happy to meet you at last, my darling girl!"

"I am delighted to meet you, as well, Lady Pen—"

"Oh, do call me Alice, dear! Everyone does." Still smiling, the older woman gazed up at Tessa. "My, you look nothing at all like your dear mother!" She laughed gaily, then sobered. "I do *so* wish I could have seen Helen once more before she . . ."

"It was Mother's dearest wish to return again to London to see you," Tessa replied warmly.

Lady Penwyck blinked back an errant tear. "And you have come in her stead. I am thrilled beyond saying!"

Lady Penwyck turned to lead the way toward a cluttered sofa. After brushing aside a number of ladies' magazines, she gestured for Tessa to sit down. Then, still chattering nonstop, she drug up a pretty japanned chair and repositioned it opposite the sofa.

"—But you do resemble your father," she nattered on. "He was *very* tall and had the most extraordinary blue eyes. All the young ladies admired Captain Benning's lovely blue eyes. My"—she clasped a hand to her breast—"but he was a handsome young man. Helen met him the night of her come-out ball and thereafter refused every other suitor. It was all very romantic!" she added with a gay laugh.

Tessa smiled. She quite liked her mother's girlhood friend. Lady Penwyck's laughing brown eyes and pleasant manner rather reminded Tessa of a small brown wren chirping happily away.

"What a glorious time your mother and I had when we were girls," Alice enthused. "The opera, the endless shopping, the balls and breakfasts. But you and I shall have a gay time of it, too, dear. I am *so* looking forward to bringing you out!"

Tessa winced. She had not come to London to while away her time in an mindless whirl of shopping and parties. She made a mental note to find a way to apprise Lady Penwyck of her true plan. Until then, she decided to remain silent.

"Was the crossing terribly tedious?" Lady Penwyck asked. "My, I cannot imagine being aboard ship for such a lengthy spell! You should have sent word to us your ship had arrived. Penny would have met you at the dock. Oh, dear." A worried frown replaced the gay smile upon the older woman's lips. "I do hope Penny will not be too terribly off-put that you . . . but then, you arrived quite safely, so where's the harm?"

"I had no trouble at all finding my way here, Lady Penwyck," Tessa hastened to say. "There were a goodly number of public carriages parked along the street. I simply told the driver where I wished to go, and—"

"How very resourceful you are! I admit I am a bit unaccustomed to looking after a young lady. Thank Heaven for Penny. He is a very proper young man. He knows precisely how to go on." She beamed at Tessa, then suddenly popped to her feet and scampered across the room to give the bellpull a smart tug. "You must be parched! I meant to ask Jenkins to bring us a nice pot of tea. Penny is expecting Mr. Winslow. I have asked the gentlemen to join us . . ." Another fretful look crossed her face. "That is, I *believe* I asked them. Dear me . . . I—"

Tessa was wondering who Penny might be when the sound of male voices in the corridor announced the gentlemen's presence.

"Ah, here are the young men now! I *did* ask them!" Lady Penwyck beamed, then looked beyond Tessa as the men entered the room. "Penny darling, this is my dear friend Helen's daughter from America, Miss Tessa Darby."

Her back to the new arrivals, Tessa drew in a deep breath before she turned full around . . . and came face to face with the same tall gentleman who had angrily chastised her on the doorstep. A wave of fresh anxiety washed over her.

But she was surprised when, despite the cool reserve in the gentleman's dark eyes, he politely said, "How do you do, Miss Darby? It appears I owe you an apology."

Alice gazed curiously from her son to Tessa and back again.

"I . . . bumped into Miss Darby on the doorstep, Mother. Apparently, I"—the aristocratic gentleman directed a speaking look at Tessa—"mistook her for someone else. My apologies, Miss Darby."

Tessa managed a polite nod. Why was the gentleman now pretending he had not recognized her from the park?

Lord Penwyck had turned to address his companion, a rather portly older gentleman.

"Miss Darby will be staying with us for the Season," he said.

"Mr. Winslow is Penny's solicitor," Alice told Tessa.

Tessa smiled at the older man as Lord Penwyck drew up a pair of chairs for himself and his guest. From the corner of her eye, she noted Penny appeared to be studying her quite intently. His long tapered fingers were now forming a contemplative steeple beneath his firm, square jaw as he glared at her.

With a disdainful sniff, Tessa lifted her chin and turned her full attention from the arrogant man eyeing her to his mother, Lady Penwyck, who was addressing no one in particular.

"Miss Darby's father is a United States senator," Lady Penwyck told the gentlemen. "He is a powerful man in America. Your father is also quite the horseman, is he not, dear?"

"Yes, that is correct," Tessa replied eagerly. "The Darbys have raised thoroughbreds for many years."

"Helen told me in her last letter that your younger brother David also had political aspirations, that he was—"

"It appears the entire family has political aspirations," Lord Penwyck remarked, his hard gaze still fixed on Tessa.

Her blue eyes cut round and, without taking thought, she blurted out, "I take it *you* do not approve of women having political opinions, sir."

Mr. Winslow laughed aloud. Then, realizing he was the only one who found the idea amusing, he hurriedly covered his outburst with a cough.

"Indeed, I do not, Miss Darby," Lord Penwyck stated firmly. "The feminine mind is not equipped to understand political concerns. A young lady who draws attention to herself by—"

"Why, whatever are you talking about, Penny dear?" Alice interrupted her son's tirade. She gazed curiously from his hardened features to her now very tight-lipped houseguest.

Tessa's pretty nostrils flared with anger but she managed to curb her upset and say nothing further.

Apparently, Penny was exactly like her stepfather, who believed women, like children, should be seen and not heard.

But, she quickly reminded herself, she was no longer under his thumb, was she?

And she would *not* be silenced in her own country. She'd come to England to speak her mind, and speak it she would.

"As it happens, sir," she stated, "I take a lively interest in politics. I grew up listening to my father and his political allies debate all the important issues in America. My opinions, sir, are not uninformed."

Lord Penwyck's dark eyes narrowed to black slits. Tessa watched the gentleman's strong chest heave with suppressed rage. Suddenly, instead of responding to her remark, the gentleman bolted to his feet and murmured something about an urgent business matter. He exited the room with a wide-eyed Mr. Winslow on his heels.

Oddly enough, Lady Penwyck seemed to find nothing amiss in her son's unexpected departure. "Penny is a very busy young man," she told Tessa brightly. "He is the earl now, you know. He has a seat in the Lords and takes his responsibilities quite seriously."

Tessa gulped. Penny was an *earl?*

Apparently her mother had not known Alice's husband had

passed on. Therefore, neither did she. Apparently Penny was the eldest of Lady Penwyck's sons and had inherited his father's title and rank. As an M.P., he was the very sort of gentleman she most wished to reach with her message. Had she already botched a prime chance to bring her message before an influential member of the House of Lords?

Four

Dinner that night was a stilted affair, at least for Tessa. Throughout the overlong meal, she was acutely aware of the dark looks aimed her way from the thundercloud seated at the head of the table. Apparently, the highborn gentleman had decided she was an undesirable and therefore unsuited for Polite Company.

He was, indeed, exactly like her stepfather, who believed women did not possess rational minds, were not to speak unless spoken to, and then were merely to smile and agree with the superior opinions expressed by their menfolk. Well, that was not Tessa Darby's way and never would be.

Tessa knew she could never be the perfect wife to any man. As a child, she'd been forced by her stepfather to read and study from the same books little boys were schooled from. Therefore her education was sadly remiss in those subjects deemed appropriate for a young girl. Tessa Darby could not sew a straight stitch, play the pianoforte, or sing. She did not know how to draw pretty pictures or paint with watercolours. She'd never embroidered a single pillow slip or handkerchief in her entire life and had no desire to learn.

She preferred simple, elegant styles in her clothing and did not wear ribbons in her hair. Although she was tall and slim, she was blessed with a shapely figure. On board ship, as she and Mrs. Benton-Caldwell promenaded about the deck, Tessa was often aware of long stares directed at her from other male passengers, as well as members of the ship's crew, and it was not because there were no other young ladies present. There were plenty.

Yet Tessa hadn't the least interest in attracting a man or forming a lasting attachment with one. She was quite happy alone. Despite the fierce disapproval her character might elicit from the high and mighty Lord Penwyck, she had every intention of pursuing her lifelong dream whilst here in England. And—she cast a challenging gaze at the gentleman seated at the head of the table, who was still glaring daggers at her—she would allow *no* man to change her.

Lord Penwyck had never felt quite so overset and was having the devil of a time deciding how to handle this prickly situation. To toss the outspoken Miss Darby into the streets was not a viable option, although he admitted it was tempting. His poor trusting mother had no idea what an unconventional miss this Miss Darby was, or that, if left unchecked, the little hoyden's actions could very well mean the ruination of them all. Ten minutes ago, when his unsuspecting mother had actually invited the young lady to remain with them indefinitely, Penwyck's jaws had ground together in consternation.

"We are your family now, Tessa dear. You will think of this as your new home. I've no doubt Helen would have taken in any one of my three boys had the need arisen. And"—she cast a helpless look across the table at Penwyck—"it very nearly did."

The earl merely cleared his throat, signaling his refusal to discuss that charged subject further. The less said about Joel Belmour, the better.

But he was mentally composing plenty to say on the subject of Miss Darby and had every intention of saying it before the situation got completely out of hand.

Once the meal had concluded and Miss Darby politely asked to be excused, Penwyck caught up to her in the corridor.

"If I may have a private word with you, Miss Darby?"

Tessa turned to gaze up at the tight-lipped gentleman, her cornflower blue eyes unwavering as she bravely held the earl's dark gaze. "I do not feel up to a coze this evening, sir. My journey has quite fatigued me."

"What I have to say will only take a moment, Miss Darby." The earl's tone was firm. A strong hand indicated a chamber to Tessa's right. "This way, if you please."

Tessa pursed her lips obstinately but obediently stepped into the room. From the rows and rows of books lining the dark paneled walls and the large kneehole desk in the center of room, she judged it to be the gentleman's private study.

She watched Lord Penwyck slide the door shut behind him and silently stride across the room to stand before the huge desk.

Feeling his cold gaze again fix on her, Tessa involuntarily shivered and edged a few steps closer to the lowburning fire in the hearth.

After a contemplative pause, the earl finally said, "I have decided the best approach to take with you, Miss Darby, is straight out."

Tessa thrust her chin up as Lord Penwyck's cool dark eyes continued to bore into hers. For the first time, she noted that, with his thick dark hair and strong square jaw, he was not unattractive. Although, having seen but one expression grace those aristocratic features, and that not a *pleasant* one, she could not in all honesty call the gentleman handsome.

The look of displeasure she'd beheld on his face since she first met him this afternoon remained unchanged as he spoke. "It appears, Miss Darby, there is a good deal you do not yet know about propriety."

Tessa's blue eyes widened in surprise. No one, not even her stepfather, had accused her of being improper. She was about to make an angry retort when the earl held up a silencing hand.

"I am not yet finished, Miss Darby. First off, a proper young lady does *not* go about Town unchaperoned. I realize you must have felt compelled to find your own way here this afternoon, but the proper thing for you to have done upon arriving in London was to have got word to us that you required assistance."

He paused, as if to allow her to say something on her own

behalf. When she did not, he added, in a slightly altered tone, "I was quite pleased to learn from your conversation at dinner that you had *not* made the crossing from America unchaperoned. I had begun to fear colonists hadn't the least notion of decency."

Indignation exploded within Tessa. "Colonists are perfectly decent!" she cried. "At least the majority of them are." She inhaled a fitful breath and was about to elaborate further when an authoritative bellow cut her off.

"Nonetheless"—Lord Penwyck folded his arms across his broad chest, the angry scowl again furrowing his brow—"I *cannot* overlook your scandalous behaviour this afternoon in Hyde Park."

Tessa's chin shot up and heated words spilled from her lips before she could even think of halting them. "I have no idea what you are referring to, sir. Furthermore, I do not apprecia—"

"My point exactly, Miss Darby. You haven't the least notion to what I am referring! Despite whatever charitable cause you are forwarding, the fact remains that proper young ladies do *not* hand out leaflets in Hyde Park!"

Tessa's breasts rose and fell, an action which the toplofty earl took note of. His gaze dropped for the veriest second to her bosom before his scathing stare bore once again into hers. Though she hadn't the least idea why, she felt a measure of satisfaction that her femininity had distracted him.

"Whilst you are a guest in my home," the arrogant gentleman continued, "you will conduct yourself with the utmost propriety and seemliness."

"I am perfectly seemly, sir," Tessa retorted angrily.

The earl glared at her. "Whether or not that is true, Miss Darby, remains to be seen." He paused, his dark head shaking from side to side. "Thank God the incident in Hyde Park took place before the fashionable hour. I shudder to think what the consequences would be if the *ton* had seen you." His well-shaped lips pursed with annoyance. "It is my mother's express wish to bring you out, Miss Darby, to introduce you to people of high consequence in London. It is becoming quite evident to me, however, that to see you married and well set up will require more than a good bit of—"

"Are you saying I am unsuitable?" Tessa cried indignantly. Without thinking, she blurted out, "For your information, sirrah, I am at this moment betrothed to the son of a United States senator!"

A dark brow arched. "Ah. So, you *do* have plans to return to America?"

Tessa's own lips pursed and the toe of her boot began to tap impatiently against the hearth. *Why could she not remember to think before she spoke?* She had *no* intention of marrying George Hancock *or* returning to America. "I did not say that. What I meant was . . . no, sir; I do not plan to return to America."

Lord Penwyck's condescending gaze further incensed Tessa. Now she'd done it. The infuriating man thought her a complete ninnyhammer!

She hurried to explain. "What I meant to say, sir, is that I am not the least bit ashamed of my conduct in the park this afternoon. As it happens, I have an absorbing interest in humanitarian causes and as an English citizen—I was born in this country, you know—I feel I have every right to—"

"Enough!" The earl's angry bellow again silenced her. "Proper young ladies are *not* interested in political issues, Miss Darby."

"Why ever not?" Tessa demanded. "I know a great deal about what is going on politically in this country and I—"

"I will listen to nothing further on the subject!" the earl exclaimed and turned to angrily shuffle some papers on his desk. A few seconds later, upon again hearing her toe tapping impatiently against the hearth, he turned toward her once more. "Have I made my position in this matter clear, Miss Darby?"

"Quite clear, sir." Tessa directed an innocent blue gaze up at him. "So long as I am a good little girl and do exactly as I am told, all will be well. Am I free to go now?"

"You are free to do as you like, Miss Darby, so long as your actions are proper."

Tessa pulled herself to her full height of five feet, seven inches. "Thank you, Lord Penwyck." She turned and headed for the door. "I mean to retire to my suite now and spend the remainder of the evening composing my next essay, copies of which I will distribute—"

She had almost reached the door when she felt strong fingers curl about her upper arm.

"Wait just a minute, Miss Darby."

Tessa turned an icy blue gaze upward.

Lord Penwyck was standing quite near her. It registered in a part of her mind that he was quite tall, nearly a head taller than she, which would put him well above six feet. His chest and shoulders were excessively broad. She felt a strange tingling sensation where his fingers touched her bare flesh. She cast a gaze that direction and noted his hands and upper arm were quite powerful. There was a pleasant woodsy scent about him she found maddeningly irritating.

"Apparently I did not make myself quite clear enough, Miss Darby." The earl's tone was lethal.

Tessa thrust his masculine woodsy scent from her mind.

"On the contrary, sir. You said I was free to do as I please, and I said I was—"

"Miss Darby"—the gentleman's dark eyes narrowed to angry slits—"I will *not* allow you to behave in a hoydenish fashion. Whilst you reside in this house, you will do precisely as I say, or I will—"

As she tossed her auburn hair, Tessa's sapphire eyes flashed fire. "Or you will *what,* sir? Banish me to my room?" It was on the tip of her tongue to add that had never stopped her before. Being forbidden to speak her mind and banished to her room because of it was precisely what had brought her here.

Lord Penwyck's strong fingers continued to grip her upper arm and the muscles in his square jaw tightened.

At length, he said, "If we are to avoid another war between our countries, Miss Darby, I suggest—"

"I am every bit as English as you are, sir! England is *my* country and I refuse to ask permission to do as I please here!"

The earl's nostrils flared angrily.

The two stood rooted in place for a long moment. At length, Lord Penwyck said, "For my mother's sake, Miss Darby, I implore you to curtail your disagreeable political activities whilst you reside in this house."

Tessa inhaled a long breath. She saw absolutely nothing wrong in what she had done this afternoon or in what she wished to do. But, apparently 'his lordship' did. Although Lady Penwyck was a bit of a skitter-wit, Tessa genuinely liked the older woman and did not wish to do anything that would displease her. To do so would be the same as displeasing her own mother.

"Very well," she finally murmured. "I will refrain from distributing leaflets in the park."

Tessa felt Lord Penwyck's strong grip on her arm relax the veriest mite. Then he let go entirely and stepped away. The movement sent the pleasant woodsy aroma that surrounded him wafting to Tessa's nostrils again. She drank in the heady scent, then quickly exhaled, as if to thrust all traces of his nearness from her.

The arrogant gentleman might have forced her hand this time, but that did not mean she would give up her dream. He was simply forcing her to find another way to carry on with her plans, one that would not attract his notice.

His anger somewhat abated, Lord Penwyck ordered his carriage brought round and a moment later, upon hearing the clatter of the wheels on the cobblestones in front of the house, took his leave.

He fully believed the impudent Miss Darby had been put firmly in her place and would now do precisely as he asked. She was a woman and, despite any small show of resistance females felt compelled to display, in the end they all obeyed. It was the way of the world. Women were meant to be ruled by men. Penwyck felt quite proud of having taken the situation in hand. By calling an immediate halt to Miss Darby's foolishness, he had once again averted disaster.

The earl felt almost jaunty as he alighted from his carriage a quarter hour later at number sixty St. James's Street and walked to the door of the prestigious gentleman's club Brooks's. Only one last item remained on his list for this evening, to apprise his good friend Lowell Ashburn of the true identity of his mother's houseguest and demand his complete silence in the matter. It would never do for the *ton* to learn that his mother, the well-liked and well-respected Countess Penwyck, intended bringing out 'The Hyde Park Spectacle.'

The butler at Brooks's greeted Lord Penwyck with a near-imperceptible nod and wordlessly relieved his lordship of his topcoat, walking stick, and curly black beaver hat.

Penwyck entered the Great Subscription Room, where later tonight the names of new members would be proposed and voted upon. The Subscription Room was the largest chamber in what was, in truth, a comparatively small building. With its high domed ceiling, elaborate scrollwork, and impressive chandelier, the Subscription Room forwarded the club's overall feeling of spaciousness and quiet elegance.

Lord Penwyck located his good friend Mr. Ashburn—who had only recently been voted into the club and who owed his good fortune to the highly persuasive earl—on the fringe of the room, engaged in conversation with a group of gentlemen who were, no doubt, promoting the qualifications of their especial favourites from tonight's roster of prospective members.

Catching sight of Lord Penwyck, Mr. Ashburn excused himself and headed toward Penwyck. "Hallo! I understand the young lady from America has arrived. Is she passing fair, or what?"

Penwyck started. This was not the first time his affable friend had stunned him with his foreknowledge of gossip or newsworthy events not yet commonly known about town. It often appeared to Penwyck that Ashburn, a mere third son of an impoverished baronet, knew as much or more about other people's affairs than they knew themselves. Regaining his composure, Penwyck said, "May I speak with you privately, Ashburn?"

Mr. Ashburn shrugged. "Of course."

Penwyck led the way to a secluded pair of overstuffed chairs drawn up before the hearth. After the men were seated, he ordered a snifter of the club's best aged brandy for himself and a glass for his companion and decided to wait until the drinks had been delivered before he broached the subject of Miss Darby. *On-dits* were quite often spread all over Town via tongue-wagging servants in gentlemen's clubs or private homes. Penwyck did not want this potentially damaging bit of news bruited about in all the drawing rooms in London.

Some minutes later, the fine brandy warming his gullet, Penwyck addressed his friend. "I've something of a rather sensitive nature to divulge to you tonight, Ash. It concerns my mother's houseguest. I demand your solemn oath that what I am about to tell you will *not* be repeated to another soul."

The utmost respect shone from Mr. Ashburn's clear blue eyes. "I would never betray your confidence, Penwyck. You have my oath."

Penwyck cocked a somewhat suspicious brow. "Mark my words, Ash. If I hear one word of this bandied about, I'll call you out."

Mr. Ashburn leaned so far forward in his chair his knees all but touched the earl's. "My God, Penwyck, what are you hiding?"

Penwyck inhaled a sharp breath. "I wish it were that simple."

"Spill it, man. I confess I am as anxious as a cat in a fishery." Mr. Ashburn took a long draught from his own glass of brandy, apparently hoping it would give his companion courage.

Penwyck inhaled another deep breath before plunging in. "It appears, Ashburn, you have already met—that is, you have already seen my mother's houseguest."

Mr. Ashburn's brows drew together thoughtfully. "Must be mistaken, old man. I have no recollection of ev—"

"Damn it! I do not mean you have been formally presented to the young lady. I said you have *seen* her."

The puzzled look on Mr. Ashburn's face deepened. "Say what?"

Penwyck's lips pursed with exasperation. "Devil take it, Ash, this afternoon in the park." The earl's dark head shook. "I regret to say my mother's houseguest is the"—he cast a surreptitious glance over one shoulder, then lowered his voice to a mere whisper—"The Hyde Park Spectacle."

Mr. Ashburn's blue eyes widened, then he threw his head back and a burst of hearty laughter spilled from his lips. "Damme, Penwyck, that's rich! What did your mother say when you told her what her protégée'd been up to?"

"I am not a complete fool," Penwyck sputtered. "I saw no need to burden mother with such fustian. I extricated a promise from Miss Darby to leave off distributing her radical literature in the park and elsewhere so long as she is in town. The poor girl was not even aware she had committed a social blunder."

"I understand her father is a United States senator."

The earl's scowl deepened. "What else have you learned about her?"

Ashburn's head shook vigorously. "Nothing. I swear, that's the whole of it. I know only that she arrived this afternoon and that your mother is set to bring her out." He grinned rakishly. "And that she is demmed pretty. You don't mind if I spread that around, do you, old man?" His lips twitched with high amusement.

"Not at all." Penwyck exhaled. "The sooner Miss Darby is married and becomes the responsibility of another man, the easier I shall breathe."

"The chit can't be so bad as all that, Penwyck. Apart from her shocking display of impropriety in the park this afternoon, what could you possibly find so displeasing about her?"

Penwyck cocked a brow. "Suffice to say, the young lady's interests are not in the common way. Her pretty head is stuffed full of political rubbish and misguided notions about . . . about . . ." The earl's voice trailed off as he shook his head, presumably to clear it of all lingering images of the perturbing Miss Darby.

"I see," Mr. Ashburn murmured. "I presume you set her straight?"

"I did. I expect Miss Darby will soon become as missish and giddy as any other female on the Marriage Mart. With her extraordinary good looks—"

"Ah, so you did notice."

"Notice what?" Penwyck demanded.

Mr. Ashburn's blue eyes twinkled merrily. "I predict your fetching Miss Darby will soon become the talk of the town, old man."

Mr. Ashburn's prophetic words were still ringing in Lord Penwyck's ears when he went down to breakfast the following morning and discovered his mother pouring over a handwritten document given her by Miss Tessa Darby.

"Penny darling!" his mother cried. "You simply *must* read this!"

Five

Tessa had worked till the wee hours of the morning on her essay, documenting a true story tearfully told to her by a distraught young woman aboard ship. Because the tale had touched Tessa so very deeply, she had decided last evening that if this poor woman's tale had moved her to tears, it would surely have the same effect on Lady Penwyck, and she, in turn, would tell her friends about it.

"Penny darling," Lady Penwyck exclaimed again, "our Miss Darby is quite imaginative! She has written a lovely story!"

Tessa winced as Lady Penwyck directed a bright smile at her. "Why, this is every bit as dramatical and entertaining as anything fabricated by Mrs. Radcliffe!"

Fabricated! Tessa cried to herself. She thought she'd made it perfectly clear that the story was *true!* That it was told her by a young lady she and Mrs. Benton-Caldwell had met on the crossing from America.

The poor woman was returning to England because she'd received word that two of her three children, whom she'd been forced to give over to the parish authorities in England because she could not provide for them, had consequently been put to work in a local cotton mill and had died there.

The overset woman had told Tessa her small children, two boys and a girl, were required to be at their posts at five of the clock every morning and to work all day long, sometimes all *night* long, with only half an hour off twice a day to take their meals. Tessa thought it an abominable practice, and hoped by exposing the awful truth, something could be done to stop it.

True, she'd begun her paper last evening in anger, a vengeful reaction against the unfair accusations Lord Penwyck had leveled at her. But as she wrote, her outrage quickly became aligned once again with those helpless victims of neglect and abuse whose own voices could not be heard, whose plaintive cries went unheeded.

Unless *someone* told their stories, unless *someone* stood up for them, nothing would be done to alleviate their misery and suffering. Tessa could not abide that. The truth had to come out, and despite the fact that Lord Penwyck thought her wrong to want to help these defenseless women and children, she still had to. She *had* to!

Until a scant second ago, she thought she'd made her first inroad with Lady Penwyck, but apparently not. Her spirits dipped lower when the countess said, "I have read every last one of Mrs. Radcliffe's novels."

Tessa's eyes darted to Lord Penwyck, who was standing before the sideboard helping himself to generous servings of kippers, creamed eggs, and hot buttered scones. When he took his place at the head of the table, a servant stepped forward, silver pot in hand, to fill his lordship's coffee cup.

"Of course," Lady Penwyck went on, carelessly pushing the sheaf of papers aside, "if you have any hope of getting your stories published, Tessa dear, you will have to do so anonymously. I do not believe young ladies can be authoresses. Is that not true, Penny dear?" She looked a question at her son, who Tessa noted now wore a bemused expression upon his face.

With a flourish, he draped a fine linen napkin across his lap. "You are quite right, mother." He directed an innocent look at Tessa. "So you have literary aspirations, do you, Miss Darby?"

Tessa's lips tightened. She would not answer the odious man's question. Even if his mother did not know the story she'd penned was true, surely he did. He was simply goading her. He was contemptible, more contemptible than her stepfather.

She could not halt the pained look that settled on her face as she gazed imploringly at Lady Penwyck, only to cringe inwardly when she noted the countess had actually set her teacup down on the top page of her carefully penned essay. Already the damp cup had blurred the words beneath it beyond all recognition.

"—mean to take Tessa shopping with me this morning," Lady Penwyck was saying, having already skittered off to another topic of conversation, "and then to accompany me on my round of calls this afternoon. I am so looking forward to our adventure!" she enthused. With a gay laugh, she reached blindly for her teacup, but instead of grasping it, she knocked it over entirely. "Oh, dear me!"

Tessa lunged for her essay, but was too late. The pages were soaked clean through, every last one completely unreadable now.

"Oh, dear me!" Lady Penwyck laughed again. Tessa watched as a stone-faced servant scooped up the dripping pages and wadded them, along with Lady Penwyck's soaked napkin, into a soggy ball. With a clean cloth, a second footman hastily sopped up the ever-widening puddle of tea. Lady Penwyck—talking all the while—reseated herself across the table. "You must write another story, Tessa dear." She laughed. "I will make certain Penny reads it before I ruin it next time!"

Her heart pounding in desperation, Tessa worked to keep her hurt feelings in check. It was beginning to appear that despite her best efforts to forward her Cause, she had a very long way to go.

She hadn't the heart now to listen to a single word Lady Penwyck was saying. Tessa had already surmised that the bulk of her conversation centered around *ton* doings—parties, routs, breakfasts, and the like—none of which interested her.

At length, Lord Penwyck laid his napkin aside and rose from the table. His dark eyes pinned Tessa. "I should like to see you in my study this morning, Miss Darby." He directed a fairly pleasant look at his mother. "There is a matter of some urgency I must take up with the young lady before the two of you take the *ton* by storm." His aristocratic features relaxed into a half smile.

"Oh, dear me." His mother laughed again. "I daresay I have been nattering on a bit, haven't I?" She turned to address Tessa. "Do you go along with Penny now, dear; I must speak with the housekeeper, Mrs. Hipley, before we set out and also with"—she gazed about—"now where has Jenkins got to?" She, too, pushed up from the table. "I declare, I cannot stay abreast of those two!" She scampered off, chattering distractedly to herself as she did so.

"Miss Darby." Lord Penwyck stood at the top of the table, an expectant look on his face.

Her lips tight, Tessa rose and again followed the earl down the corridor and into his private study. Apparently she was in for another royal setdown this morning.

With a self-righteous sniff, Tessa lifted her chin and leveled a contemptuous gaze at 'his lordship.' But there was something about his demeanor today that disarmed her. He looked . . . well, almost handsome in a forest-green coat with brass buttons, a biscuit-coloured waistcoat, and buckskin trousers. Walking beside him in the corridor, Tessa had again been assailed by distracting whiffs of the pleasant woodsy aroma he wore, but she thrust aside the arresting memory of that and fixed her attention on the present moment.

The same as last evening, the aristocratic gentleman was standing with his back to the large kneehole desk in the center of the room, his arms folded across his massive chest. Tessa noted a somewhat odd look on his face as he gazed at her and could not help wondering what the look meant.

Finally, he said, "It has suddenly occurred to me, Miss Darby, that I have yet to see a genuine smile upon those pretty pink lips of yours."

Tessa started.

"Well?"

She sniffed again. "Perhaps I have not yet found anything to smile about, sir."

A brow quirked. "This is your first trip to England, is it not? One would think that would be reason enough to cause a young lady to smile." A glint of humor shone from his dark eyes.

Growing uncomfortable beneath what she perceived to be the gentleman's mocking gaze, Tessa lowered her lashes. "I am . . . quite pleased to be in London, sir."

"Ah." He nodded, then, with a dismissive shrug, said, "Well, perhaps browsing in the shops this morning will serve to lift your spirits, which is the reason I wished to speak with you just now."

Tessa glanced back up.

Lord Penwyck walked around the desk and pulled open a drawer. "I received this missive from your father a few days back, and—"

"My *step*father," Tessa corrected him.

"Yes, well, your stepfather. At any rate, Senator Darby has authorized me to deposit a quite generous sum of money in a London bank expressly for your use whilst here." Penwyck unfolded the letter. "Per your stepfather's instructions, I am also to set aside an amount sufficient for your return passage to America."

Tessa's blue gaze became defiant. "I will not be returning to America, sir."

"Well, in the event that you change your mind, Miss Darby, I will be most happy to handle the arrangements for you." The earl dropped the packet onto the desk. "In the interim, you have leave to purchase whatever fripperies strike your fancy—new bonnets, gowns, ribbands, gloves, whatever." He cast an appraising look at Tessa, his eyes roaming from the top of her auburn head—today her long hair was pulled into a tight knot and pinned at the nape of her neck—down the length of the rather plain blue merino frock she wore.

"It appears," he muttered with some distaste, "that young ladies in America get themselves up a bit differently than do young ladies in London."

Tessa's eyes widened. Was he now telling her she looked *unpresentable?* On impulse, she decided to toy with him a bit. "I haven't the least notion what you mean, your lordship."

A sudden scowl of disapproval crossed his face. "It is entirely inappropriate for you to address me as 'your lordship,' Miss Darby," he stated firmly. "You are neither a servant nor a housemaid."

"And how would you have me address you, sir?"

The earl considered a moment, then said, "Since we share a common roof and are likely to bump into one another quite frequently in the weeks to come, you have my permission to use my given name, which is—"

"Penny darling?" Tessa parried innocently.

Penwyck's eyes narrowed. Then, upon noting the veriest hint of amusement playing about the young lady's lips, he smiled.

It was the first outright smile Tessa had beheld on the uppity man's face, and it completely transformed his features. He was, indeed, a handsome man.

"I daresay you are larking with me, Miss Darby," the earl exclaimed with high satisfaction. "That is quite a good sign."

Tessa stared at him as if dumbstruck. A good sign of what, she wondered, but chose not to question his oblique remark. To say truth, she didn't care a fig what he thought of her. She continued to gaze steadily at the irritating earl, who had turned his attention to straightening the few items on his desk—an inkstand, a crow-quill pen, three or four fresh sheets of cream-coloured paper, a ledger, and a lead pencil.

Presently, he glanced back up. "I have nothing further to take up with you this morning, Miss Darby. I merely wished you to know I had received your fath—your stepfather's missive and that your financial needs have been provided for. You may purchase whatever you like. Mother will help you select the appropriate items." He paused, but continued to gaze at her. Presently, his brow furrowed. "If you will forgive my boldness, Miss Darby, I was wondering, what is your age?"

"I am nineteen," Tessa replied warily.

"Ah, I had thought you were a good bit older."

Tessa's outrage came again to the fore. "Are you now saying I look *old?*" she cried.

A small smile played at his lips. "That was not my meaning at all, Miss Darby. Due to your . . . ah, serious nature, you simply seemed more mature than your years, that is all. The trace of humor I detected in you a bit ago was quite refreshing. If I may give you a bit of advice, Miss Darby"—he paused, then continued on—"what I mean to say is, if it is your desire to attract the notice of a gentleman whilst you are in London, with an eye to matrimony, you would do well to cultivate that lighter attitude. Honey will draw a good many more flies than vinegar."

Tessa's stomach churned. She fought the impulse to make another angry retort, and in the end was unable to entirely quell her tongue. "You presume a great deal, sir," she finally said.

He glanced up again, a fresh glint of interest shining from his dark eyes. "I presume since you have no intention of returning home to America to be married, you mean to find a husband here and live in England. Are you saying that is untrue?"

"Indeed, I am," Tessa replied smartly. "I have no intention of marrying . . . at least, I am in no hurry to do so."

Lord Penwyck's lips pursed as he reached absently to pick up the ledger from atop his desk. "Of course you will marry, Miss Darby. All young ladies marry. What would you do with your time otherwise?"

Tessa inhaled sharply. It was on the tip of her tongue to enlighten this thick-skulled man as to precisely what her true purpose was in coming to England, but another part of her mind told her there wasn't a shred of merit to the idea. The toplofty earl disliked her as much as she disliked him. He would simply poke fun at her ideals and limit her freedom to the point where she'd be unable to accomplish a thing.

In an effort to forestall further censure from him, she tried to soften her tone when she said, "I simply do not feel I am ready yet to become a wife or a mother," she replied, a good deal more contritely than she'd intended.

Fresh interest shone from Lord Penwyck's dark eyes. After a pause, he put down his ledger and, in a thoughtful tone, said, "I am beginning to understand what you are trying to tell me, Miss Darby." A considerably kinder look replaced the hardened gaze in his eyes. "If you will sit down, please." He gestured to a comfortable-looking leather chair opposite the desk.

Lord Penwyck watched with satisfaction as Miss Darby obediently perched on the edge of it. Perhaps he had been hasty in his judgment of the young lady. She was as English as he, but the truth was she had not been nearly so fortunate. Instead, she had had the distinct misfortune to be raised in a foreign country, a country populated with the dregs of every society in the world—criminals, half-wits, lowlifes, and naked savages wielding tomahawks and bows and arrows. The obvious trouble between Miss Darby and her stepfather explained why she was so vehemently opposed to returning to America.

He suddenly beheld the young lady in a new light. In truth, she was dashed courageous to come here alone. She did not need his censure, she needed his help.

"Miss Darby," he began magnanimously, "I see you are in a quandary. You have come to England with the idea of making a fresh start, and yet . . ." He stepped from behind the desk and casually seated himself on a corner of it, his expression now quite warm as he gazed down upon her. "It is perfectly clear to me you haven't the least notion what is expected of young ladies in England. Although I fear Mother may not be of the greatest help to you in that quarter—she raised only sons, you know—as it happens, I can be of service to you. I am well versed in the intricate rules and regulations that govern young ladies in London. I will be most happy to help you, Miss Darby, and to answer any questions you may have." He regarded her expectantly. "Have you any questions, Miss Darby?" he asked in a patient tone.

The blank look he beheld on Miss Darby's face puzzled him. He waited, and still she said nothing.

"Well, there are times," he began, his tone kindlier still, "when one is so very unaware of what one does not know that to formulate a question seems a formidable task."

He returned to stand before his desk again and withdrew a crisp sheet of cream-coloured linen paper from a drawer. "As it happens, I recently compiled a list of traits and qualities that I believe will be of benefit to you. I call it 'Acceptable Behaviours for a Young Lady.' " He glanced over the top of the page at her. "I will be most happy to read it to you."

Deciding that the deepening blue of her eyes signaled her eagerness to learn what she could from him, the earl drew in a long breath and proceeded to read.

"A proper young lady always conducts herself in a quiet and ladylike fashion. She is not given to loud talking or laughter. She is virtuous in both public and private, is of a cheerful disposition, and displays a generous sensibility—meaning she places the welfare of others before herself," he explained.

"She passes her time well and does not exhibit herself unseemly, nor does she"—he could not refrain from glancing up and pinning Miss Darby's round blue eyes with quite a stern look this time—"make a *spectacle* of herself." Although he did not wish to destroy the element of commonality that had sprung up between them by bringing up the unfortunate incident in the park yesterday, the infraction was still quite fresh in his mind.

His eyes scanned the balance of the list. "The remainder deals with items such as mastery of certain feminine skills—sewing, playing the pianoforte, dancing, the like—all of which I presume you to be adequately schooled in, Miss Darby. Some things are the same the world over, are they not?" He laid the page aside and fastened a look of genuine approval upon her. "I heartily commend you for your desire to improve yourself, Miss Darby. Have you any further questions?"

Tessa stared at him. At length, she murmured, "N-no, sir."

"Well, then." Penwyck drew in another breath. "I shall have my secretary make a copy of this list for you. I carry a copy with me at all times. Perhaps you might like to do the same." Again, he gazed at her with expectation.

"T-that will not be necessary, sir. I have quite a good memory."

"By jove!" There were times when the young lady's astuteness quite astonished him. "A good memory, eh?" He reached to dip the crow-quill pen into the inkwell and hurriedly scratched an item at the end of the list.

"I wonder I did not think of that myself, Miss Darby. A gentleman carries such a lot on his mind these days; it would be an invaluable help for a woman to assist him in such a fashion. Thank you, indeed." He blotted the notation, then dusted the page with powder.

Wearing a very pleased expression on his face, Lord Penwyck glanced up again. "I feel quite gratified after our talk, Miss Darby, but if you will excuse me now, I have an important business matter to attend to."

Tessa sprang at once to her feet. "Thank you, sir."

"In future, you must not hesitate to come to me whenever you find yourself in a quandary." He watched as the young lady made her way across the room, shyly casting one or two backward glances at him before she disappeared into the corridor.

She was an odd one, he decided. A curious mixture of pride and stubbornness, and yet there was a vulnerability about her that was . . . well, quite appealing.

And she was really very pretty, he allowed. He had never seen such creamy, flawless skin and shiny auburn hair. He trusted his mother would take her to a reputable salon to have those overlong tresses cut into a more becoming style. He supposed it was fortunate she did not wear her long hair in a single braid down the middle of her back as did the squaws of American Indians.

As Mr. Ashburn had noted yesterday in the park, Miss Darby also had a handsome figure—a full bosom and shapely hips—although she was a bit tall for Penwyck's taste. Still, her features were quite attractive. She had a beautifully shaped mouth and a small nose. Her most striking feature, however, were those incredible cobalt blue eyes, prettily framed by thick dark lashes and delicately arched eyebrows. Penwyck nodded thoughtfully to himself. Properly rigged out, she would be a very appealing young lady.

She merely required direction, that was all.

It had been unfair of him to judge her in the same way he did those young ladies whose names appeared on his list of prospective marriage partners. They had had the benefit of the best tutors in the land, whereas the unfortunate Miss Darby had not—although her table manners last night at dinner had been astonishingly correct. Even in her present state, Penwyck concluded, Miss Darby already knew enough to be able to conduct herself in a seemly fashion whilst taking tea with his mother's friends.

Still, Penwyck decided it best to keep a close watch on her, not with an eye to punishing or censuring her, but to guide and to help. After all, when all was said and done—meaning when Miss Darby had made a sensible match and was provided for—the effort would, indeed, be well worth it.

Six

Not even her stepfather carried a list of acceptable behaviours for a young lady in his coat pocket, Tessa fumed as she hurried away from the library. Lord Penwyck was surely the strangest man she'd ever met. That he thought she needed him to show her how to go on was the outside of enough!

Gaining her bedchamber, she decided her only course was to put as much distance as possible between herself and the contemptible man. Surely there were other gentlemen in London with as much or more influence in the House of Lords as 'Penny darling.' She would simply have to meet them.

One week later, Tessa was forced to admit meeting other English peers was considerably more difficult than she'd first imagined. Drawing on her gloves yet again, Tessa thought back over the week just behind her. Standing beside her in the foyer of the Penwyck town house, Lady Penwyck straightened her bonnet. Every afternoon for days now immediately following luncheon, Lady Penwyck had announced, "Today I should like to introduce you to . . ." followed by the name of yet another society matron who, according to Alice, was high *ton*.

High *ton,* indeed. Tessa grimaced. She was sick to death of smiling till her cheeks hurt and sipping insipid tea whilst listening to empty-headed matrons natter on about their silly doings.

A week ago, when she'd decided to quietly go along with all

of Lord and Lady Penwyck's plans, she'd done so with the hope of meeting influential gentlemen of the *ton.* What better way to meet them, she'd thought, than by taking tea in the gentlemen's very drawing rooms? But apparently politically influential London gentlemen had the good sense to spend as much time away from home as did 'Penny darling.'

On the other hand, Tessa had been presented to quite a number of London dandies, gentlemen in buckram-padded clothes who reeked of perfume and dressed outrageously in brightly coloured coats and pantaloons, their silk blouses adorned with rows and rows of frills, their waistcoats and stockings embroidered with colourful birds and flowers and even clocks!

At the end of her tether two days ago, Tessa had boldly approached Lady Penwyck with the idea of spending a few hours in the city on her own. A shocked expression on her face, Tessa's sponsor had at once vetoed the notion and strenuously cautioned Tessa against mentioning such a scandalous thing again, especially in front of Penny.

"It is considered quite unseemly for an unmarried girl to go about on her own, Tessa dear."

The following morning, however, when Tessa broached the subject again, this time demurely implying she'd like to do a bit of personal shopping, Lady Penwyck had relented and allowed Tessa, protected by Lady Penwyck's personal abigail and a brace of liveried footmen, to go up to the shops in Piccadilly alone.

"But only for a single hour, and only so long as Betsy remains faithfully by your side."

Thrilled to the core, Tessa had immensely enjoyed her hour of freedom. She'd even purchased a few items of feminine frippery, a new pair of slippers, and a pretty bonnet with a lacy green plume. But she'd also bought a current copy of *The London Times,* and was overjoyed to discover a lad hawking copies of William Cobbett's publication, the *Political Register,* on a street corner.

After reading and rereading every single word printed in Mr. Cobbett's newspaper, Tessa decided her only hope of getting *her* ideas for reform heard in this country was through the famed reform leader's weekly magazine, though how she might go about meeting the renowned William Cobbett she did not know.

Today, she had dutifully dressed for another exhausting round of morning calls, which were, of course, undertaken in the afternoon. She'd donned her new bonnet again today. To her immense chagrin, Lord Penwyck had commented upon it not ten minutes after she'd returned home with it yesterday. Tessa wasn't certain if the gentleman actually liked the new bonnet, or if by purchasing the feminine gewgaw she was acting more in accord with his notions of how a young lady ought to behave.

Standing quietly beside Lady Penwyck now, Tessa tried not to let her peevishness show as she patiently waited for the countess to muddle through a fairly straightforward set of instructions to Jenkins before they departed for the afternoon.

Her back toward the interior of the house, Tessa did not see Lord Penwyck approach the small party gathered in the foyer. But upon hearing the sound of his deep baritone as he greeted his mother, her blue eyes rolled skyward.

"Ah, there you are Mother. Miss Darby."

Of late, the mere sound of the gentleman's voice was enough to set Tessa's teeth on edge. Despite the great lengths she employed to avoid him, he seemed always to be on hand to monitor her every move, as if he feared she might commit some social blunder or unforgivable gaffe. The situation was fast becoming intolerable. The worst of it was Tessa had no idea how to remedy the matter. Since coming to England in search of her freedom, she'd been thwarted at every turn. Moreover, she hadn't heard or taken part in an intelligent conversation since her arrival. In truth, she was fast losing patience with everything and everyone.

At the moment, his high and mighty lordship was attempting to straighten out his mother's muddled instructions to the butler. Everything about Lady Penwyck was so akilter that Tessa wondered how the poor woman had gotten along thus far in life, let alone raised three sons without serious mishap.

Even now, as Penwyck spoke, his long fingers absently patted the lace collar of his mothers pelisse into place. Tessa watched the action from the corner of one eye. Presently, she ventured a peek at him.

As usual, 'Penny darling' was impeccably turned out. Today he had on a chocolate brown riding coat, a tastefully embroidered tan silk waistcoat, and matching dove-coloured breeches tucked into handsome brown leather top boots. The gleaming white neckcloth at his throat was twisted into a most impressive shape.

Tessa could not help marveling over the white froth, which was another peculiarity she'd discovered about the English. They deemed to attach a great deal of importance to a gentleman's neckcloth. Why, in the past week, Tessa had actually heard young ladies in drawing rooms discussing a new twist of the linen as if it were a Reynolds painting! So far as Tessa knew, American men simply wrapped the thing about their necks and were done with it.

When Lord Penwyck turned suddenly and his dark eyes met Tessa's, she quickly looked away.

"And how are you this fine afternoon, Miss Darby?" the earl inquired pleasantly.

Tessa thrust her nose in the air. "I am very well, thank you."

A few seconds elapsed. When Tessa heard him say nothing further, she risked another sidelong look at him. Noting his long gaze slowly raking up and down her body, her blue eyes widened with outrage. "Do I pass muster today, sir?" she snapped.

Lord Penwyck seemed a bit taken aback. Still, his expression was quite pleasant when he replied, "Indeed, you look quite presentable, Miss Darby. As I remarked yesterday, the new bonnet adds a certain *je ne sais quoi.*"

Tessa's nostrils flared. Why did he get her back up so?

Lord Penwyck appeared not to notice her displeasure. "I presume you ladies are off on another round of calls today." The smile on his handsome face was broad as he drew on his gloves, obviously also preparing to leave. "It quite astonishes me how the fairer sex never seem to tire of tea and a coze."

Tessa's eye widened. *Never tire of it!* Suddenly, she sputtered, "As it happens, sir, I do not drink tea."

Both the earl's and Lady Penwyck's head jerked up.

"Do not drink tea, Miss Darby?" Lord Penwyck regarded her quizzically. "Why, I seem to recall on a number of occasions you—"

"I used to drink it. I no longer do."

Oh, why had she blurted out such an absurdity? An article in the *Political Register* had reported that William Cobbett refused to drink tea. And since thus far Tessa had been unable to make any sort of political statement in England, she had decided the very least she could do was follow suit. But why did she feel compelled to inform the uppity earl about it?

A thoughtful look on his face, Lord Penwyck appeared to be trying to decide whether or not this infraction was serious enough to warrant censure. Tessa's ire grew as she watched his aristocratic jaw tighten.

Presently, in a measured tone, the earl said, "Would you mind telling me, Miss Darby, why you have suddenly decided not to take tea?"

"Because I—I . . ." Why did she let him irritate her so? The article had given no specific reason for Mr. Cobbett's abstinence, so, of course, she had no reason either. "I just do not," she replied tartly.

"Well." Penwyck glanced at his mother. "I suppose if you cannot tell me why, that will have to do, so long as refusing to take it in polite company does not cause comment."

"I know how to conduct myself in polite company!" Tessa sputtered.

"I am quite certain you do, Miss Darby." The earl's tone had become somewhat irritable. "Though allow me to suggest that when calling upon the *ton,* a more pleasant countenance would not be amiss. If you persist in displaying such a Friday face, Miss Darby, everyone is likely to conclude that, on the whole, your disposition is quite disagreeable. While both Mother and I know that to be untrue, other people do not."

Tessa's blue eyes flashed fire.

A fleeting moment of satisfaction washed over her when, beside her, Lady Penwyck put in, "Why, Penny dear, whatever are you talking about? Miss Darby has quite an agreeable disposition. Everyone says so!"

Lady Penwyck stared reproachfully at her son. "I cannot imagine what has got into you of late, sweetheart. You were never the critical sort. I daresay you have been appointed to far too many House committees. You simply must tell your friends they are overtaxing you."

Lord Penwyck's lips pursed with annoyance. "I am not the least bit overtaxed, Mother." He cocked one dark brow. "At least, not with my House duties."

Tessa sniffed piously.

"All the same," Lady Penwyck continued, "our Miss Darby is quite a delightful companion. She has a very pretty smile. Both ladies *and* gentlemen have remarked upon her beauty."

"Gentlemen?" One of Lord Penwyck's arched brows shot up again.

"Well, of course gentlemen. Not every young man spends all his days attending to House business. In the past week, Miss Darby has met a number of London's most eligible bachelors. She shall not want for partners at her come-out ball," she added with conviction. "Come along, Tessa, dear." She took Tessa's arm and, in a swish of silk, steered her charge through the front door and down the marble steps.

Lord Penwyck's footfalls crunched behind them as he strode across the yard to the curb where a footman waited with his employer's chestnut stallion.

"Penny dear!" Lady Penwyck called again to her son. "Will you be joining us for dinner?"

The busy earl did not glance up. "I have a long list of things to do today, Mother. Having dinner with you and Miss Darby is one of them."

As a footman handed Tessa into the carriage, a chuckling Lady Penwyck climbed in after her.

"I daresay Penny is growing more like his father every day. William also had a short memory. Why, neither one would get up in the morning if it weren't jotted down on a list somewhere." She settled herself on the plush velvet squabs opposite Tessa.

"I do hate to see him so overburdened with his House business, though I understand he is making quite a name for himself. Penny is quite a persuasive orator. Still," she fretted, "I do believe he is overtaxing himself."

Unable to summon an appropriate response, Tessa merely tried for a pleasant countenance. As Lady Penwyck continued to natter mindlessly on, Tessa directed a wistful gaze from the coach window. Watching Lord Penwyck spur his high-spirited mount into action, envy enveloped her as horse and rider galloped off down the street. She'd give her right arm to know precisely what House committees the eminent earl been appointed to. But she knew very well to ask him would only net her another setdown.

Over dinner last evening, when she'd brought up an item she'd read in the *Times* about a new bill being proposed to halt rising criminal activity in the city, he'd quickly informed her polite young ladies did not discuss such things.

"Are you saying I am wrong to want to stay abreast of what is taking place in my own country?" she'd boldly inquired.

Lady Penwyck had tittered nervously while her son retorted, "I am saying the state of the kingdom is in the capable hands of gentlemen lawmakers and there is no need for you or any other young lady to concern herself with such matters."

He'd given Tessa a hard, speaking look which clearly told her the conversation was at an end.

Tessa was jarred from her reverie now as the carriage lurched forward and Lady Penwyck addressed her.

"Did I mention the Montgomerys have just returned to Town?" Alice asked brightly. "Their daughter is about your age. Deirdre is a lovely girl, but her mother is quite overset by the fact that she"—her voice lowered—"didn't *take* last season. Gracie, that's Mrs. Montgomery, has her heart set on Deirdre's snagging a title. If you ask me, I believe she has her sights set a tad too high. The Montgomerys are not peers, you know. Still, Gracie is one of my dearest friends. She is so capable! Gracie quite takes my breath away. At any rate"—Lady Penwyck's voice took on a conspiratorial quality—"rumor has it Deirdre has acquired a suitor. No one knows who the gentleman is, but it stands to reason if the girl is trying to keep the young man's identity a secret, it is certain her parents would not be pleased."

With thoughts of the grandiose earl still swirling in Tessa's mind, she was experiencing great difficulty concentrating on Lady Penwyck's chatter.

"I think it high time Penny married, as well," Alice went on, "but I wouldn't dare issue an ultimatum to a young man. Penny will make the right choice when he is ready. I did tell you that Stephen, my youngest, is starting his nursery, did I not? The babe is due this coming autumn."

"Yes, you did mention that," Tessa murmured. To herself she added, *at least a dozen or more times.* "You must be quite a-tremor."

"I am thrilled to pieces." Lady Penwyck clapped a gloved hand to her breast. "I am so looking forward to holding a babe in my arms again." She reached to touch Tessa's knee. "I can assure you there is nothing like it! At any rate, I am certain you will find Deirdre to your liking. She is a good deal like you, dear. You are both a bit out of the common way."

Tessa was somewhat startled by the astuteness of the older woman's remark, but realized she simply hadn't the interest or inclination to inquire what prompted it. She only hoped Alice was right about Deirdre Montgomery. She certainly needed a friend right now.

An endless number of calls later, Tessa and Lady Penwyck were finally ushered into a lavishly appointed three-story red brick house that stood like a regal monument on the outskirts of London. The circular drive in front gave way to an immense marble staircase that led to a covered portico which seemed to encircle the entire house. The grand estate quite impressed Tessa.

Moments later, ensconced in an enormous carpeted withdrawing room, she was vastly pleased to discover she liked both Mrs. Montgomery and her daughter, Deirdre. The older woman's friendly manner reminded her of her own mother, and Deirdre, who was close on Tessa's age, also seemed quite genuine. Tessa thought the girl not the least bit puffed up or consumed by her own importance, as were so many other young ladies to whom she had been presented in drawing rooms all over London.

Moments after the Montgomery butler appeared in the large chamber carrying an impressive silver service, a uniformed maid silently served tall glasses of lemonade and small plates of tarts and biscuits to the four women clustered at one end of the cavernous chamber.

Tessa had taken only a few sips of the lemony brew when Lady Penwyck launched into a colorful recitation of the latest *on-dit* regarding the party thrown for Lord Byron and his sister at Almack's during which Augusta was ignored, and as soon as Byron arrived, the room emptied.

Tessa had heard the story numerous times already and so was vastly relieved when, only minutes into it, Deirdre leaned over to whisper in her ear.

"Shall we take our lemonade in the garden? I do so hate listening to gossip." The smile on her pretty face, and her words, quite pleased Tessa.

"I should like that very much!" she mouthed back, her blue eyes shining.

The girls quickly excused themselves and Tessa happily fell into step beside her new friend, who, not quite as tall as she, had soft brown curls and lively brown eyes.

Once outdoors, the girls settled themselves on a cushioned bench inside a picturesque gazebo situated amid a veritable carpet of bluebells and sunny yellow daffodils.

"It is quite lovely here," Tessa enthused, gazing about at the well-tended grounds. The air felt crisp and cool and smelled of fresh earth. "It rather reminds me of my home in America," she added softly, then worked to push down an unexpected sting of homesickness.

"Do you also live in the country?"

Tessa nodded tightly. Not wanting to enlarge upon the subject, she hurriedly changed it. "I like London very much."

"I expect England must seem quite different from America,"

Deirdre remarked. "I understand people are a good bit . . . *freer* there."

Tessa bit her lower lip to stem the sudden flood of emotion rising within her.

"Sometimes there seems nothing for it here but to go along," Deirdre added on a sigh.

Tessa nodded, still fighting for control. "I confess, I have quite had my fill of tea and—"

She was startled when her reply was interrupted by a burst of merry laughter spilling from Deirdre's lips.

"I knew you felt the same as me!" she cried. "I *abhor* tea parties! I refuse to waste away my afternoons sitting woodenly in a drawing room, sipping cup after cup of watery tea and listening to the same dull *on-dits* again and again! And if I ate every apricot tart served to me I should become as fat and ungainly as Prinny!"

Immense relief washed over Tessa, causing her also to laugh aloud. How wonderful to simply relax and be herself. "I confess I quite agree with you! I do like England—it is my *true* home, you know—but it has not been quite what I expected."

"I am quite looking forward to being married and on my own," Deirdre said. "Once I have my own home, I intend to host a weekly salon and invite only learned people to discuss literature and *important* topics."

Deirdre's words were like music to Tessa's ears. She had met a kindred spirit at last! "Lady Penwyck mentioned you had settled on a suitor."

"Indeed, I have. And he is not the sort of gentleman my parents would have chosen for me."

"Do tell me about him," Tessa urged, quite enchanted by her new friend.

Her brown eyes sparkling happily, Deirdre set her glass of lemonade onto a pretty japanned table. "His name is Jeffrey Randall, and he does not have a title. He has his own business," she declared with pride.

"How ever did you meet him?" Tessa asked, marveling to herself over the immense courage it must have taken for Deirdre to go against her parents' wishes. "And how do you manage to see him without your parents' knowledge?"

Over the next quarter hour, Deirdre told Tessa all about her young man, how her father—who busied himself acquiring dilapidated country estates and refurbishing them to sell—had hired Mr. Jeffrey Randall to manage his vast holdings. Because Deirdre's father spent a good deal of time abroad searching out properties to purchase, Deirdre had taken on the task of penning the weekly letters which kept Mr. Randall abreast of what needed to be attended to on each estate. Through the many letters the two had exchanged, a warm friendship had developed. When the young people finally met in London the previous year, the friendship quickly escalated to love.

"And your parents know nothing of it?" Tessa marveled.

Deirdre's soft brown curls shook. "They are quite fond of Jeffrey and trust him implicitly. Although," she grinned mischievously, "they do not yet know it is he I love."

Tessa was vastly intrigued by this real-life drama.

"Jeffrey is coming to dinner this evening," Deirdre went on. "He and Father will spend the bulk of the evening in the study, but afterward, when my parents have retired for the night and Jeffrey has gone . . . that is, when they *think* Jeffrey has gone . . ." She grinned impishly as her voice trailed off.

"You will rendezvous here in the garden!"

Deirdre's brown eyes twinkled merrily. "I am *so* pleased we met! I have longed for a friend to share my secret with."

Tessa's breath grew short. She, too, had longed for a friend to confide in. "There is something I have been *aching* to tell someone since I arrived in London," she began breathlessly.

"Tell me!" Deirdre cried, her cheeks flushed with joy.

In minutes, the words tumbling from her lips in a rush, Tessa told Deirdre all about her Cause, about her desire to get a reform bill on the floor of the House, how she'd secretly read William Cobbett's newspaper and learned about the revival of the Hampden Club meetings, how she longed to attend a meeting and speak with the famed reform leader herself.

"Apart from distributing those few copies of my lovely pamphlets in Hyde Park the day I first arrived in London, I have shown my literature to no one. I feel so dejected. I did so wish to do something to help." A long sigh of frustration escaped her.

Deirdre reached to squeeze her new friend's hand. "I gather Lady Penwyck also refused to listen," she said compassionately.

Tessa's chin began to tremble as she haltingly relayed the story of the spilled tea on her essay. "I worked so very hard choosing precisely the right words. I was quite proud of it."

"I am certain it was wonderful." Deirdre's tone was sincere. "I should have liked to read it."

Tessa blinked back the sudden droplets of moisture that were welling up in her eyes. "Lady Penwyck is a dear friend, but she . . . she appears unable to keep her thoughts fixed on any topic for any length. Even her home is a bit of a jumble."

Deirdre's merry laughter rang out again. "I recall the first time I visited there. The furniture is all askew."

A watery smile wavered across Tessa's face as she nodded vigorously. "I cannot imagine how she and my mother got on so well together. They are as different as chalk and cheese. Mother was quite precise, and Lady Penwyck is so caper-witted."

"People change," Deirdre said solemnly. "I used to believe my parents were right about everything. Now I know in order to be truly happy, I must follow my own heart."

Tessa's heart swelled with admiration for her newfound friend.

The two girls fell silent for a spell. At length, in a thoughtful tone, Deirdre said, "Jeffrey and I may be able to help you with your Cause, Tessa. May I call you Tessa?"

"Of course, you may, if I may call you Deirdre." Tessa's blue eyes glistened with warmth.

At that second, a servant appeared, summoning the girls to rejoin the ladies in the drawing room, where the women were discussing plans for Tessa's debut.

That night at dinner, the ball to be held in Tessa's honor was uppermost in Lady Penwyck's mind.

"I cannot say how relieved I am Gracie offered to host the *affaire,*" she enthused. "I should never be able to organize it, and the Montgomerys' ballroom is the envy of the *ton,* you know. Their lovely home formerly belonged to the Duke of Gravewater," she told Tessa. "Penny darling, you recall Deirdre's come-out last season, do you not? It was simply *nonpareiled."*

Lord Penwyck glanced up from his plate. "I take it you have introduced Miss Darby to all the right people, Mother."

"Indeed, I have. She has been presented to every last person on the list you gave me, sweetheart. I simply proceeded from top to bottom."

Tessa listened in silence as the pair of them discussed her *entrée* into society as if she were not present. Why did it not surprise her 'Penny darling' had been instrumental in her being carted all over town this past week? Did he hope the sooner she met and married someone, the sooner she would disappear? How very strenuously he must object to her being here.

"And what of the vouchers to Almack's?" he inquired, in a matter-of-fact tone. "Did a sufficient number of patronesses find nothing amiss?"

"Indeed." Alice smiled happily. "Lady Cowper, as well as the others, were quite impressed." She beamed at Tessa. "You recall meeting Lady Cowper, do you not, dear? She was the pretty dark-haired lady who engaged you in conversation that day at the Countess Lieven's home."

Tessa did recall meeting the attractive woman. It was at the same tea party where she'd met Madame de Staël's daughter. The two of them had had an agreeable conversation in French. Tessa recalled thinking it odd that the Countess Lieven seemed so very intent on probing into her past.

"I feared there might be a problem," Lady Penwyck was saying, "until dear Lady Sefton arrived. It was she who finally convinced the others. Of course, I reminded Lady Castlereagh who Tessa's mother was, and when she recalled having met Tessa's father and had actually attended their wedding, we were set." Lady Penwyck again addressed Tessa. "Did I not tell you every last one of us were a bit in love with your handsome papa, Captain Benning?" She laughed gaily. "He was the third son of a viscount," she told her son.

"Well." Lord Penwyck slanted an appraising look at Tessa. "It appears you have done very well for yourself, young lady."

Tessa hadn't the least idea what she had done to gain 'his lordship's' approval. Of course, she had heard many young ladies speak of Almack's with almost reverential awe, but as she had no desire to go there, she hadn't given the matter much thought. She pasted a set smile on her lips and turned again to the roast pigeon pie and buttered vegetables on her plate.

She bristled a moment later, however, when she heard Lord Penwyck mutter beneath his breath, "I had rather expected we would have to employ a battery of tutors in order to bring Miss Darby up to the mark."

"Penny!" his mother scolded. She flung an apologetic look at her protégée.

Tessa pretended not to notice. If she took umbrage at every insult the highborn gentleman leveled at her, she'd be in a perpetual snit. Meeting Deirdre Montgomery today and finding her quite to her liking had the added effect of helping Tessa put the disagreeable earl from mind. From the corner of her eye, she directed a disdainful look at him. He had set his knife and fork down and indicated to a nearby servant that he desired more coffee.

"I take it you and Mrs. Montgomery decided on a theme for Miss Darby's ball?" he inquired of his mother.

"Indeed, we did!" Lady Penwyck laughed gaily. "Of course, I knew we could not possibly come up with anything to rival the Egyptian theme at Deirdre's debut."

She turned a smile on Tessa. "Gracie had a replica of Cleopatra descending the Nile erected on the veranda. She imported miniature palm trees from Egypt and all the draperies were edged in a pretty zigzag braid. The effect was stunning!" She continued to gaze at Tessa. "Why don't you tell Penny what we decided for you, dear?"

Tessa nearly choked on the buttered asparagus in her mouth. She had no desire to tell the arrogant earl anything. Still, she managed to swallow convulsively and in a small voice said, "It is to be a wilderness theme to represent the New World."

"With Indians!" cried Lady Penwyck.

"Yes." Tessa nodded tightly.

"Well, not *real* Indians," Alice clarified, "but we shall darken the servants' skin and they shall all wear buckskin breeches and feather headdresses!" She cast another apologetic glance at Tessa. "Do forgive me for interrupting, dear. I confess I am all atwitter!"

Tessa's long lashes fluttered nervously. She was not looking forward to being presented to all of London at a silly soiree. In addition, something else was beginning to nag at her, something she must very soon reveal to Lord and Lady Penwyck, something one or both would find reprehensible.

"Go on, dear," Lady Penwyck urged.

Tessa's stomach churned. "Mrs. Montgomery is to have an artist paint a mural of Christopher Columbus and the Nina, the Pinta, and the Santa Maria—"

"Which is why we had to tell Tessa and Deirdre the plan after all," interjected Lady Penwyck. "Neither Gracie nor I could recall the names of all the little boats, so we sent for Tessa to come and tell us! I was certain she would know."

Lord Penwyck cocked a brow and gazed with renewed interest at Tessa. "Indeed."

Tessa thought she detected a glimmer of something akin to respect in the earl's dark eyes, but she couldn't be certain. It could have been merely a reflection from one of the many silver serving dishes littering the table.

"Well, it appears you ladies have the matter of Miss Darby's debut well in hand. If you will excuse me?" He placed his napkin beside his plate and made as if to rise from the table.

"Penny dear, you mustn't go yet!" his mother cried. "We have not decided on a date for the ball. I wished to consult with you first. You shall be required to lead Tessa out for the first set, you know."

Lead her out? Tessa's heart plunged to her feet and she felt her breath desert her. Apparently she would be obliged to reveal her secret sooner than she thought.

"Which do you prefer, dear?" Lady Penwyck inquired of

Tessa. "A quadrille, or perhaps a dance that is popular in America?"

A blinding panic gripped Tessa.

How was she to tell them *she did not know how to dance?*

Seven

"Is something the trouble, Miss Darby?" Tessa felt Lord Penwyck's penetrating gaze upon her. "You suddenly seem quite pale."

"You do look a bit ashen," Lady Penwyck chimed in. "You are not taking ill, are you, Tessa dear?" Concern was as evident in her tone as it was missing from her son's. "Oh, my," she fretted, "I do hope we shall not have to postpone the—"

"I have not taken ill, Lady Penwyck," Tessa managed to say. "I . . . I . . ." She *had* to tell them. "I do not know how to dance," she blurted out abruptly. She lowered her lashes, fully expecting Lord Penwyck to severely chastise her for this shocking lapse in her education.

"So." The gentleman's lips pursed. "There it is."

"Well, what of it?" Lady Penwyck exclaimed. "We shall simply hire a dance master!"

"No, we shall not hire a dance master," Lord Penwyck flatly contradicted his mother.

"But why ever not, Penny dear? Tessa must learn to dance. There would be no point in throwing a ball if she is not to dance. What would everyone think?"

"That is precisely my point, Mother. Once it is known Miss Darby does not dance, all manner of speculation regarding the absence of other important feminine accomplishments will arise, which, you may rest assured, will destroy all chances of her making a proper match. No," he stated quite emphatically, "we shall *not* hire a dance master."

"Then what?" his mother asked, quite at a loss.

Lord Penwyck cleared his throat. "I shall teach Miss Darby to dance."

Tessa's head jerked up, her blue eyes wide with alarm.

Across from her at the table, Alice cried, "What a perfectly splendid idea!" She clapped her hands together with glee. "No one shall be the wiser and Tessa will most certainly make a brilliant match. Penny is an excellent dancer, Tessa dear."

Tessa squirmed in her chair. No doubt he was, but that did not mean she wished him to teach her.

"Shall we begin tonight?" Lady Penwyck asked brightly.

Tessa was about to protest when Lord Penwyck replied solemnly, "I have a previous engagement tonight, Mother. We shall begin tomorrow evening following dinner."

Tessa did not sleep at all well that night. When she still felt out of sorts the following afternoon, she toyed with the idea of pleading a megrim in order to avoid accompanying Lady Penwyck on her daily grind of calls and all the other scheduled activities. But not being one to give way to weakness, she refused to do so now. No doubt her failure to show up for the dance lesson tonight would simply provide the trussed-up earl with further reason to dislike her.

When the dreaded hour was finally upon her, Tessa's megrim was no longer a figment of her imagination. In addition, she was plagued with a churning stomach and clammy palms. At least proper decorum, in the form of clean white gloves, allowed her to disguise the latter. Otherwise she was certain 'his eminent lordship' would berate her for that, as well.

As Lord Penwyck rose from the table at the close of dinner, he said, "I have asked a good friend of mine, Mr. Lowell Ashburn, to provide the music for us tonight."

He and the ladies exited the dining chamber and moved down the corridor.

Tessa wasn't certain where the dance lesson was to take place. When the three of them reached the stairwell and the earl and his mother trooped upward, Tessa wordlessly followed suit.

"Our ballroom is quite small," Lady Penwyck remarked.

"Our ballroom is adequate," the earl stated firmly.

Just then, the stilted conversation on the stairwell was interrupted by the sound of the heavy brass door knocker rap-rap-rapping.

"That will be Ashburn," Penwyck said. "We will join you ladies shortly. No doubt Ash will want a brandy before we begin." He cast an unreadable gaze at Tessa. "As do I."

Lord Penwyck turned to retrace his steps back to the ground floor. Minutes later, Lady Penwyck showed Tessa into a long narrow room that extended across the entire front of the house on the third floor.

Because the chamber was less than half the size of the Montgomerys' cavernous withdrawing room, Tessa surmised that the Montgomery ballroom must be stupendous. She glanced about at the admittedly small chamber. A row of cane-bottomed chairs and benches lined three of the four walls. Long mullioned windows, partially covered by heavy green velvet draperies, took up the fourth. At one end of the long room stood a small square pianoforte. It suddenly occurred to Tessa that, compared with the rest of the house, this chamber looked positively orderly. The thought brought a nervous titter to her lips.

She was still ruminating on the silly subject when the sound of approaching footfalls from the corridor reached her ears. The pair of gentlemen entered the room and Tessa waited quietly as Lady Penwyck and Mr. Ashburn exchanged greetings. The stockily built, blond-haired man presented a stark contrast to his tall, dark-haired companion, both in looks and in that he seemed quite agreeable. The pleasant smile on Mr. Ashburn's lips as the earl introduced them put Tessa more at ease than she'd felt all day.

"Ash has agreed not to reveal a word of this . . . ah . . . business to anyone," Lord Penwyck remarked.

Tessa wasn't entirely certain to whom the earl was speaking—

not that it mattered. Lady Penwyck was already nattering away at Mr. Ashburn as he and Lord Penwyck headed toward the pretty little pianoforte. Still talking nonstop, Lady Penwyck slipped onto a nearby chair as the earl handed several pages of sheet music to his friend.

Fearing the humiliation of her life was fast upon her, Tessa felt her breath grow short as she watched Mr. Ashburn leaf through the music.

"What shall we begin with?" he asked without looking up.

"I expect we will need to start with the basics," Lord Penwyck replied. "The minuet—"

"Oh, I quite recall the first time I danced the minuet," Lady Penwyck exclaimed. "I was fifteen and the young man was a—"

"Mother." Lord Penwyck's firm voice halted his mother's no doubt convoluted tale. He turned and advanced to Tessa's side. "The minuet is seldom performed these days, Miss Darby, but the steps form the basis of many of today's modern dances."

As he drew closer to her side, he reached to take her hand.

Her heart pounding wildly in her ears, Tessa instinctively stepped backward.

Lord Penwyck advanced another step forward, and just as Tessa was about to move a corresponding step away from him, he bellowed, "Miss Darby!"

Tessa's blue eyes became quite large and round as a deafening silence filled the room.

"Lesson number one, Miss Darby. Do not back away when a gentleman approaches you for a dance. It not only makes for a poor impression, it makes dancing together impossible!"

"I was not backing away," Tessa snapped. "I was"—she flicked a glance over one shoulder—"um—m-moving toward the center of the floor where we might have more space to maneuver about," she concluded in quite a strong tone, considering her supreme agitation.

"I see. Well, in that case, I beg your pardon."

Tessa forced her body to remain stationary as Lord Penwyck—looking sinfully handsome tonight in a maroon coat, mauve satin waistcoat, and distractingly tight gray woolen trousers—reached to place a large hand at her back and guide her to the center of the floor. Once there, he turned to face her.

"The patterns that comprise the minuet, Miss Darby, are—"

Tessa did not hear him. The only thing she was fully aware of now was the lingering warmth at her back where his hand had been. It was as if the flesh beneath the thin fabric of her gown was actually *tingling.*

"—thusly," Lord Penwyck concluded. He reached to grasp one of Tessa's gloved hands in his and, holding her arm aloft, formed an arc of sorts. He extended one long leg slightly apart from the other, the toe of his black evening pump at a point. "You will position yourself thusly, Miss Darby," he instructed.

Tessa tentatively followed suit.

"The opposite foot, Miss Darby," Penwyck said patiently. "Yes, that's it. Ash?" His glance toward the gentleman at the pianoforte signaled the music to begin.

"Now, follow my lead through the first pattern."

First pattern? Tessa started. That meant there were more patterns to follow, and she hadn't the least notion how to perform this one.

She did her very best, but since she hadn't heard a single word Lord Penwyck had said, her very best proved deplorably wide of the mark. Before the music halted, she'd trod upon Lord Penwyck's shiny black toes more times than either of them could count.

"Oops . . . I am so sorry, sir."

"Quite all right, Miss Darby. Carry on. To the left. *Your* left."

"Oh! Do forgive me."

"Now, the right. Under. Pass to the side. The *other* side. Yes, that's it."

"Oh, dear. I fear I'm not at all—"

"Penny dear." Lady Penwyck spoke over the music, her voice bringing the melodic sounds to a halt. "Perhaps we should engage a—"

"Let us try once again, Miss Darby."

Tessa had never felt so mortified in all her life. She desperately wished she'd listened to her mother when she had pleaded with Tessa to attend dance classes, but it had been the winter her mother had become ill and Tessa had been in no humor to learn how to dance.

She felt her cheeks flaming now and her palms, beneath their soft kid covering, were swimming with perspiration. She hadn't expected Lord Penwyck's nearness to befuddle her quite so thoroughly. She was behaving quite foolishly indeed.

"Perhaps if I were to"—she flung a helpless look at Mr. Ashburn seated before the piano, a friendly smile upon his lips—"try the dance with Mr. Ashburn as my partner and you instructing us?"

Hearing Tessa's proposal, Ash sprang at once to his feet. "Capital idea!"

"Ash!" The single word from Lord Penwyck's lips silenced his friend. "We shall try it again, Miss Darby. The pattern is quite simple. An arc, step forward, step back—I *know* you can do that," he chided. "Step once to the side, then to the other side, then follow through. Repeat the sequence three times. There, you see? Quite simple."

Tessa inhaled an uneven breath and, with effort, managed to ignore the distracting sensations inspired by the attractive gentleman standing so very near her. She would not be made to look the fool. She would not!

A half hour later, Tessa was gliding with ease through not only the first pattern of the dance, but three others, as well.

"And there it is," Lord Penwyck declared.

Spontaneous applause erupted from both Lady Penwyck and Mr. Ashburn.

"Miss Darby is quite a quick study, after all!" Mr. Ashburn enthused as he approached the pair still clasping hands on the dance floor.

"You were splendid!" cried Lady Penwyck as she, too, rushed forward.

Relief flooded Tessa as she smiled prettily at her appreciative onlookers. "I did start off rather poorly," she began. Then, with a start, she realized Lord Penwyck was still holding her hand tightly in his. She cast an upward glance at him . . . and noted a quite peculiar look upon his handsome face.

Miss Darby was indeed a quick study. Astonishingly quick! After she'd blundered her way through the first set, Penwyck had had serious doubts about the venture, but suddenly she'd rallied and all he'd had to do was *tell* her the sequence of steps he'd jotted down on a list of basic patterns to teach her and she performed them to perfection.

In addition, she looked quite lovely tonight. She had on a pretty blue and melon striped gown, the neck and sleeves trimmed in blond lace. On a number of occasions as they'd danced, the low-cut bodice revealed to his eyes a good bit of soft ivory flesh. He'd had to drag his gaze away from the alluring sight more than once lest the rise and fall of her ample bosom cause him to forget what he was about.

Her shiny auburn hair was drawn back from her flushed face in an upswept style with a few wispy tendrils dangling before her ears. And those shining blue eyes . . . Penwyck inhaled sharply. It would be quite easy for a gentleman to become lost in . . .

"What do you say, Penwyck?"

The sound of Mr. Ashburn's voice cut through Penwyck's reverie. "Beg pardon, Ash. You were saying?"

"I asked if you'd like to join me at the club for a brandy."

"Ah . . . ummm." Penwyck flung a wild glance at Miss Darby and then at his mother. "Perhaps we might *all* have a brandy. Here," he suggested magnanimously. "You will join us, won't you, Mother?"

"Why, Penny dear, I would—"

"Miss Darby?" He turned an open gaze on the upturned face of the attractive young lady standing quietly by his side.

Although the kind invitation caught Tessa completely off guard, she had to admit to enjoying the pleasurable half hour spent in the drawing room with Lord Penwyck, his mother, and Mr. Ashburn. The good-natured Mr. Ashburn was quite likable, indeed. His humorous remarks and easy laughter kept them all entertained.

By the end of that week, Tessa had received several more dance lessons from the earl and felt proficient enough at every dance on the list he'd drawn up for her—the quadrille, the lancers, and one or two popular country dances—to actually perform them in public with partners other than her esteemed instructor. Adjourning to the drawing room for refreshments afterward became habitual with the foursome and, Tessa noted, seemed to have the additional effect of mellowing the cold-hearted earl. To Tessa's immense astonishment, he actually complimented her on more than one occasion that week.

"You look very nice this evening, Miss Darby," he said once, his dark eyes almost warm as he gazed down upon her.

Another time he remarked on her quickness at picking up the steps to the quadrille. So unaccustomed was she to hearing appreciative remarks from a man that Tessa couldn't help feeling gratified to have earned the least bit of praise from Lord Penwyck. His change of attitude toward her was almost enough to make her wonder if she hadn't misjudged the highborn gentleman at the outset.

Each day that week, Lady Penwyck kept Tessa busy with a dizzying round of calls, fittings for new gowns, and shopping for accessories and other items necessary to complete her coming-out toilette. Although she scarcely had a moment to think her own thoughts, her burning desire to meet William Cobbett and solicit his advice on forwarding her Cause was still never far from mind.

One morning at breakfast, a week before Tessa's come-out ball, Lady Penwyck announced they had all been invited to a small dinner party to be held that evening at the home of Lord and Lady Chalmers and she very much wished to attend.

"But Miss Darby is not yet out, Mother," Lord Penwyck protested quietly. "I do not think it entirely proper that she attend any society functions just yet." He flicked a look at Tessa. "Perhaps an additional dance lesson might be—"

"But, Penny, I see no harm in it. The Chalmers are leaving for Paris at week's end. They will be unable to attend Tessa's come-out ball and they are quite atremor to meet her." Lady Penwyck directed an affectionate smile at her protégée. "Tessa has favourably impressed a goodly number of our friends. I predict quite a brilliant career for her."

One of Lord Penwyck's dark brows cocked. "Very well. You may send word to the Chalmers that we shall all be present this evening."

Tessa experienced a slight twinge of annoyance following the earl's declaration. To be honest, she would have much preferred another dance lesson tonight, but apparently the time had come for her to test her wings in society and, as usual, she had no say in the matter.

She cast a somewhat shy glance at the earl. Though she could scarcely believe it herself, she had to admit to being immensely grateful he would be along. She had become quite accustomed to his strong, confident air and believed his presence would go a long way toward easing her apprehension tonight.

Tessa chose the favourite of her new gowns to wear that evening, a lovely lavender satin slip with a matching silk overdress, lavishly trimmed in delicate silver lace. Lady Penwyck sent her own dresser up to assist Tessa and to do up her hair in a fashionable new style. Her thick auburn tresses were piled into a mass of curls atop her head and a soft feathery plume nestled amongst them.

Taking one last peek at her transformed image in the looking glass, Tessa astonished herself when she realized the thought uppermost in her mind was whether or not Lord Penwyck would think she looked pretty.

Eight

Rubbish! She didn't care a fig what he thought. She wished only to have the evening got behind her and to be allowed to carry on with her own plans. Surely once she was *truly* out, she would be allowed more freedom to go about on her own. She had heard many young ladies speak of shopping or making calls or even riding in the park with only an abigail or footman in tow.

Indeed, she looked forward to that day.

Squaring her shoulders, Tessa departed her bedchamber and made her way to the stairwell. Halfway down the steps, she became aware of Lord Penwyck standing quietly in the foyer, the familiar penetrating look in his dark eyes as he intently assessed her.

An unexpected pang of anxiety shot through Tessa. Tonight was her first real foray into London society, and suddenly she realized Lord Penwyck was right on yet another score: She hadn't the least notion how to go on.

Because the Darbys had resided year-round in the country, Tessa had had very little occasion to venture out in society. Her mother had often accompanied her stepfather to Philadelphia or to Boston, and upon arriving home took great delight in telling Tessa all about the lavish dinner parties and glittering balls they'd attended, but Tessa had had no firsthand experience. It alarmed her now to suddenly feel at such a great loss—and to realize the only person she had to rely on was Lord Penwyck.

Reaching the bottom of the steps, she half hoped he would

deliver a quick lecture on proper decorum before they set out tonight. She risked a somewhat apprehensive peek up at him and was startled to find the granite-hard expression in his dark brown eyes considerably softened.

"You look positively enchanting, Miss Darby," he murmured.

A nervous smile flickered across Tessa's lips. "T-thank you, sir." She caught herself before she could blurt out how anxious she felt.

Instead, she tilted her chin up proudly and turned her face away, but not before noticing how very attractive he looked tonight in his elegant evening attire. Nipped in at the waist, his black cutaway coat accentuated the broadness of his shoulders and his narrow hips. He had on a charcoal-gray silk waistcoat, form-fitting black trousers, and shiny black evening pumps. He looked splendid.

She was glad when Lady Penwyck at once appeared in the foyer. The countess's nonstop chatter carried the three of them through the front door, down the marble steps, and into the high-sprung carriage that awaited them at the curb.

It was but a short drive to Lord and Lady Chalmers fashionable town house in nearby Berkeley Square. The four-story building was ablaze with light. Once inside, a fraction of Tessa's apprehension dissolved when she discovered that during the past fortnight, on the endless round of calls she'd made with Lady Penwyck, she'd already been presented to nearly all of the ladies present here tonight.

They each greeted her quite pleasantly, most remarking on how pretty she looked. Tessa found it effortless to truthfully return the compliments, for she'd never beheld such beautiful gowns and exquisite jewels in all her life. Everyone, men and women alike looked smashing.

By the time the guests assembled in the dining chamber for dinner, Tessa felt veritably relaxed. Flanking her at the table were a pair of contrasting gentlemen; both in age and looks. On her left sat a young gentleman, who, judging from his colourful dress and the fact that his cheeks were brightly rouged, Tessa determined to be a bit too dandified for her taste. To her right, however, sat an elderly gentleman named Lord Dickerson, whose warm gray eyes and unassuming manner reminded Tessa of one of her stepfather's longtime friends, Mr. Thomas Jefferson.

Although the former president of the United States shared in Senator Darby's firm belief that women shouldn't wrinkle their brows with politics, Tessa had always liked the kindly old man. Tonight she found herself warming also to the gentle Lord Dickerson.

His faded gray eyes twinkled as he addressed Tessa over a glass of blood-red Madeira. "I understand you hail from America, Miss Darby."

"Indeed, I grew up abroad, sir, although I was born right here in London." Tessa reached for her delicate long-stemmed glass and took a small sip of the fruity wine.

"Lived in London most of my life," Lord Dickerson replied, a bit thoughtfully. "City ain't been the same since the war."

"Which war would that be, sir?"

Lord Dickerson leveled an interested gaze at his pretty young companion. "Well," he laughed, "I guess it don't matter which one. War always changes things, for better or worse." He set his wine glass down and dipped his spoon into the plate of cold turtle soup that had just been placed before him.

Tessa also tasted the soup. "I have never heard war likened to marriage before, sir," she replied with a charming smile.

"Beg pardon?" The old gentleman looked up.

"You said 'for better or worse.' Is that not a phrase one repeats in one's wedding vows?" Tessa asked innocently.

When Lord Dickerson's watery eyes held her gaze for quite a length, she felt herself colour. Had she inadvertently said something improper? Relief washed over her when the old gentleman suddenly laughed aloud.

"Indeed it is, Miss Darby. You are quite right. In many ways, marriage can be likened to war." He chuckled.

Tessa gazed almost shyly at him from beneath long lashes. It was an odd conversation, but she was heartily enjoying it. To her left, she could hear the dandy discussing his colourful wardrobe with a simpering young lady seated to his other side. She quickly cast about for a way to draw Lord Dickerson out further. If she were lucky, she might learn something important from him.

"Are you . . ." She pondered how best to phrase the question even as she was speaking. "As a gentleman"—she started afresh—"I expect you have had ample opportunity to influence the state of things in this country."

Lord Dickerson's blue-veined forehead puckered. "Don't quite take your meaning, Miss Darby," he said.

"Parliament, sir. Surely you have had occasion to . . ." She grew a trifle flustered as echoes of Lord Penwyck's stern warnings against broaching such topics grew louder in her head. She flung a quick glance about the crowded table and spotted him sitting quite a distance from her, too far away to overhear anything she might say. "Do you not have a seat in the House of Lords, sir?"

"Are you inquiring after my politics, Miss Darby?"

Tessa's blue eyes widened as she nodded eagerly.

The old man's white head shook as if he couldn't quite fathom what he'd just heard. "I daresay you are quite unlike any young lady I have ever met before, Miss Darby. Must be your American upbringing." His thin lips twitched as he continued to gaze at her with interest. Presently, he said, "Whig. Reform. I may be an old man, but it is quite plain to me the old ways ain't serving England in the same way they once did."

His attention was momentarily diverted as a servant stepped forward to whisk away their soup plates and replace them with sparkling clean dinnerware. Once their plates had been filled with piping hot servings of buttered lobster and compote of crab and asparagus, Lord Dickerson turned again to Tessa.

"Tell me, Miss Darby, are most young ladies in America as interested in the law as you are?"

Tessa turned a pleasant smile on the elderly gentleman. "My stepfather is a United States senator. I grew up listening to political debates. You rather remind me of one of my father's close friends, Mr. Thomas Jefferson."

"Ah." The tone of Lord Dickerson's voice told Tessa the comparison pleased him. "I understand Mr. Jefferson authored the

American Constitution." He grinned. "Of course, that took place long before you were born. Did your stepfather take part in the Continental Congress?"

"Yes." Tessa nodded tightly. "Both he and his father attended." She chewed up a bite of the lobster in silence, then turned again to Lord Dickerson. "Do you happen to be familiar with the writings of Thomas Paine, sir?"

Lord Dickerson's white head jerked up again. "Indeed, I am. Paine was an Englishman. Brilliant young man, despite being a commoner." His voice lowered. "Make no mistake, the boy's radical notions were none too popular in England at the time. However, he made quite a name for himself in America."

Tessa's breath grew short with excitement. How serendipitous to be placed next to this gentleman whose opinions so closely aligned with hers. "I have read everything Mr. Paine wrote," she enthused. "His writings are very popular in America." She longed to broach the topic so dear to her heart, but not here. Perhaps later, in some secluded spot, she and Lord Dickerson might continue their talk uninterrupted.

Her blue eyes wide, Tessa leaned close to the older man's ear. "There is something I would very much like to discuss with you, sir," she whispered breathlessly, "but I fear I mustn't bring up the subject here."

He turned and nodded knowingly at Tessa. She decided the speaking look in his eyes meant he understood perfectly.

"May I suggest a stroll in the garden following dinner, Miss Darby? Or perhaps a coze in the library, if you prefer."

"The library would be lovely," Tessa murmured. A flush of scarlet warmed her cheeks. She was enormously pleased she had come to the dinner party tonight!

Although he was managing to keep up with several conversations at once, Lord Penwyck was also keenly aware of his mother's protégée, Miss Tessa Darby, seated across the table and down a bit from him.

Earlier that day, after it had been decided they would all attend the dinner party tonight, he had given some thought to drawing her aside and inquiring if she had any questions regarding the proprieties or social protocol observed at formal gatherings. After further thought, he'd dismissed the notion. In the past week, Miss Darby's eagerness to please him in learning how to dance, coupled with the impeccable manners she displayed toward himself and Ash had caused him to rethink his initial assessment of her.

Miss Darby was a quite well-mannered young lady. Apparently her daily exposure to other young ladies in Town and to his mother and her friends had taught her a great deal. Despite the slight tinge of an American accent that, Penwyck allowed, was hardly noticeable once one grew accustomed to it and could even be thought charming, she had easily gained the approval of the haughty Countess Lieven and Princess Esterhazy, who in Penwyck's estimation possessed a superior knowledge of etiquette. This very evening, Penwyck had observed Miss Darby conversing quite splendidly with both those patronesses and other fearsome lionesses of the *ton*. It was the first time he'd had the opportunity to watch the young lady in a social situation, and he confessed to being quite pleased with her performance.

There was just one minor thing he'd noted tonight at dinner that he must remember to caution her against. Thus far during the meal, she had completely ignored Mr. Templeton, seated to her left, and was instead monopolizing the elderly Lord Dickerson. The ripple effect of that *faux pas* was that he was ignoring the other of his dinner companions, who was consequently forced to remain silent, or monopolize one of hers, and so on. No doubt the old earl was highly enjoying the attention from the attractive Miss Darby, but to show favouritism with one or another of one's dinner companions was not the done thing. Miss Darby *must* be made aware of the rules on that head.

Penwyck kept a sharp eye on his charge as the meal wound down. He lost track of her for close on half an hour when the ladies repaired to the drawing room for coffee and the gentlemen lingered at table for brandy and a smoke. But because she was in the company of his mother, it did not occur to him anything might go awry. Not even Lord Dickerson's leaving the table ahead of the other gentlemen and disappearing into the corridor gave Penwyck pause. However, upon returning to the drawing room, and finding neither Miss Darby nor Lord Dickerson there set off an alarm bell in Penwyck's head.

The layout of the Chalmers's lovely home, although somewhat larger than Penwyck's, was a good deal like every other town house in London, with the public rooms on the ground floor, the private and family rooms on the floors above, a ballroom—if there was one—above that, the servants' quarters in the attic, the kitchen and pantry below ground, and a small knot garden in the rear.

Penwyck began his search for the errant Miss Darby and her wily companion—for that is how he viewed the experienced older man, who most certainly knew by now the young lady he'd lured away from the others was as innocent as a schoolgirl—in the small garden behind the house.

Finding a few of the Chalmers's guests taking the air, but Miss Darby and the rakish old earl not amongst them, he reentered the house and proceeded boldly into every room he came upon. A sitting room just inside the rear door proved empty, as did a secluded little music room adjacent to it. Across the corridor, he flung open the door of a dimly lit chamber where books lined the walls and a low-burning fire sputtered in the hearth. Hearing a murmur of voices from inside, Penwyck charged in.

"Ahem!" he bellowed, by way of announcing his presence.

Two heads, in close proximity to one another—one topped with shiny auburn curls, the other a thinning, whitish thatch—popped round the side of a free-standing revolving bookcase.

"Miss Darby!" Lord Penwyck's eyes narrowed as he advanced with great haste toward the pair. "And Lord Dickerson!" His tone was decidedly accusatory, the scowl of displeasure on his face clearly directed at the elderly man.

"Evening, Penwyck," the older gentleman said. "Miss Darby and I were just—"

Penwyck's black eyes narrowed in anger. "I will receive you tomorrow, Dickerson. You will kindly take your leave now."

The elderly gentleman bent a polite nod. "Very well, Penwyck." He flung an apologetic glance at Tessa. "Good evening, my dear."

Saying nothing further, Lord Dickerson crossed the room and closed the door gently behind him.

Her mouth agape, Tessa stared up at Lord Penwyck. "How dare you barge in here and insult that dear old man?"

Penwyck's chest heaved. "We will be leaving now, Miss Darby." He made a move as if to take her arm and guide her to the door.

But Tessa jerked angrily from his grasp. "You are not my guardian, Lord Penwyck! Lord Dickerson and I were merely discussing—"

"Whatever you and Dickerson were discussing does not signify, Miss Darby. What does signify is that Lord Dickerson has knowingly succeeded in compromising your virtue."

Tessa stared at the misguided earl with disbelief. "That is rubbish and well you know it. My virtue was perfectly safe just now. Why, that . . . that poor old man is incapable of . . . of . . ."

"No man is *in*capable of, Miss Darby."

Tessa coloured. "Well, at any rate, the . . . the fact remains we were simply talking about . . ." She paused, her promise to abandon her political interests whilst residing with the earl's family echoing loudly in her head. She clamped her lips shut and tilted her chin up self-righteously. "Well, I don't suppose what we were talking about signifies, either, does it?"

"You will have plenty of time for talk *afterward,* Miss Darby."

Tessa looked a question at the tight-lipped earl.

"You could do worse," he said on a resigned breath.

"Excuse me?" Tessa murmured.

"Dickerson is unmarried at present," Penwyck stated matter-of-factly. "And he has no heir—at least, not a legitimate one. I expect you will be required to provide one. Thereafter, you will be free to—"

"I am free now!" Tessa cried, beginning to take the gentleman's meaning, but refusing to believe he could be serious. "I have no intention of marrying Lord Dicke—"

"You have no choice, Miss Darby," Penwyck stated flatly, "just as I will have no choice but to accept his suit on your behalf when he calls tomorrow."

Tessa gasped. "You cannot be serious!" A moment later, her flashing blue eyes narrowed. "If you are trying to scare me, Lord Penwyck, it will not work. I am not the least bit frightened." She folded her arms beneath her bosom and glared stubbornly at him.

"I am not trying to frighten you, Miss Darby. I am merely apprising you of the facts. I've no doubt Lord Dickerson is, even now, consulting with his man of business. The financial arrangements alone will require a good bit of straightening out."

"I will not marry that elderly man. The very idea is unthinkable! You cannot *make* me marry him!"

She almost added, *can you?* but caught herself. She was not conversing with her stepfather, after all! The powerful Senator Darby eventually got his way, but Tessa was no longer under his thumb and she would not acquiesce to this absurdity without putting up the fight of her life.

She moved to angrily skirt past the misguided earl, but he was too quick for her. Catching her wrist in his hand, he forced her to a standstill. In her struggle to escape, Tessa became aware of his strong forearm pressed firmly against her breasts. She could feel her cheeks begin to burn as a scorching ripple of *something* raced through her veins.

"You are hurting me!" she ground out.

Penwyck held fast. Miss Darby's sudden show of temper and the glittering blue fire in her eyes both angered and aroused him. The white-hot passion rising within him was unlike anything he'd ever felt before. Her willfulness made him want to tame her, to savagely kiss her into submission and then to . . . to . . . oh, what the deuce? Her reputation was already in shreds. He could take her right here and no one would be the wiser.

But he was a gentleman. No amount of passion would cause

him to take advantage of a lady, no matter how badly he—or she—might wish it. He pinned the obstinate young lady with a scalding hot gaze. Something in her fiery blue eyes told him she wished it every bit as much as he.

He slowly released his tight grip on her arm. "Let this be a warning to you, Miss Darby. A young lady cannot play ducks and drakes with her virtue and expect to come away unscathed."

Still glaring with fury at him, Tessa stood rubbing her wrist with her other hand. "I am not a liar, sir, and I will stake my good name against that of any young lady in England. If Lord Dickerson is half the gentleman you say he is—and I do not doubt he is—he will not do or say anything to cast a shadow of disgrace upon me. You, sir, on the other hand . . ." She tossed her auburn head saucily. "I am, at this moment, sequestered in here alone with you." Her tone mocked him. "Does that mean *you* are prepared to offer for me?"

Penwyck glared down at her. She was, indeed, unlike any woman he had ever known before. Vast numbers of young ladies would give their right arms to be caught in just such a compromising situation with him. Even if there were not a shred of truth to it, they would embellish the facts to the point that any self-respecting man would jump to offer for them. But not Miss Darby. She was goading him for sport.

He watched a slow, smug smile curve those tantalizing pink lips of hers. Then, she lifted her long silk skirts and, without a backward glance, swept regally from the room.

"I thought not," she flung tartly over one shoulder.

Staring after her, Penwyck worked to calm his temper and cool his passion. *What was it about the infuriating Miss Darby that was so dashed intriguing?*

Attempting to sort out the riddle, Penwyck became aware of the faint aroma of the lilac sweetwater she wore lingering on the air. The appealing fragrance had muddled his concentration more than once this past week during the surprisingly pleasurable hours he'd spent teaching her to dance. Now it again taunted him.

Swallowing convulsively, he worked to tamp down his body's involuntary reaction to the attractive young lady's charms.

A sudden image of her deeply engrossed in conversation with Lord Dickerson at the dinner table filled his thoughts. She'd appeared to have eyes for no one but him, which, in and of itself, was an oddity, since she'd staunchly denounced any such designs on the man. The thought did not allay the prick of jealousy Penwyck felt.

He commenced to pace. He would not allow himself to become infatuated with the infuriating Miss Darby! Still, there was *something* about her that set her apart from any woman he'd ever known before. What could it be?

His thoughts skimmed over the events of the past several evenings she'd spent in the company of himself and Lowell Ashburn. She'd appeared quite pleasant to both of them, conversing congenially and laughing readily at Ash's quips. It was obvious he was completely smitten with her.

"She's a diamond of the first water," Ash had declared to Penwyck more than once, "but it's clear she has no interest in me."

Penwyck's brow furrowed with consternation as he continued to pace, moving now to stand before the low-burning fire.

Until tonight, Penwyck had thought Miss Darby had no interest in him. She did not treat him in the same way scores of women—young ones and not-so-young ones, married and unmarried ones—did. They flattered, they simpered, they . . . suddenly it struck him.

Miss Darby did not flirt!

He reached into his coat pocket and jerked out the list of "Acceptable Behaviours for Young Ladies" he always carried with him. He quickly scanned it. Nothing there about flirting. Damn it! Women were *supposed* to flirt. It was expected. To fail to live up to what was expected of one was . . . well, it was akin to subterfuge, that's what.

To say nothing of being dashed disconcerting!

A fresh wave of irritation engulfed the suddenly very confused earl.

To instruct Miss Darby in the fine art of flirtation was beyond his capabilities. And his mother's, he suspected.

Damn the wench!

She was making mice-feet of his well-ordered life. How was he to go about the business of living day to day, keep up with his exhausting schedule of House committee meetings, find time to monitor the behaviour of those candidates he'd chosen as prospective brides for himself, and keep a daily—nay, *hourly*—watch upon the unpredictable Miss Darby?

It would not do for her to monopolize her dinner partners, engage in clandestine rendezvous, or flatly refuse all offers to salvage her reputation. It simply would not do.

Devil take it! Penwyck sputtered to himself. In a sudden uncharacteristic fit of rage, he wadded the crisp sheet of linen paper in his hand into a tight ball and flung it into the fire.

Muttering another, stronger oath beneath his breath, he stormed from the room.

To shirk duty was not in his character. He had no choice now but to step up his vigilant watch of his mother's protégée. There was no saying what sort of scandalbroth the unconventional young lady would land them in next.

Nine

"I have never felt so frustrated!" Tessa fumed.

She and Miss Deirdre Montgomery were seated beside one another on the plush velvet squabs of the Montgomerys' tilbury, a single horse clip-clopping in front them as they tooled down a shady lane on their way to Hatchards Book Shop. Tessa had rejoiced that morning when the note arrived from Miss Montgomery inviting her on the excursion.

As expected, Lord Penwyck had balked, but Lady Penwyck had maintained there'd be no harm in it.

"I am certain the girls will be properly chaperoned," she said. "To be sure, Gracie rarely let's Deirdre out of her sight these days!" Lady Penwyck lowered her voice. "The identity of the girl's suitor is still unbeknownst to anyone, you know." She flung a quick glance across the breakfast table at Tessa, the look saying she highly suspected Tessa might know something and, instead of telling, was choosing to protect her friend.

Although Tessa was gazing directly at her hostess, she was far too fearful that permission to accompany Deirdre would be denied to care what suspicious thoughts were running through Lady Penwyck's mind.

When at last it was agreed nothing untoward could possibly result from the outing, Tessa was so elated she literally bounded up the steps to her room to change her clothes and await the Montgomerys' carriage.

Now, on their way toward Piccadilly, where the famous bookseller and print shop was located, Tessa was unable to refrain from telling her friend all that had transpired at Lord and Lady Chalmers's dinner party a few nights earlier.

"Lord Penwyck insisted I marry poor Lord Dickerson! He said my reputation would be ruined otherwise!" she cried.

Deirdre's soft brown curls shook sadly. "I am quite certain you were innocent of any wrongdoing, Tessa. Yet it does not surprise me that Lord Penwyck would be so adamant. He is quite staunch now in his desire to avoid further scandal."

"*Further* scandal?" Tessa's smooth brow puckered.

Deirdre glanced at her friend, then looked quickly away.

"Deirdre," Tessa began softly, "I dislike gossip as much as you do, but if something untoward has happened, perhaps I might better understand Lord Penwyck's motives if I knew what the trouble was." She paused. "I came to England to escape my step-father's fierce grip on me, and now I find Lord Penwyck every bit as tenacious. I have very nearly reached the end of my tether. The truth is I do not wish to marry anyone. I wish only to be allowed to pursue my own course, to conduct my affairs as I see fit. Instead, I find at every turn I am confronted by others who insist I live my life to *their* liking." When her lower lip began to tremble, Tessa bit down hard on it. "My only wish is to be free!"

"Perhaps you should have stayed in America," Deirdre replied dryly, "where there are fewer rules to abide by."

"There may be fewer rules, but it is no different where men are concerned," Tessa cried. "We are still at their mercy."

Deirdre inhaled sharply. "Well, that is not the case where Jeffrey is concerned. He does not try to force his ideas or opinions on me. He allows me to be myself and he loves me, even when our thoughts are decidedly dissimilar." She smiled impishly. "We fall into quite heated debates at times."

"And he does not . . . punish you, or berate you . . . or declare you a silly female?" Tessa asked incredulously.

"No. Jeffrey listens to me. On occasion, he even changes his views to coincide with mine."

Tessa sighed wistfully. "Well, that does give one hope."

Deirdre cast a sympathetic look at her friend. "Perhaps I *should* tell you about Lord Penwyck's troubles."

"I shan't breathe a word of it to anyone!"

Deirdre laughed. "There is no need for such a promise now. Everyone in London already knows!" She settled back, absently arranging the long pink ribbons of her reticule in her lap. "Has Lady Penwyck ever mentioned her middle son, Joel, to you?"

Tessa thought back, then shook her bonneted head. "No. She has told me about Stephen, the youngest, that he recently wed and that his wife is . . . increasing."

Deirdre nodded, but before beginning again to speak, she flung a glance over one shoulder as if to ascertain that they were indeed alone. As the small open tilbury was occupied by only the two girls; that anyone would overhear their conversation was not a likely prospect. A pair of liveried footmen clung to the rear of the vehicle, but with the wind whistling in their ears, the young ladies had little to fear from that quarter.

Presently, Deirdre began. "Joel Belmour was a scoundrel of the first order." She scooted so close to her companion the brims of their bonnets actually touched. "Rumour has it he sired enough by-blows to fill his own orphanage."

Tessa drew back in shock, her pink lips forming a small o.

"He gambled recklessly. A cousin of mine told me that Joel Belmour's name appears on virtually every page of the betting book at White's, often two or three times in the same day! It was said he lost or squandered away the entire Penwyck fortune. And it was quite vast. The gentleman was a walking scandal."

"Oh, my," Tessa murmured. "I had no idea." Suddenly, she felt quite guilty for imposing herself upon her unfortunate host and hostess if their circumstances were as dire as Deirdre suggested.

"But," Deirdre added, her tone rising with respect, "in only one year, Lord Penwyck has single-handedly turned things around."

A relieved sigh escaped Tessa. "I am glad to hear that. But how did he manage? And where has his brother got to?"

"Joel was killed in a duel. The circumstances surrounding his death were somewhat mysterious. Some say he died a hero, but

I have my doubts." She paused, a speaking look on her face. "I rather suspect Lord Penwyck twisted the facts in order to protect his mother. As to the other, I haven't the least notion how he recovered the family fortune. He and my father made a number of investments together, but beyond that . . ." She turned her palms upward. "I know Father advised him on the managing of one of their north country holdings. Stephen and his wife, Caroline, now live on the estate." She paused. "Lord Penwyck is quite brilliant, and he is greatly admired and respected."

Tessa exhaled a long breath. Knowing the dreadful truth did help her better understand the man, but did not lessen the immense vexation she felt with his vigilant watch over her. She had no intention of embarrassing the family or causing any sort of scandal whilst in Town. So why did he refuse to trust her?

Tessa tried to put the gnawing irritation from mind when, some minutes later, she and Deirdre alighted from the tilbury and entered Hatchard's Book Shop.

The establishment was far more spacious than Tessa expected. It looked to contain upward of a thousand books and a vast assortment of caricatures and prints. It surprised her to note a goodly number of ladies and gentlemen milling about, many talking and laughing quite loudly with one another.

"It is a bit noisy in here," Tessa remarked as she and Deirdre approached a floor-to-ceiling wall of books.

"A good many people frequent Hatchard's, and *not* because they wish to purchase a book."

Tessa had already drawn down a volume from the shelf and was leafing through it. "I noticed another book shop nearby," she offered. "Ridgeway's, I believe it was called. Perhaps we might go there instead."

Deirdre pulled a face. "Ridgeway's would be no less congested. Lord Byron shops there."

Tessa hadn't the least notion what that had to say to anything. She'd heard a goodly number of *on-dits* regarding the wicked poet. Perhaps scandal plagued that unfortunate man as surely as it had Joel Belmour.

"In any case," Deirdre whispered, "we shan't stay here long." She cast a wary glance about.

"Are you feeling unwell?" Tessa asked, a quizzical look on her face.

Deirdre grinned sheepishly. "I feel wonderful. Forgive me; I should have told you the truth straight out."

Tessa's curious gaze deepened.

"I often come here to meet Jeffrey. I thought he would be here today, but . . ." She glanced down at the book she held.

Tessa couldn't make out the title, but apparently it didn't signify. What was tucked inside the book was far more interesting.

Deirdre held up a small square of paper. "Jeffrey left this note for me. He wishes me to come to his office." She clapped the small volume shut and hastily returned it to the shelf. "Have you found a book you'd like? I should purchase something—perhaps a print or a Minerva novel—to assure Mother that we were indeed here."

Deirdre's agitated tone and the fact she was even now headed for the circular counter in the center of the shop told Tessa their excursion was fast drawing to a close. With some dismay, she reshelved the book she'd been perusing and hurried after her friend.

Tessa thoroughly enjoyed the half-hour ride to yet another part of London. As the tidy carriage twisted and turned up and down numerous cobbled lanes, it occurred to Tessa they were now tooling through what appeared to be the business sector of Town. The faint odour of salt in the air and the fact it suddenly felt a good bit cooler told her they were not far from the waterfront and the busy quay where she'd got her first glimpse of London.

"Many land agents office here," Deirdre told Tessa as the tilbury drew up before a row of austere-looking sandstone buildings.

Tessa gazed about with interest. Although the cobbled street had become quite narrow, there were a good many coaches and carriages lining the curb. Most bore the coat-of-arms of titled families. Many fashionably dressed gentlemen strode purposefully along the flagway, but Tessa noted not a single female amongst them.

"Perhaps it would be best if I go in alone," Deirdre said, somewhat apologetically. "If we should happen to be seen, I shouldn't wish to cause you any trouble. I can always say I am delivering important papers from my father."

"Of course." Tessa nodded absently. "I don't mind a bit waiting in the carriage. I am quite enjoying the outing."

The split second the Montgomery tilbury drew to a standstill and the steps were let down, Deirdre scampered to the ground.

"I shan't be gone overlong!" she called brightly, then disappeared from sight.

Tessa settled back to wait. It was a lovely afternoon. Despite the aborted trip to Hatchards, she was vastly enjoying her freedom. The lazy call of a gull circling overhead claimed her attention, and she glanced up and over one shoulder for a long, lingering look. At that moment, a high-sprung carriage parked alongside the opposite curb jerked into motion and afforded Tessa a clear view of the sign on the plate glass window in the front of the building across the way.

In plain block letters, the sign read, "The Political Register."

Tessa gasped. The *Political Register!* As if possessed, she sprang to her feet and, in her haste to depart, fairly stumbled down the steps before she bolted across the busy cobbled street.

Her eyes round, Tessa stepped into the cool, dank interior of the somewhat ramshackle office building and gazed about with wide-eyed wonder.

She spotted two gentlemen, both busy at work: one a fresh-faced young clerk bent over a large oaken desk littered with papers; the other an older, white-haired gentleman dressed in a rather shabby dust-coloured coat, grimy breeches, and blue garters. The faint odour of sweet-smelling tobacco from the older gentleman's pipe filled the room.

In moments he glanced up, his alert black eyes seeming to pierce clean through to Tessa's soul. When he nodded pleasantly, the butterflies in Tessa's stomach ceased fluttering at once.

She gulped. "I-is it *you?*"

A smile on his lips, the older man stood. "William Cobbett at your service, ma'am. May I help you with something?"

"Oh, sir. I cannot say how *very* pleased I am to finally meet you!" Tessa enthused. "I am Miss Tessa Darby, come from America. I do hope I am not intruding, but when I spotted your sign in the window, I simply *had* to come in."

Mr. Cobbett's smile was friendly. "I am pleased you did, Miss Darby. Might I offer you a . . ." He glanced about, then shrugged. "Well, it appears I have nothing to offer you, Miss Darby, since I don't drink—"

"Tea," Tessa murmured. "I know. I no longer drink it either, sir."

The older gentleman laughed aloud. "Is that so? Well, in any event, you are welcome to come in and chat a bit, Miss Darby. From America, you say?"

Feeling as if she'd been invited inside the Heavenly Gates, Tessa moved with reverential awe into the paper-littered room. She'd never been so happy in her life.

"I still maintain landowners are doubly guilty when they fail to educate themselves to good managerial practices and to appoint qualified agents," remarked one of three well-dressed gentlemen riding horseback alongside Lord Penwyck that afternoon.

The four men had lately been appointed to a new Parliamentary Committee for the purpose of investigating fraudulent land agency practices in London. As chairman of the committee, Lord Penwyck had drawn up a list of land agents he and three of his committee members meant to interview that afternoon.

"Employing a good manager does not mean a landowner can divest himself of all responsibility for his estate," Penwyck stated now. "I admit when I inherited, I knew little to nothing in regard to managing my father's property. I daresay the same holds true for many young men today. If during the course of one's life one has not had the opportunity to live a great many years in the country, one cannot be expected to know all that is required in order to properly manage either the land or tenants."

The other gentlemen solemnly nodded assent.

"Without a keen knowledge of one's property and the worth

of the soil to be farmed," Lord Penwyck went on, his voice strong with authority, "it is next to impossible to determine what to charge in the way of rents or what expenditures to allow in the way of improvements."

"I have it heard it said," one of his companions, Lord Combe, added, "that many tenants actually prefer to farm the estates of nonresident owners, since the property is more likely to be mismanaged."

"Nonetheless," put in Sir Glower, "when rents continue to fall and gross irregularities are easily spotted in the accounts, it cannot all be laid at the feet of a negligent landowner."

"You are quite right," Penwyck replied with conviction. "There have been far too many complaints from far too many gentlemen of late for there not to be some havey-cavey business afoot, which is why we will not stop until we have investigated every last land agent in Town."

The four men had ridden a good distance beyond Lincoln's Inn Fields, where they had questioned two of the wealthier land agents on Penwyck's list. They were now closer to London's dockside, where the bulk of London's resident land agents officed.

"We shall split up here," Lord Penwyck instructed his companions. "I am personally acquainted with Mr. Jeffrey Randall. Whilst I suspect nothing amiss in his business practices, I mean to question him about others on the list with whom I am not so well acquainted. You and Glower may interview Mr. Hughes and Mr. Ewart," he said to Lord Combe. "I drew up a list of other agents for you to visit with, did I not, Villiers?" he asked the fourth gentleman riding with them.

Lord Villiers nodded assent.

"Very well then, gentlemen, we shall reconvene on the morrow to discuss our findings."

Lord Penwyck directed his high-spirited chestnut onto a narrow cobbled lane and cantered toward the sandstone office building that housed Jeffrey Randall's Land Agency Office.

His mind fully occupied with the business at hand, he did not notice the small tilbury waiting at the curb when he slipped from the saddle and absently tethered his horse to the railing in front.

Stepping into the building, however, Penwyck was at once jarred to awareness by the remarkable sight of a fashionably dressed young lady animatedly engrossed in conversation with Mr. Jeffrey Randall; so engrossed, in fact, neither one noticed another person had entered the building.

"Ahem." Penwyck loudly cleared his throat.

When the young lady spun about, a dark scowl marred Penwyck's handsome features he recognized Miss Deirdre Montgomery.

Penwyck glared at the young lady. "It was my understanding you and Miss Darby were to spend the afternoon at Hatchards."

"We left there a scant second ago," Deirdre replied hesitantly. "F-father wished me to . . . to deliver a message to Mr. Randall. Mr. Randall is my father's land agent. You recall meeting him when you and Fath—"

"Indeed." Penwyck nodded perfunctorily in Mr. Randall's direction, then aimed a long gaze through the plate glass window in front. This time, he took keen note of the Montgomerys' neat tilbury, the sleepy-eyed footmen lounging on the curb, and the driver on the bench, the ribbons listlessly dangling from one hand. The carriage, however, was quite remarkable in that it was quite empty. "And precisely where is Miss Darby now?" he demanded of Deirdre.

Deirdre's soft brown eyes were large and round. "She is waiting for me in the carriage, sir. Did you not see her when you came—"

His business with the land agent momentarily forgot, Penwyck had already turned and was now striding purposefully back through the door to the street.

Gazing anxiously after him, Deirdre watched as both footmen sprang to life and, when questioned by the tall, elegantly dressed gentleman, gestured toward the ill-kept building opposite.

Deirdre's eyes rolled skyward. "Oh, no. Tessa has gone to see Mr. Cobbett!" she exclaimed, even as Lord Penwyck angrily charged across the street.

Ten

Lord Penwyck entered the dank rooms that housed William Cobbett's radical newspaper The *Political Register* in time to hear the end of Miss Darby's tale. The unexpected passion in her voice compelled him to listen.

"Two of Mary Black's three children perished, sir. Those dear innocent children departed this world without the loving arms of their mother about them to comfort them.

"Mary Black's children were ill-used. They were sent to the workhouse for the simple reason that their mother, who loved them dearly, was unable to care for them. They were forced to work long hours in appalling conditions, without fresh air to breathe or enough food in their bellies to sustain them."

Miss Darby's voice nearly broke. "Nothing can be done now to alter what happened to Mary Black's children, but I refuse to sit idly by as long as there is breath in me and do nothing to help other women and other children who are being forced to endure such atrocities in the mills and factories of this country. I refuse to do nothing, sir. I *refuse!"*

In the silence that followed Miss Darby's heartfelt plea, an indefinable something snapped inside Penwyck. He hadn't the leisure, however, to sort out his feelings. By calling on the newspaperman at his place of business, Miss Darby had once again committed a serious blunder. It was Penwyck's duty not only to point out the impropriety of her actions, but to rescue her.

Moving from inside the shadowy doorway where he stood,

he made his presence known. From the corner of his eye, he noted Miss Darby's bonneted head turn toward him.

"Forgive the intrusion," Lord Penwyck addressed Mr. Cobbett.

His eyes cut to Miss Darby's, and the prick of guilt that stabbed him when he saw shock and anger replace the fire of passion that had surely been present in those shining blue eyes nearly caused him to shrink back into the shadows. Again an odd mix and stir of emotions beset him.

"We will be going now, Miss Darby," he said firmly. He directed another gaze at the admittedly pleasant countenance of London's most radical citizen. "Good day, Cobbett. I trust you will forgive the intrusion," he said again.

Tessa's fury was so great she fairly trembled with it. She dared not speak lest her pent-up anger with Lord Penwyck destroy the last vestige of civility she could possibly muster toward him.

Back across the street, he calmly handed her into the Montgomery tilbury, where a round-eyed Deirdre awaited them.

"I will escort you young ladies home," Lord Penwyck said firmly.

Following the pronouncement, Tessa did permit herself a glower of contempt. How she loathed the self-righteous earl!

After Lord Penwyck voiced his intentions to the driver, he determinedly strode in the direction of his tethered horse.

The Montgomery carriage jerked forward and wheeled to the end of the street, where it circled around and headed back in the opposite direction. Astride his horse, a stern-faced Lord Penwyck fell in beside the little coach. Once they'd gained a busier thoroughfare, horse and rider fell a bit behind.

Apparently feeling it safe now to speak, Deirdre addressed her overset companion. "Tessa, I am so very sorry."

Her chin at a stubborn tilt, Tessa's breath was still coming in fits and starts.

"I should have told you Mr. Cobbett's newspaper office was

nearby." Deirdre's brow furrowed with consternation as she twisted her gloved hands together in her lap. "I fear I am *so* in love with Jeffrey I am unable to think of anything else. We are *desperate* to be married!"

A sob caught in the distraught girl's throat. "Jeffrey says we have no choice now but to tell my parents the truth, but I am so afraid, Tessa. If Father dismisses Jeffrey, we shall have . . . we *must* have the income Jeffrey realizes from my father if we are to live together as man and wife. What are we to do?"

Tessa's eyes squeezed shut as she worked to thrust aside her vexation with Lord Penwyck and focus her thoughts on Deirdre's problem. "Perhaps Lord Penwyck will not tell. It is possible he saw nothing amiss in finding you at Mr. Randall's office."

Deirdre considered. "I told him I was delivering a message from Father. He did seem more intent upon discovering your whereabouts than wondering at my being there."

Tessa's stomach churned. "I daresay he will ring a royal peal over my head."

"He did not seem terribly angry with you just now," Deirdre pointed out.

"He can appear quite contained on the surface, but beneath that calm veneer . . . he is very like my stepfather in that regard."

Deirdre's tone was sympathetic. "Was your stepfather very harsh with you?"

Tessa blinked back the sudden moisture that sprang to her eyes. "He was excessively harsh. I have never told anyone, not even my mother, the whole of it." Her voice had become quite small.

Deirdre reached to squeeze her friend's hand. "I am so sorry for all you have endured, Tessa. I am certain Lord Penwyck will not be nearly so cruel. He has no right," she concluded simply.

The painful lump in Tessa's throat had become large enough to strangle her. "My stepfather also had no right," she murmured. "I wish only to be free," she cried.

Deirdre exhaled a long sigh. "And I wish only to marry Jeffrey. Perhaps you are right. Perhaps Lord Penwyck did not suspect. Perhaps he will not betray us." Despite her hopeful words, the concerned look in her brown eyes and the worried frown on her lips remained fixed in place.

When the tilbury drew up before the Penwyck town house, Lord Penwyck did not dismount. Instead, the spirited stallion danced beneath him as he watched Tessa alight from the carriage.

Because she could feel his penetrating gaze upon her and because she could not refrain from doing so, she flung another contemptuous look at him before voicing her good-byes to Deirdre.

But Lord Penwyck's firm voice interrupted the girls' soft murmurings. "I will speak with you this evening, Miss Darby."

Fresh apprehension shuddered through Tessa as she watched horse and rider gallop away. Her anxious gaze returned to Deirdre. "I did break my promise to him," she admitted.

"I suppose my parents will eventually learn the truth," Deirdre wailed.

Tessa regarded her friend sadly. "Perhaps I can be of assistance."

"How?" Deirdre exclaimed, her pretty face contorted with anguish.

"In exchange for Lord Penwyck's silence, I will renew my vow to abandon my Cause."

"Oh, Tessa, Jeffrey and I would be ever so grateful! It would only be for a short while," she rushed on. "Just until we decide what to do. We are *desperate* to be married," she said again.

Tessa reached for her friend's gloved hand and pressed it to her cheek. "I am very happy for you, Deirdre. I am certain things will work out for you and Jeffrey."

Tessa was unable to think of anything else for the remainder of that day. By dinnertime, she was near sick to her stomach with worry. By breaking her promise to Lord Penwyck, had she overstepped the bounds to such a degree that he'd insist she return to America? It was a possibility she hadn't considered when she'd burst into William Cobbett's office that afternoon.

When she'd caught sight of the sign in the window, it was as if she were possessed by a compulsion beyond her control to enter the building and meet the man she'd read and heard so much about. Nothing could have prevented her from doing what she did. *Nothing!* Yet it had all come to naught. Her glorious interview with Mr. Cobbett had ground to a halt the second Lord Penwyck barged in. Tessa's lips tightened with renewed annoyance as she thought back on it. She fervently hoped that someday, someday *soon,* she'd be granted another opportunity to visit with the famed reform leader.

Uppermost in her mind tonight, however, was what sort of punishment Lord Penwyck would mete out.

She took great pains as she dressed for dinner that night, choosing to wear a simple but elegant gown of pale blue sarsenet, the sleeves and neckline edged with lace embellished with delicate rosebuds of peach silk.

A maid had dressed her hair in a style Tessa especially favoured, her rich auburn tresses pulled back from her face and secured on either side with jewelled combs. A fringe of wispy curls lined her forehead, while long, soft waves of hair brushed her bare shoulders. She hoped Lord Penwyck would think her appearance proper . . . and pleasing.

Lord Penwyck thought Miss Darby looked exquisite. Her pale blue dress intensified the deep blue of her eyes, and the peach rosebuds on the sleeves and bodice of her gown complemented her thick auburn hair.

This afternoon, however, he had not thought she looked quite so charming or alluring. In truth, he was having the devil of a time reconciling the bold young woman he'd heard speaking this afternoon with the vision of feminine loveliness seated before him at the dinner table.

He cast a quizzical glance at her. She was nibbling at the

food on her plate in silence, her eyes downcast, her manners impeccable.

Miss Darby was, indeed, an enigma whose strange behaviour both alarmed and puzzled him. What could possibly cause such a beautiful young woman to thoughtlessly risk everything important in her life—her reputation, her future, everything?

On the surface, Miss Darby appeared to be all that was proper. For the most part, in Polite Company her bearing was above reproach. With her smooth ivory skin, her glorious eyes, and that shiny hair, she was far prettier than most young ladies on the Marriage Mart today. Despite her American upbringing and her admittedly less than impressive credentials, she still showed great promise. Were she to set her mind to it, Miss Darby could easily aspire to and attain any height. She could most assuredly snag a title. Why, she could even become a . . . countess.

Penwyck's gaze flitted to his mother, who *was* a countess. A dark brow cocked. Well, suffice to say his own mother, who had spilled several droplets of blood-red wine on the tablecloth and now wore remnants of the lobster soup and curry sauce on the bodice of her lovely gown, was not the sort of pattern card he would hold up for any young lady to emulate.

Still, Miss Darby was an intelligent young woman. Surely she was aware of the limitless possibilities stretching before her. Surely she desired a bright future. So why did she seem so intent upon ruining her career before said career was officially launched?

Penwyck's thoughts turned to the imaginary woman he envisioned as his future countess. In both face and figure, she would be every bit as perfect as Miss Darby, although *she* would possess a superior knowledge of the proprieties and in all circumstances would exhibit the grace and style Society demanded of a woman of such exalted rank. She would be the perfect counterpart to himself. She would bear his children, serve as his helpmeet, oversee a smooth-running household, and when they were alone together . . . he swallowed convulsively as, of their own accord, his eyes flitted again to Miss Darby.

Damn the wench! She was becoming an annoying intrusion. Now that he had made up his mind to seek a bride and to marry, he instead found himself obliged to look after a headstrong hoyden who refused to listen to or obey him. It was enough to drive any man over the edge.

He considered the idea of finding her a husband first. She had already had one offer. The elderly Lord Dickerson had, indeed, called and properly discharged his duty toward her. But Penwyck had allowed Miss Darby's protests to sway him and sent Dickerson on his way.

His breath again grew short with annoyance. What would it take to set the misguided chit on the right course and keep her there?

Immediately following dinner, Penwyck politely requested a private audience with his mother's protégée.

Walking quietly beside the tall gentleman as they made their way once again to his private study, Tessa was grateful that at least the arrogant earl had not brought up her misdeed at dinner. Had he apprised his mother of the events of the afternoon or his suspicions regarding Deirdre and Jeffrey, Alice would have spent the whole of the meal discussing Deirdre's unfortunate choice. Instead, she had spent the bulk of the meal chattering non-stop about nothing.

Gaining the study, Tessa watched Lord Penwyck close the door behind himself and turn to face her. That his features did *not* resemble a thundercloud only increased her sense of foreboding.

He crossed the room to the hearth and after gesturing for her to take a seat on the small leather sofa positioned across from his own comfortable wing chair, he sat down. A moment later, he began to speak.

"I am experiencing great difficulty trying to understand why you seem so intent upon ruining yourself, Miss Darby."

Tessa looked a question at him.

"Surely you are aware, Miss Darby, that William Cobbett is

an irrational human being who does not think clearly. The man champions no real cause. His prejudice against the British government is widely known, and, unfortunately, becoming quite widespread. It is fierce, unreasonable, and unrelenting. Why in God's name would an intelligent young lady such as yourself seek to associate with such a vulgar man?"

As Tessa listened to the earl malign her political hero, her ire grew by leaps and bounds. Unable to stop herself, she blurted out, "Mr. Cobbett is quite literary! He champions a number of causes. He has a remarkable command of the language and he is not afraid to speak his mind. I am not alone in my admiration of him or his ideals!"

Lord Penwyck's face contorted angrily. "For God's sake, Miss Darby, the man has been *imprisoned* for his seditious views!" He leaned forward in his chair. "Trouble follows the old fool like a loyal puppy. The recent Luddite riot springs to mind."

Tessa's blue eyes glittered with rage. "William Cobbett *rebuked* the Luddites. It was he who explained to the rioters the necessity of the very machinery they had set out to destroy!"

"Which proves my point exactly," Penwyck retorted. "Cobbett is a man without a clear-cut cause."

"What he aims for is noble—to see every labourer with plenty to eat and drink. He is fighting for the rights of Englishmen who have been made victims by profiteering manufacturers and shortsighted politicians like yourself."

Penwyck's nostrils flared. "Ah, yes. Cobbett is a simple man, a beer drinker whose ale is, no doubt, brewed from his own barley. Cobbett is for everything *old!*"

Tessa eyed her adversary coolly. Suddenly, she realized she was actually enjoying their heated debate. Speaking her mind for the first time in weeks felt exhilarating.

Forming the perfect rebuttal to the earl's last comment in her head, she delivered the set-down with aplomb. "If you are saying all the old ways are wrong, sir, then it appears to me you are every bit as radical as Mr. Cobbett."

She watched the haughty gentleman cock a dark brow as

he contemplated her remark. He looked elegantly attractive tonight in a forest-green waistcoat and brown superfine coat over biscuit-coloured breeches. His brilliant white neckcloth perfectly matched the gleaming whiteness of his teeth and set off to perfection the appealing bronze of his skin. Tessa's breath grew short as she realized again what an attractive man the earl was. She almost regretted the fact they had plunged full tilt into a genuine disagreement. Still, she could not deny the strong attachment she felt to the outcome of this debate.

It went far beyond her childhood desire to make her stepfather see reason. It was as if she could not disengage from this battle of wills until the infuriating Lord Penwyck completely and fully acknowledged her views had merit.

Presently, the earl said, "You might be right, Miss Darby. But as a gentleman, I choose to fight the uphill battle for reform in a more acceptable fashion than your friend Mr. Cobbett."

Tessa's chin shot up. That the arrogant man had conceded on even one small point felt supremely satisfying. She listened raptly as the earl again spoke.

"I, too, believe England's modern manufacturing plants are necessary for the progress of our country and society at large. And I further believe not everything within our present Parliamentary system is as it should be."

Tessa felt *quite* gratified. "So you agree there *is* a need for reform?"

A scowl suddenly marred Lord Penwyck's handsome features as he abruptly stood and began to pace. "What I believe, Miss Darby," he ground out, "is . . ." He paused, his jaws grinding as he attempted to keep his temper in check.

Tessa could only wonder what was going through the gentleman's mind now. The familiar penetrating look was once again evident in his dark eyes.

"What I believe, Miss Darby," he concluded, "is that a proper young lady should not endeavour to speak on topics unbecoming to the feminine sensibility and beyond a woman's capacity to understand."

Tessa's nostrils flared with renewed anger. Without uttering a word, she, too, rose to her feet. The two stood nearly toe to toe. Again the unexplained attraction she felt toward this man reared its ugly head, but she angrily thrust the feeling aside. How dare he accuse her of speaking on topics above her capacity to understand!

"For your information, sir, I am *extremely* well-read on the reform ideas presently being circulated in England. Regardless of what *you* intend doing about the matter in your capacity as an esteemed statesman, I hereby renew *my* vow to do whatever I am capable of as a woman." She glared stubbornly at him. "Furthermore, I will not allow you or anyone to sway me from my course."

To Tessa's immense astonishment, Lord Penwyck said nothing. She elected to continue speaking. "I do admit, sir, that I broke my promise to you to leave off my 'disagreeable political activities.' As it happens, I feel far too strongly about the position I have aligned myself with to abandon it. In short, sir, I *cannot* abandon my Cause. I do, however, renew my promise to act in a discreet manner whilst pursuing my course. Contrary to what you believe, it is not my wish to tarnish my reputation or to bring scandal upon this house."

In a small show of contriteness, she dropped her gaze. "I beg you to forgive my lapse today, sir, and ask that you say nothing to Lady Penwyck about anything you saw or overheard this afternoon."

Tessa took heart from the fact that instead of striking her, as her stepfather might have done, she heard only Lord Penwyck's deep intake of breath. She raised a solemn blue gaze to meet his still shuttered one.

He drew in another long breath before speaking. "I accept your apology, Miss Darby. I see no call to speak of this matter to Mother or to anyone." After looking at her for a long moment, he nodded. "Good evening, Miss Darby."

Left alone in his study, Penwyck again pondered the perplexing puzzle posed by his mother's protégée.

The arresting quality he'd observed in her voice this afternoon in William Cobbett's office had struck him again tonight as she spoke. The fervent, self-assured tone was one he had never before heard from a woman. Until now, he had not thought women capable of such passion or depth, which only added to the riddle. Miss Darby was unique for a number of reasons. One, she did not flirt; two, she clung to her beliefs with a stubborn tenacity that was every bit the equal of any man.

Further complicating the riddle was the disturbing realization that he and Miss Darby actually shared something in common.

When Penwyck delivered a speech on the floor of the House, especially when the subject was dear to his heart, when the principle was one he believed to be right and just—believed in it strongly enough to fight for it—he knew his words exuded the same sort of electrifying current he'd felt this afternoon and tonight when Miss Darby spoke. The energy emanating from his body, and from hers, fairly crackled with life.

At such moments, he felt his very being suffused with the magic of the moment, breathless with an aura of expectancy as he waited for each vote to be laboriously taken and counted, until at last it was revealed that each and every mind in the room was in perfect concert with his.

There were no words to properly describe the exalted feeling. It was, Penwyck realized, closely akin to the explosion that terminated a sexual encounter with a woman. The aftermath left one feeling exhausted but exceedingly satisfied.

What plagued Lord Penwyck now was the certainty that if a vote had been taken this afternoon in William Cobbett's office following Miss Darby's heartfelt recitation, the outcome would have been unanimous in *her* favour.

Because Penwyck recognized the fervour generated in a human being by a passionate belief in anything he knew precisely how Miss Darby felt about her Cause, however off the mark it was. Despite his belief that as a woman she should not act in an unseemly fashion, he could not, *would* not be responsible for squelching that fire within her.

That as her self-appointed guardian he ought to silence her, that for her own good she should be silenced, was quite obvious. Yet Penwyck realized that if, as a young man, someone had tried to destroy the budding passion within him which today defined him as a gentleman whose life was dictated according to his duty and his precepts, he would not be here. The entire Penwyck family and fortune would simply not exist. To destroy his passionate belief in what was good and right would be the same as destroying him.

A nameless something inside Penwyck refused to let him destroy the passion that existed within Miss Darby. To do so would reduce her to the same sort of simpering milk-and-water miss that, in all honesty, Penwyck detested.

He sat alone, pondering the oddity long into the night. When at last he slowly climbed the stairs to his bedchamber, a single thought stood out in his mind: As things now stood, he hadn't the least notion what to do about the perplexing Miss Darby.

Eleven

Only a few days remained before Miss Darby's debut. Lady Penwyck and Mrs. Montgomery stayed busy meeting with one or another of the several firms engaged to oversee the decorations, the flowers, the food preparation, and the musicians who would provide music for dancing as well as entertainment whilst the guests partook of a lavish midnight supper. New ball gowns were also being made for all four of the women.

Because everyone was kept so very busy, Tessa was accorded only a few moments alone with Deirdre before the actual night of the ball.

"Lord Penwyck gave his word he would say nothing to anyone about finding you at Mr. Randall's office," Tessa hurriedly whispered to her friend as the two girls waited in an anteroom while Lady Penwyck and Deirdre's mother were being tended to by the modiste. It was the ladies' final fitting before the new ball gowns were to be delivered.

Deirdre smiled serenely. "Jeffrey and I appreciate all you have done for us, Tessa." She placed a gloved hand on her friend's arm. "Once we are wed, we want you to be the first guest to join us for dinner in our new home.

Tessa smiled appreciatively. "Why, thank you, Deirdre. I am quite looking forward to meeting Jeffrey. Will he be coming to the ball?"

"Oh, no." Deirdre's soft brown curls shook. "Jeffrey is

not . . . Mother wouldn't . . . no, he will not be coming," she concluded firmly.

Grasping the reason why Mr. Randall's name had been omitted from the guest list, Tessa shifted uncomfortably. "Would you like for him to come?" she asked. "It is *my* party, after all. I will simply tell Alice I wish—"

"No, really. Everything is quite all right as it is. Jeffrey understands completely, truly he does."

Tessa paused. Something in Deirdre's tone struck her as a bit odd. However, not until the night of the ball did she fully understand what it was.

The Montgomerys' grand ballroom, located on the third floor of their palatial estate on the outskirts of London, had been transformed to resemble an outdoor vista complete with artificial trees, a small pond, and footpaths that meandered through a plush green carpet that represented grass. Earthen pots full of colorful spring flowers bloomed alongside the paths and clustered at the base of the silk-leaved trees. At the bottom of the room, a three-tiered waterfall spewed forth sparkling champagne that splashed merrily into a bubbly pool at its base. Hundreds of tiny lights twinkled in the treetops, and more glittered like stars in the painted midnight-blue sky overhead.

In the rotunda at the top of the room, the orchestra was housed in the largest of the three ship hulls representing Columbus's maiden voyage to America. Each was painted in bright hues of red, blue, and green. The remaining two facades, resting on opposite sides of the room, hid platforms containing high-back chairs upon which persons who did not wish to dance might sit and comfortably watch the proceedings.

"It is lovely!" Tessa breathed, gazing about with wonder when she and her party entered the room following an early supper provided for them by Mr. and Mrs. Montgomery.

"Yes, it is lovely, isn't it?" Lady Penwyck murmured. "I do so wish your Mother could be here."

"Mama would be very pleased," Tessa agreed, gazing up at the stars and then around the perimeter of the room, her vivid blue eyes taking in the spectacular sight. "Thank you for all you have done for me, Lady Penwyck."

Because Lady Penwyck, elegantly attired in a gray satin gown, a multitude of diamonds twinkling at her neck and ears, had already turned to address someone else, she did not hear Tessa's heartfelt reply, but her son did.

"I have never seen Mother quite so happy or so content as she has been since you arrived, Miss Darby," Lord Penwyck remarked quietly.

Both the kindness of the gentleman's words and the sincerity of his tone stunned Tessa. She had seen precious little of the earl the past few days and had to admit to rather missing him. He had surprised her the other evening by not chastising her roundly for her improper call upon Mr. Cobbett. Instead, she had vastly enjoyed the discussion they had fallen into. While she was still certain he did not approve of her broaching the seditious subject of Parliamentary reform, he had not rebuked her for doing so, all of which caused Tessa to wonder at his abrupt change of heart.

He looked quite handsome tonight in black evening clothes, a brilliant white cravat at his throat and spotless white gloves on his hands. The delicious sandalwood scent that wafted about him made Tessa want to edge closer and draw in a deep breath.

The two stood eyeing one another a bit warily.

"You look—" Lord Penwyck began, at the same moment Tessa opened her mouth to speak.

"You look quite handsome tonight, sir," she said softly when he deferred to her.

He inclined his dark head a notch. "Thank you, Miss Darby. I was about to voice the same sentiment in regard to your appearance. Although I would have chosen the word *pretty* as opposed to *handsome*."

Tessa smiled sweetly. With one gloved hand, she brushed an imaginary wrinkle from the silken skirt of her lovely new gown. She'd picked the exquisite cream-coloured fabric over all the others presented to her at one of the many shops she and Lady Penwyck had visited. The low-cut bodice of the gown and the small cap sleeves featured an intricate floral pattern embellished with pearls and delicate golden threads. The slim skirt fell to the floor in a single column of silk, interrupted only by a handful of pleats in the back which allowed for ease whilst walking or dancing. It was the most beautiful gown Tessa had ever seen. She felt quite feminine—even elegant—wearing it. That Lord Penwyck had complimented her appearance tonight pleased her immensely. Although she would never have admitted it, she was quite looking forward to dancing with the attractive earl.

When the great hall finally filled up with guests, Lord Penwyck sought out Tessa to lead the first set, a French cotillion.

"I do hope I have not forgotten the steps," Tessa whispered with genuine concern.

Lord Penwyck smiled down into her anxious blue eyes. "You have nothing to fear, Miss Darby. Had I thought you required another dance lesson before your debut, I would have insisted upon it."

Once the music began, Tessa relaxed and found moving through the simple pattern that comprised the dance a fairly easy prospect. She bowed, turned, stepped forward and back, circled beneath another gentleman's arm and returned again to her esteemed partner, Lord Penwyck.

"There, you see?" He smiled into her glittering blue eyes once more. "You are doing splendidly."

Throughout the lengthy dance, Penwyck could not help noticing the multitude of admiring glances being directed at his mother's lovely protégée. Miss Darby indeed looked a vision tonight. Her shiny auburn curls piled atop her head added several inches to her impressive height. With her chin held high, she looked as proud and regal as a princess. Penwyck did not expect the lovely Miss Darby would suffer from a lack of dance partners tonight.

Indeed, when the music ground to a halt, he was quickly shunted aside as half a dozen young men rushed forward to claim her hand for the next dance. Penwyck moved to the sidelines and stood quietly watching her.

" 'Evening, old man," came a gentleman's voice to Penwyck's left.

His dark eyes cut round. "Ashburn."

"Any of the young ladies on your list present tonight?" his good friend inquired jovially.

Penwyck's dark brow cocked. "Only one."

"Oh?" Mr. Ashburn gazed about with interest. "Must have added someone new. I don't recall seeing either Miss Carruthers or Lady Amabel when I—"

"I was referring to Miss Darby," Penwyck snapped.

Mr. Ashburn's blue eyes widened. "You have added Miss Darby's name to your list of eligibles?"

Penwyck shot his friend a dampening look. "Miss Darby is on the list of things I am obliged to take care of. The chit is proving . . . well, she is proving . . ."

"What?" Ashburn asked, his lips beginning to twitch with amusement. His daze sought out the young lady in question. "Doesn't appear to need taking care of to me," he remarked candidly. "Although she may soon require a secretary to help sift through her many offers. I daresay the whole room is buzzing about your mother's fabulous new find. Recall telling you Miss Darby was destined to become the talk of the town. She is in splendid looks tonight."

Lord Penwyck's lips pursed irritably.

"She speaks French, you know," Ashburn remarked.

Penwyck snorted. "I sincerely doubt that, Ashburn. Talk about Miss Darby appears to be getting out of hand. I assure you, she speaks no foreign languages, and most assuredly not French."

Ashburn shrugged. "Well, everyone declares she is a diamond of the first water. And rightly so, unless I miss my guess."

Penwyck flicked a curious gaze at his friend. "Precisely what is being said about Miss Darby?" he inquired.

"That she is somewhat a mystery. That she has already turned down a Russian count and a—"

"Dickerson is the only chap I am aware of who has offered for her," Penwyck put in dryly.

Mr. Ashburn's brow puckered. "Old Lord Dickerson?" He laughed. "Can't say as I blame her for refusing him."

"She should have accepted." Penwyck's tone was firm.

Mr. Ashburn said nothing as he stood quietly watching Tessa. "She's unlike any other young lady I've ever met," he observed quietly. "Just look at her."

Penwyck was. Standing with his gloved hands clasped behind his back, he hadn't been able to drag his eyes from Miss Darby the past half hour. At the moment, she was again surrounded by at least a dozen admirers, each young man preening and posturing in the vain hope of garnering the merest whit of attention from her, and every last one failing miserably.

"She don't seem to favor no one," Ashburn pointed out. "Rumour has it Miss Darby is"—he cast an appraising look at his companion—"already in love."

Penwyck cocked a dark brow. "Not possible," he stated flatly. "Rumour mill has run amok."

Noting a certain wistful quality in Mr. Ashburn's tone, Penwyck flicked another curious gaze at his friend. "Are you saying *you* fancy her?" he asked, but even as he spoke, an unexpected prick of . . . *jealousy* stabbed him. With calculated interest, he watched Ashburn's shoulders rise and fall nonchalantly.

" 'Course I fancy her. Miss Darby is clearly the sort of woman any young man would dream of marrying. I daresay I would find it hard to deny Miss Darby anything."

Penwyck started. Miss Darby had already caused *him* to give in to her demands, first with Lord Dickerson and second by causing him to not censure her over the impropriety of calling on Mr. Cobbett.

"Allow me to caution you against pursuing the young lady too strenuously, Ashburn," Lord Penwyck declared firmly.

His companion regarded him suspiciously. "Why? Because you have aspirations?"

"Good God, no!" Penwyck sputtered, a bit too loudly and adamantly.

Ashburn studied him, then grinned. "Methinks thou dost protest too much, old man."

"Cut line, Ash. I am far too sensible. Miss Darby may be lovely to look at, but it is quite obvious the young lady is garnering attention simply because she is foreign. She is without artifice or affectation for the simple reason that colonists have none. They are simple people with simple ways."

"Miss Darby is English," Ashburn pointed out stubbornly.

"True, she was born in England. But she was raised in America amongst savages and lowlifes. Unfortunately, there is no escaping that."

With a curt nod to his friend, Penwyck strolled away.

He was making a cake of himself watching Miss Darby like the proverbial hawk. What rubbish that Ashburn would think he had aspirations that direction! He had cautioned Ash against pursuing the young lady for the simple reason that he had uncovered certain alarming qualities in Miss Darby that were, indeed, unlike other young ladies in Town, qualities which Penwyck knew full well a decent man would find not only distasteful, but which he would be unprepared to deal with. Penwyck was simply sparing his good friend the trouble.

At least, that was the explanation he clung to now.

With a singleness of purpose, he strode across the room to one of the painted ship facades. Deliberately approaching one of a number of milk-and-water misses seated there, he politely inquired if she would like to stand up with him. Miss Darby was not the only young lady in the room, after all.

But she was the only one who had danced every dance and whose slippers had begun to pinch her toes. As the fourth quadrille of the evening commenced, Tessa gazed longingly at the few vacant chairs inside the Nina and the Santa Maria.

As the guest of honor at her own debut, she wondered if she were allowed to sit out a dance or two—or even three. Suddenly, she caught sight of Deirdre gesturing agitatedly to her from the edge of the dance floor.

Tessa did not wait for the dance to end, but politely extricated herself from her partner and scurried to her friend's side.

"What is it, Deirdre? You look positively stricken!"

"Tessa, I need your help," Deirdre whispered. Tossing an anxious gaze over one shoulder, she drew Tessa behind an especially large painted tree. "I mean to . . . to run away tonight and—"

"Oh!" Tessa's blue eyes widened with alarm.

"I told Jeffrey I would slip away from the ball and come to him. I am certain my parents will never consent to our marrying. I mean to persuade Jeffrey to elope with me tonight."

"Oh, Deirdre!" Tessa sucked in her breath.

"I did not expect finding a carriage to take me to Jeffrey's such a daunting task. The drive and grounds are completely ranged-in with coaches. Not a one of Father's carriages can be got from the mews. I need your help, Tessa," she begged.

"But what can I do?"

"Please ask Lord Penwyck to drive me into the city. I am convinced he knows about Jeffrey and me, and as he had not yet betrayed us, I thought it safe to trust him tonight."

"Oh, Deirdre," Tessa began dubiously, "I cannot think that wise. Lord Penwyck is—" At precisely that moment, Tessa's eyes met Mr. Lowell Ashburn's smiling blue ones. An idea seized her. "Wait for me in the foyer, Deirdre. I know someone who can be trusted."

Driving home from the ball that night, Lord Penwyck was again caught up in what he feared was becoming an obsessive fascination with the intriguing Miss Darby.

As usual, she was not behaving as expected. Most every young lady who had just made her debut in as spectacular a fashion as Miss Darby would be as atremble with excitement as the evening drew to a close as she had been for the weeks preceding it.

But Miss Darby was huddled in one corner of the dimly lit coach, her somewhat crumpled satin cloak drawn tightly about her shoulders as she stared—one might even say sullenly stared—from the coach window into the night.

Take a Trip Back
to the Romantic
Regent Era of the
Early 1800's with
4 FREE
Zebra Regency
Romances!
(A $19.96 VALUE!)
4 FREE
books are
yours!
PLUS YOU'LL
SAVE ALMOST $4.00
EVERY MONTH
WITH CONVENIENT
FREE HOME DELIVERY!

Twelve

Tessa hardly slept at all that night. She had hoped now her debut was behind her and she was officially out, she'd be accorded more of the freedom she so desperately craved. Instead, by assisting Deirdre to run away tonight, she feared she had further imprisoned herself.

It was almost morning before she finally drifted off to sleep and barely a quarter hour later when she was quite rudely awakened.

"Miss Darby!"

The sound of a deep male voice calling to her penetrated her consciousness. Tessa at once recognized it to be Lord Penwyck. That he sounded inordinately angry sent a sharp pang of fear racing through her.

"Miss Darby!" The insistent summons was punctuated by a loud rapping at her bedchamber door.

Flinging back the coverlet, Tessa drove her toes into her slippers and snatched up her wrapper, which she shrugged into as she scampered across the room.

Opening the door a crack, she aimed a wide-eyed gaze upward.

"W-what is it?" she asked innocently.

"Deirdre's father is belowstairs," Lord Penwyck replied curtly. "He wishes to speak with you."

"Oh." It was more of a squeak really. "I-I'll just be a—"

"At once, Miss Darby!" the irate earl commanded.

It was Penwyck's mother who was nattering mindlessly on and on and on about the thrilling events of the evening.

"I declare I never expected Gracie to actually have the servants' heads shaved! But how better to display the brightly coloured feather headdresses? And where do you suppose she got all those exquisite feathers? I don't doubt she had them imported. We shall simply have to throw a lovely dinner party, or several dinner parties, for Gracie and Charles. I declare, this evening was a stupendous success. Tessa darling, you were splendid! Both the Princess Esterhazy and the Countess Lieven were in raptures over your gown. In fact, everyone demanded to know who made it! You were quite right to refuse the insipid white most young ladies wear. You looked simply stunning. Did she not look stunning, Penny?"

By way of answer, Penwyck merely cleared his throat, his dark eyes cutting again to the shadowy figure of Miss Darby seated on the coach bench opposite him. Were it not for the fact her head was still erect, he would think her fast asleep.

Suddenly, he was seized by an almost overpowering urge to take her by the shoulders and shake her. Why did she not behave as other young ladies her age did? And why did her stubborn refusal to conform irritate him so? It was as if she had some strange hold on him—a grip so powerful it compelled him to watch her, to note her every move, to censure her when her actions did not please him and yet, at the same time, he found her lovely and fascinating, and did not wish to change the least thing about her.

It was most confusing and most irritating. What was worse, his inability to drive the confounded young lady from his thoughts was keeping him awake nights and thoroughly disrupting his days.

As Tessa hurried up the stairs to her bedchamber that night, she couldn't help wondering how very angry Lord Penwyck would be with her once he learned she had helped Deirdre Montgomery run away to be married.

Tessa attempted to gulp down the large lump of anxiety in her throat as she flung open the door and fell in beside the outraged earl. Clutching at the loose edges of her cotton wrapper, she nervously fumbled with the ties in an attempt to secure the garment across her nearly bare breasts.

"Montgomery declares his daughter has taken flight," Lord Penwyck informed Tessa as the two hurried to the stairs. "He fears she and her . . . ahem . . . young man have run away to get married. He is convinced you know who the fellow is and something of the couple's whereabouts."

Tessa's breath was coming in fits and starts. From the corner of one eye, she saw Lord Penwyck cast a sidelong look at her half-exposed bosom. The effrontery of the man only added to her upset. No doubt he would now chastise her for appearing abroad in so shameless a state.

"I would have dressed had you accorded me the time!" she snapped, in answer to his imagined rebuke.

A dark brow quirked. "We are all of us in a state of undress, Miss Darby. I doubt anyone will especially remark upon your . . . choice of apparel." The gentleman sniffed piously. "Miss Montgomery's disappearance is quite a serious matter. The girl has succeeded in ruining herself. The scandal will not only follow her the rest of her days, it will also adversely affect her family. She has behaved in quite a foolhardy manner."

Tessa had no time to defend her friend, for the very second Mr. Montgomery and Lady Penwyck heard the earl's deep voice in the corridor, the angry man, with an anxious Lady Penwyck close on his heels, rushed into the foyer to meet them.

Tessa blanched at the sight of Mr. Montgomery's face. He was quite a large man with piercing black eyes. When he spoke, his brusque manner put Tessa in mind of her fearsome stepfather.

"What do you know of my daughter's whereabouts?" Mr. Montgomery demanded furiously.

Tessa flung a helpless look up at Lord Penwyck.

"You will tell the gentleman what you know, Miss Darby,"

the earl commanded, his tone very nearly as harsh as Mr. Montgomery's.

Lady Penwyck at once cut in, in a far gentler tone. "You and Deirdre are bosom bows, Tessa dear."

Tessa's blue eyes grew frightened as the assembled company waited for her to speak. She truly did not wish to be the one to divulge Deirdre's secret to her father, but it appeared she had no choice.

"I demand you tell me at once where my daughter is!" Mr. Montgomery insisted.

"I-I . . . she . . . I do not know where she is, sir," Tessa replied haltingly.

"I refuse to believe you know nothing, young lady! Tell me at once what you know of Deirdre's disappearance!"

"I do not know where she is, sir. Truly, I do not." It was not a lie. Deirdre had not said *where* she and Jeffrey were headed. And because, thus far, neither Mr. Montgomery nor Lord Penwyck had inquired with *whom* Deirdre had taken flight, Tessa felt no obligation to divulge that vital piece of information. If asked, she would, of course, not lie, but she would also say no more than was absolutely necessary.

With a huff of exasperation, Mr. Montgomery bellowed, "The two of your were seen huddled together at the ball, Miss Darby. I refuse to believe that you know nothing!"

"Charles, our Miss Darby would not tell a falsehood," Lady Penwyck put in patiently.

"Do you deny that you assisted in my daughter's disappearance?" the overset man demanded.

Tessa thrust her chin up. "I deny nothing, sir. I am merely attempting to answer your questions as truthfully as I can."

"So I am to drag it out of you, am I? Well then, I shall begin again!"

"Charles, you really mustn't—" Lady Penwyck began. She was also clothed in her nightrail and wrapper, her graying hair concealed beneath a very pretty lacy nightcap. She turned a sympathetic look on Tessa. "Everyone knows Deirdre has formed a *tendre* with *someone,* Tessa darling. You must tell us if you are acquainted with her young man."

"I-I have never met him," Tessa replied, shaking her head. Her long auburn curls dangled loosely about her thinly clad shoulders.

"Randall," suddenly announced Lord Penwyck. Standing with both arms folded across his chest, he tapped his chin thoughtfully with one forefinger. "Caught the pair of them together in his office only last week. Thought then it seemed a trifle odd."

Mr. Montgomery's brows snapped together angrily. "Are you saying Deirdre and my *land agent* are—"

"Is this true, Tessa?" Lady Penwyck asked calmly. Of Tessa's interrogators, Alice was, by far, the most collected, which was a bit odd, considering the woman was generally a bona fide skitter-wit.

Tessa nervously chewed on her lower lip.

"Well?" bellowed Montgomery. "Has Deirdre gone off with Jeffrey Randall?"

Her blue eyes shuttered, Tessa slowly, *very* slowly, nodded assent.

"I'll kill the reprobate! I'll *kill* him!" Fuming, Mr. Montgomery pushed past a frightened Tessa on his way to the front door.

Lord Penwyck fell into step behind him. "Perhaps you should calm yourself a bit first, man. If you'd allow me a moment to dress, I shall be happy to accompany you. They may still be in London. We shall try Randall's flat first and then—"

Suddenly, in a firm voice, Tessa announced, "I am coming along."

Scowling, Lord Penwyck wheeled to face her. "You will do nothing of the sort, Miss Darby."

Tessa's blue eyes snapped fire as she glared at the uppity earl. "You are *not* my father and you will *not* tell me what to do! I said I am coming along and that means I am coming along. Deirdre will need a friend to comfort her, and I intend to be there."

In the moment of strained silence that followed Tessa's outburst, she added, "You will please wait for me while I change into more appropriate clothing."

That said, she imperially brushed past a somewhat subdued Lord Penwyck and marched regally up the stairs.

From the foyer, she heard the earl instruct his mother to see that Mr. Montgomery received either a cup of coffee or a brandy, and then he, too, ascended the stairs some distance behind Tessa.

Beginning to feel the effects of the sleepless night she'd just endured, Tessa nonetheless hurriedly dressed and scurried back downstairs. Not until she and her gentlemen companions, a tight-lipped Lord Penwyck and a still fuming Mr. Montgomery, stepped outside and headed for the Montgomery coach did she realize a storm of another sort was brewing outdoors.

Although it was close on seven of the clock, the sky was still quite dark. Large blue-gray clouds hung low over the city. Thunder rumbled in the distance, and when a sudden crack of lightning startled the handsome bays harnessed before the Montgomery coach, Tessa, too, jumped with alarm.

"Appears to be cutting up nasty," Mr. Montgomery muttered irritably. "We'd best make haste."

Tessa swallowed her fear and turned to address the man. "I expect we shall find Deirdre safe and sound at Mr. Randall's flat, sir."

"So!" Deirdre's father sputtered angrily. "You do know where she is!"

Tessa thrust her head up and said nothing further.

Wearing a deep scowl, a silent Lord Penwyck handed her into the carriage.

"Spring 'em!" Montgomery called to the driver as he, too, clambered inside.

Tessa scooted as far from Lord Penwyck on the carriage bench as she could and pretended an absorbing interest in watching huge droplets of rain begin to slide down the coach window. In truth, she'd never been abroad in London this early before, and she did find the sight arresting. What with the fog swirling about the lampposts and cold rain splattering onto the cobblestones, the sleeping city had an eerie feel about it. She prayed wherever Deirdre and Jeffrey were, they were safe and warm.

As the high-sprung coach rumbled over the slick cobblestones, Tessa noted what appeared to be phantoms, shadows moving in slow motion on one or another street corner. Ignoring the rain, the vendors were busily arranging their daily wares—flowers, fruit, cabbages, and potatoes—atop rickety carts. Tessa grimaced when she saw numerous ill-clad children huddled together on various rain-soaked stoops as the luxurious carriage wheeled past.

Some minutes later, the shiny black coach turned onto a narrow lane and drew up before a not ill-kept town house squeezed in amongst a row of similar tall red brick structures.

Before the carriage had shuddered to a complete standstill, Mr. Montgomery scrambled to the ground and, in a rush to avoid a drenching and to extricate his daughter as quickly as possible from her abductor's clutches, rushed up the flagway. He pounded loudly on the door. Lord Penwyck followed at a somewhat slower pace, one gloved hand holding his black beaver hat in place as rain-laden wind threatened to whip it off.

Her heart in her throat, Tessa anxiously watched the proceedings from the coach window. She barely had time to wonder if Deirdre were, indeed, inside when the door to the flat burst open and Mr. Montgomery and Lord Penwyck rushed inside.

Mere seconds later, a scarlet-faced Montgomery reappeared, one arm protectively encircling the slim shoulders of a sobbing Deirdre.

"Oh!" Tessa sucked in her breath as she watched the threesome—Deirdre, her father, and Lord Penwyck—brave an angry downpour of rain on their way back to the carriage. As each climbed into the coach, a shower of raindrops dampened Tessa's pelisse and boots.

"Oh, Tessa!" Deirdre cried. Upon catching sight of her friend, she at once fell onto the bench and buried her head in Tessa's shoulder, her sobs increasing in volume.

Once the two gentlemen had taken their seats and the coach again lurched forward, Montgomery blurted out, "I'm not the least bit sorry I called the reprobate out! The man does not deserve to live!"

"Oh-h-h, Papa!" Deirdre cried.

"There, there." Tessa tightened her arms about her friend's shoulders. "Everything will be all right."

"You will stand as my second, Penwyck," Montgomery commanded, furious, his black eyes mere slits in his face.

After a pause, Penwyck said, "No, sir. In all fairness, I find I cannot take part in—"

"What are you saying?" Montgomery demanded. "The blackguard has ruined my daughter and I will not—"

"I am not *ruined,* Papa!" Deirdre cried.

Penwyck added, "Randall swore that he did not touch her, sir." He cast a guarded glance at Tessa. "And I believe him. Jeffrey Randall is a truthful man."

"I will *never* forgive you if you kill him, Papa! Jeffrey and I love one another. I *will* marry him. I don't care what you say, I *will!"*

"I will deal with you later, girl!" Deirdre's father sputtered angrily.

"Papa . . . please; Jeffrey did *nothing!* I swear it!" Deirdre turned a pleading look on Lord Penwyck. "Help me, sir, please!"

The earl solemnly addressed the overwrought Mr. Montgomery again. "To say truth, sir, Randall seemed quite unruffled. It was almost as if he were relieved to see us."

"He was!" Deirdre cried. "Jeffrey wouldn't listen to me last night. It was *I* who wished to run away. Jeffrey said he refused to begin our married life by . . . by dishonoring me. I am being truthful, Papa, truly I am!"

"Then why did he not send you home?" her father demanded suspiciously. "You spent the night with hi—"

"I am pure, Papa. I am *pure!"*

A moment of strained silence followed Deirdre's heartfelt confession. Tessa's eyes were quite large and round as she took in the drama unfolding before her.

At length, Lord Penwyck said, "With your permission, sir, I would be happy to deliver a note of apology to Mr. Randall."

Montgomery huffed his exasperation.

"Please do not kill him, Papa! *Please!"*

Montgomery turned a stern look on his only daughter. "You will never leave the house unchaperoned again; and if you ever lay eyes on that reprobate again, I swear I will run him through!"

Deirdre's bedraggled curls shook. "I will never see him again, Papa; I promise." Her bosom rose and fell as with fright she drew in quick gasps of air. Her cold fingers tightened around Tessa's.

"Very well," Montgomery muttered reluctantly. "I will spare his life. This time."

Deirdre's father insisted on taking his daughter home at once. A half hour later, the Montgomery coach rumbled back into London carrying a silent Lord Penwyck and a now rather sleepy Miss Darby back to Portman Square.

Hard sheets of rain slowed the horses progress as they slogged through debris-filled rivers of running water on the outskirts of the city.

Inside the noisy coach, Tessa and Lord Penwyck were seated opposite one another on the bench. Despite the storm raging outdoors, which made hearing one another all but impossible, Tessa felt compelled to thank Lord Penwyck for his intervention on Mr. Randall's behalf that morning.

"It was good of you to calm Mr. Montgomery," she began.

Penwyck aimed a distracted gaze out the coach window. "Montgomery was a deal too overset to see Randall was being truthful."

"Deirdre was also being truthful."

Penwyck directed a caustic look at Tessa. "Indeed."

"She loves him very much," Tessa added firmly.

Penwyck turned again to the window. "Loves her father, or Randall?"

"Both, I expect. But she is in love with Jeffrey." She paused. "They are desperate to be married."

Penwyck's gaze remained fixed on the fuzzy blur of images speeding past the coach window. "The girl's head is full of romantical notions. She would do well to forget she ever knew Jeffrey Randall. Despite the Montgomerys' less than exceptional consequence, I expect Deirdre could land a younger son, a baronetcy, perhaps better. She must allow her father to select a proper young man for her to marry."

Which sounded precisely like something Tessa's stepfather would say. Tessa flew into a rage. "You are the most unfeeling man I have ever known!" she cried. "I daresay you have never, *ever* been in love! I daresay beneath that calculating, aristocratic veneer you have never experienced *strong* feelings in your life!"

A dark brow cocked as the earl appeared a trifle amused by Tessa's outburst. "You are presuming a great deal on a subject about which you know nothing, Miss Darby."

"Your actions have told me a great deal!" she cried. With a pious sniff, Tessa thrust her chin up and glared at the odious man.

How was it possible she had enjoyed dancing with him only a few hours ago at her come-out ball? She had thought he looked quite handsome and dashing then, and he had appeared genuinely kind and solicitous. But today he had once again assumed his infuriatingly aloof persona.

The earl's lips twitched as he gazed lazily at her. "Precisely what have you observed, Miss Darby?" he inquired.

Tessa clamped her lips tightly shut. She should have known better than to attempt a proper conversation with the starched-up earl. Why did she let him rile her so? And why did she feel so compelled to rip away that self-righteous mask and uncover the real man beneath? Of course, she did not truly know how he felt about anything, but the maddening part, the irksome part, was that she *wished* to know him, and know him well. There was something undeniably attractive about the disagreeable Lord Penwyck. It had succeeded in drawing her in and now it held her quite against her will. Because she did not wish to find the irritating man attractive, she loathed him for making her feel what she did not wish to feel!

"Well?" Lord Penwyck prodded. His taunting gaze locked with hers.

Tessa's blue eyes narrowed and, because she could not help herself, she blurted out, "In the short time I have known you, sir, I have observed enough about you to know I do not like you the least little bit!"

It gratified her that the uppity Lord Penwyck seemed taken aback.

Penwyck was taken aback. Not only had no woman ever spoken so candidly to him before, no woman had ever told him straight out she did not like him. Miss Darby's words stung him to the quick.

Suddenly he felt exactly as he had felt as a boy of five when an elder cousin of his, whom he had looked up to, had mean-spiritedly pushed him into the lily pond in the meadow. Penwyck's cousin knew very well he did not know how to swim.

It had further stunned Penwyck when, after tossing him into the water, the older boy had simply turned and run away. Penwyck had learned to swim that day, but he had very nearly drowned in the process.

He felt as if he were drowning now, that if he did not do something to right things between himself and Miss Darby, she would run away . . . and leave him.

"So," he said hesitantly, "you do not like me."

The young lady's auburn head sat at a stubborn tilt. She had on a dark-blue toque bonnet that perfectly matched the deep blue of her eyes. Suddenly, Penwyck was beset by a tantalizing image of her in her nightclothes this morning. She'd looked quite alluring with her long auburn hair flowing about her bare shoulders and her lovely breasts bouncing beneath her thin wrapper as she hurried alongside him. Waiting for her to speak now, Penwyck worked to ignore the effect that vivid image was having on his body. He was glad when she began to speak.

"Perhaps I did not mean I do not like you, sir. What I meant to say was I . . . there are *qualities* about you I do not like."

Penwyck digested that and decided she had given him something to cling to. He felt a whit better.

"I see. Well, then . . ."

He cast about for something further to say. But because nothing further occurred to him at the moment, he simply cleared his throat and turned again to stare from the coach window. Sheets of bitter rain were sliding down it.

He became aware of the persistent splat, splat, splat of raindrops pelting the roof of the coach. The angry sounds grew louder and louder.

Suddenly, blurred images began to dance before his eyes: Miss Darby passing out leaflets from the side of a hansom cab in Hyde Park. Penwyck had been appalled at his first glimpse of her . . . and yet he'd been strangely fascinated with the tall beauty. She was so very unlike any other young lady in Town.

Another image formed before his eyes. Miss Darby looking extraordinarily pretty the night he drew her into his arms and attempted to teach her to dance. She'd been shy at first, but her confidence grew as the lesson progressed. She'd smiled often, then.

Had she liked him then?

That image dissolved and a picture of her laughing over dinner with old Lord Dickerson took its place. Penwyck squirmed uncomfortably on the coach bench.

He had observed her laughing a good deal last evening with Lord Chesterton and Sir Richard Warwick and Lords Marchmont, Fenwick, Powell, and Kirshfield. Penwyck's eyes narrowed jealously. She'd even laughed with the new Frenchman in town, Monsieur de la whatever-his-name-was.

Penwyck's chest grew tight as his nostrils flared with rage.

Miss Darby had danced and danced and danced and laughed and laughed and laughed. She appeared to like every last one of her many suitors.

But she did not like him.

Which felt bitterly painful, as painful as icy water filling his lungs.

There must be some way to right things!

At length, he turned to face her.

"Perhaps I might speak with Mr. Montgomery again," he began quietly, "on Deirdre's behalf."

One of Miss Darby's finely arched brows lifted as a puzzled look flitted across her pretty face. "Speak with him?"

"If Deirdre truly loves Mr. Randall, I see no reason why they should not be allowed to marry."

Miss Darby's sapphire blue eyes widened with joy. "And you will tell her father that?"

"I will do my best to persuade him, Miss Darby."

"Oh, thank you, sir! I am certain you can persuade him. You are a very persuasive man. I have never known a man as strong and sure as you are, sir. Deirdre will be very happy!" Her pretty mouth softened. "As am I."

Penwyck drew in a long, relieved breath. The sight of Miss Darby's lovely features once again smiling felt like the sun bursting through the clouds and chasing the rain away.

It was turning out to be a glorious day after all.

Thirteen

Penwyck thoroughly enjoyed the few minutes of lighthearted conversation he and Miss Darby fell into as the Montgomery coach returned them to Portman Square.

He listened with genuine interest as she told him about a time when she and her brother, David, got caught in a downpour as they were returning home from visiting a neighbour who lived adjacent to their father's plantation.

Penwyck asked several more questions about Miss Darby's life in America about what sort of crops Senator Darby cultivated on his plantation and if there were Indians in close proximity to the farm. Tessa smiled before telling him most American Indians now lived further inland, on the central and western plains of the continent, a good distance from the more civilized eastern cities.

Apart from the Indians, Penwyck was pleased to note Miss Darby's upbringing was, in essence, not so very different from his. One exception was that he had been shipped away to school and she had been educated at home, as were a good many young ladies in England.

Penwyck's spirits were so elevated following their pleasant discourse that by the time they arrived home and discovered the flagway in front of the Penwyck town house a veritable gully, he very gallantly swept an only mildly protesting Miss Darby into his arms and carried her the few steps up the path and into the house.

Once the earl had set Tessa down inside the marble-tiled foyer, she, feeling a trifle dazed by the experience, hurriedly excused herself and fled up the stairwell to the safe haven of her bedchamber.

What had come over Lord Penwyck just now? And what had come over *her?* After he had announced in the carriage he would speak to Mr. Montgomery on Deirdre's behalf, the two of them had begun to converse as if they were friends. The high-born earl had never before expressed an interest in her life in America or asked about her brother, David. Tessa realized with a sudden pang she missed her brother quite dearly. It would be *wonderful* if David could come to London. She would love to introduce him to Lord Penwyck.

What had she just thought?

A frantic look on her face, Tessa began to pace nervously before the hearth in her bedchamber. A minute later, she realized she was so overset she had not yet removed her rain-soaked pelisse or bonnet!

Catching a glimpse of her reflection in the oval looking-glass atop the dressing table, she realized she looked inordinately flushed.

She stared with wonder at her own image in the glass. Had Lord Penwyck actually scooped her into his arms and carried her up the walk into the house?

She'd never been carried by a gentleman before. The experience was quite disarming, but it was very chivalrous of him. The hem of her gown and pelisse would have been soaked with mud otherwise.

She hurriedly slipped out of her damp garments and absently removed a dry gown from the clothespress.

She had quite enjoyed the light banter she and the earl had exchanged in the carriage. A small smile softened the anxious look on her face. The arrogant earl really was a nice man.

No! He was not a nice man!

Recalling the disquieting feel of his powerful arms holding her aloft and her soft bosom pressed to his chest, her insides suddenly began to tingle. *What is the matter with me?*

When the odd tingling sensation became a shudder of longing, Tessa fell weak-kneed onto the bed. Was she taking ill? Pondering the oddity, she lay flat on her back, staring up at the ceiling.

Some moments later, a light scratch sounded at her bedchamber door. A fresh pang of alarm stabbed Tessa as she lurched upright, but disappeared the instant she opened the door and a housemaid stepped inside.

"Lady Penwyck be asking after ye, Miss. Will ye be coming down for breakfast this morning, or would ye like a tray sent up?"

"I confess I am feeling a bit chilled. You may tell Lady Penwyck I would prefer to breakfast in my room, thank you." Tessa ran her hands up her damp arms. "You may also tell Lady Penwyck that I—I would like to rest a bit this morning."

"Very well, miss." The maid bobbed a quick curtsy.

Lady Penwyck received Tessa's message as she was seating herself at the breakfast table. Although she was sorry Tessa was not feeling well, the extraordinary events of that morning had not diminished her spirits the least little bit.

"Not yet ten of the clock," she exclaimed joyfully to her son, who, having changed into dry clothing, was joining her for the morning meal, "and more than a dozen invitations have already arrived and twice as many cards!"

Penwyck, taking his customary place at the head of the table, merely nodded. That following Miss Darby's successful debut last evening a barrage of invitations had already been delivered did not surprise him. Apparently his good friend Ashburn had the right of it when he predicted Miss Darby would become the newest darling of the *ton.* Indeed, she was a diamond of the first water. Penwyck's initial assessment of his mother's protégée had been quite wide of the mark. Miss Darby was not only lovely to look at, she was charming and intelligent. Penwyck had found their conversation this morning in the carriage both enlightening and delightful. It was easy to see why so many gentlemen flocked to such a charming young lady.

"I can hardly wait to read about Tessa's debut in the morning papers!" Lady Penwyck added. She snatched up the small crystal bell that reposed near her plate and gave it a resounding jingle.

When a servant appeared at her elbow, she sent the fellow off in search of the *The Times* and *The Morning Post.*

"I declare I am all atwitter!" she announced gaily.

"Miss Darby's debut was indeed a resounding success, Mother. I am certain the papers will give it quite a glowing account. You and Mrs. Montgomery are to be commended."

"Well, the bulk of the credit belongs to Gracie. I am not nearly so organized as she—or as you, for all that. But it was a marvelous party, was it not, Penny dear? Tessa looked splendid!"

"She did, indeed."

"Of course, our work is not yet done," Lady Penwyck added smugly. "We have yet to accomplish our most important goal."

Over the rim of his coffee cup, Penwyck aimed a question at his mother. "What goal would that be, Mother?"

"Why, marriage, of course. Our work is not done until Miss Darby is affianced."

Penwyck's coffee cup seemed of its own accord to escape his grasp and drop with a loud clatter onto the saucer. "I-I see."

"Why else would one go to such lengths to present a young lady to Society if not to land her a husband?" Lady Penwyck laughed gaily. "For all your brilliance, Penny dear, you can often be quite . . . well, *silly.*"

Penwyck's lips thinned with sudden annoyance.

"I predict Tessa will receive upwards of a dozen offers! Several young men showed quite a good deal of interest in her last evening. What do you think, dear?"

Penwyck had managed to regain himself somewhat but was not yet prepared with a definitive answer to the question. "Well . . . I . . . I rather expect she will receive her share of offers, in due time."

"In due time?" Lady Penwyck echoed. "Whatever do you mean by that, you silly boy?" she demanded affectionately.

Penwyck brought his coffee cup to his lips again. "I was

given to understand Miss Darby was . . . well, that her father had . . . that she was already betrothed to an American gentl—"

"Oh, my, no! That is not the case at all," his mother interjected. "Tessa has no intention whatever of returning to the colonies. She means to remain in England, you may be sure of that. Oh!" Her gray eyes widened and she gleefully clapped her hands together. "I've a perfectly splendid idea!"

Penwyck waited.

"You are quite good at drawing up lists, Penny dear. I should like you to draw up a list of young men who would be suitable candidates for our Miss Darby to wed." She paused to consider. "Although I daresay it was difficult last evening to determine what sort of young man she prefers. She stood up with so many. I declare she must have danced with every young man present. She was a genuine belle of the ball! I do so wish her dear mother could have been here. Helen would have been so proud. At any rate, you are quite good at drawing up lists," she said again.

Throughout his mother's lengthy monologue, Penwyck had been working to collect himself again. Marriage was, of course, the only sensible answer to the dilemma posed by the disturbing Miss Darby. It was just that, for some reason, the idea of *his* selecting a suitable husband for her suddenly seemed . . . well, it seemed . . .

He squirmed uncomfortably, and because of a sudden he felt inordinately warm, ran a finger along the inside of his neckcloth, which in his haste to dress this morning must have somehow got wound a bit too tightly about his neck.

Of course Miss Darby would one day marry. And that his mother should call upon him to help select a suitable candidate made perfect sense, on the surface.

So why was it that, beneath the surface, somewhere in the region of his middle, or perhaps his heart, the idea of Miss Darby's marrying sickened him?

Suddenly, the notion of his finding a husband for the delectable Miss Darby seemed the stupidest idea he had ever heard!

"—we shall be attending countless balls and soirees," his mother was saying. "I shall leave it to you, Penny dear, to present Tessa to each of the gentlemen on your list. Perhaps it would serve if you asked her if she has a preference in—"

"Confound it, madam!" Penwyck suddenly sprang to his feet, his handsome features twisted into an angry scowl. "I have far more important things on my mind than searching out a proper mate for Miss Darby!"

That said, the tight-lipped earl stomped from the room in obvious disgust.

His mother sat staring after him. Presently, a thoughtful smile lifted the corners of her lips.

"Well, well. Perhaps we shan't need a list of prospective suitors for Miss Darby after all."

Fourteen

Before the day ended, Penwyck relented and told his mother he would speak with Miss Darby to ascertain her preference, if any, in a suitor.

With a sly smile, Lady Penwyck said she thought that quite a good idea.

Afterward, Penwyck quit the house and returned again to the Montgomery mansion to speak with Deirdre's father on behalf of the ill-fated lovers.

Following dinner that evening, the earl did not retire to his study with a brandy or join one of his gentlemen friends at his club. Instead he accompanied his mother and Miss Darby to the family's cozy but not so tidy sitting room at the rear of the house. He seldom ventured into this room, although it had been a particular favourite of his as a boy. He and his brothers had been allowed to come here in the evening and freely play with their toy soldiers and other games whilst Lord and Lady Penwyck sat reading or talking by the fire.

He assumed his mother and Miss Darby sat here often. The overstuffed chairs and sofas were littered with ladies' magazines—*Ackermann's Repository,* the *Lady's Monthly Museum,* and *La Belle Assemblée*—as well as a needlepoint sampler his mother had been labouriously stitching upon this past half decade.

"Why, Penny dear, do you mean to join us this evening?"

Lady Penwyck asked brightly as he followed her and Tessa into the room.

She began to clear a place for him on one of the sofas.

"Do sit here beside m—" She cast a quick glance at Tessa. "Perhaps you would prefer to sit there beside Tessa. It is a bit chilly this evening and the aspect by the fire is especially pleasant. I shall sit"—she drug a chair over—"here."

Exchanging guarded glances with one another, Tessa and Lord Penwyck both sat down, as instructed, on the small settee by the fire.

Presently, Lord Penwyck said, "I took tea with Mr. and Mrs. Montgomery this afternoon."

"Oh, my dear, how are they faring? Has Gracie recovered from the ordeal? I really must pay a call tomorrow. What a simply horrid turn after our lovely party last night!"

"Indeed." Penwyck crossed one long leg over the other. "However, I daresay things have turned out rather well, considering."

Tessa leaned forward. "I can hardly bear the suspense, sir. What did Mr. Montgomery say? Are Deirdre and Jeffrey to be allowed to marry?"

Penwyck turned a supremely satisfied look on Miss Darby. He thought she looked especially lovely this evening in a green cambric round gown trimmed with plaid braid. A soft kerseymere shawl of a darker green was draped about her shoulders. He favoured the young lady with a pleasant smile.

"After a great deal of deliberation, the Montgomerys have agreed to announce their daughter's engagement to Mr. Randall in the newspapers."

"Deirdre is to be married?" both Lady Penwyck and Tessa cried at once.

Penwyck grinned. "By teatime, it had already become clear that despite Deirdre's promise never to see Randall again, to enforce the edict would merely hasten the pair's departure for Gretna Green."

"Did I not tell you they were desperate to be married?" Tessa put in, her blue eyes sparkling happily.

The look of joy on Miss Darby's face was as enchanting as any Penwyck had ever beheld. He drew in a long breath and settled back to bask in the sheer pleasure he alone had brought her. The glow that suffused him soon grew so warm (he *was* quite near the fire) that had he not been occupying the prime spot next to Miss Darby, he'd have sought a considerably cooler aspect. As it was, he decided the reward was well worth the discomfort.

Beside him on the sofa, Tessa was, indeed, thrilled.

"I cannot think how you managed it!" she cried. "I thought Mr. Montgomery so exceedingly angry this morning, it would take a miracle to placate him."

She turned a beaming smile on Lady Penwyck and proceeded to recount the events of the dramatic interval to Alice. Because Tessa had spent the bulk of the day in her room, she had not seen or talked to the countess all day.

When the topic had been fully exhausted, Lady Penwyck professed to a prodigious tiredness and, with a bit of a gleam in her eye, declared her intent to retire.

Tessa felt quite weary herself, but for some reason was loath to bring the evening to a close. She'd had a difficult time today thrusting pleasant but unsettling memories of Lord Penwyck from her thoughts. That he was again being as affable and congenial as he had been this morning in the carriage quite lifted her spirits.

She was further pleased when he chose not to quit the room in his mother's wake, but instead asked if she would care for a brandy or a glass of wine.

Having risen when his mother did, the earl headed toward a small sideboard and reached for one of several decanters sitting atop it.

"A dram of brandy would be nice." Tessa smiled. "Thank you, sir."

After he handed her a neat snifter, Tessa felt a bit of a pang when Lord Penwyck seated himself in the chair vacated by his mother instead of returning to the settee beside her.

Drawing in a deep breath, he said without preamble, "Mother

has asked me to draw up a list." His tone was quite solemn. "Before doing so, I thought it prudent to consult with you."

Still wondering why Lord Penwyck had not returned to sit beside her and feeling somewhat disquieted at being left alone in his company, Tessa only half heard what the earl had said. In an absent gesture, she lifted her glass to her lips and enjoyed the feel of the velvety brandy as it slipped down her throat. "A list?" she repeated. Then, when it occurred to her he was soliciting her views, her spirits lifted considerably. She directed a warm smile his way. "What sort of list?"

Penwyck took a sip of his own drink. "Of suitable candidates for your hand in marriage."

Tessa started. "M-marriage?"

"As Mother rightly pointed out to me at breakfast, the ultimate object of introducing a young lady to Society is to see her wed," Penwyck replied matter-of-factly, his gaze steady. "Before setting down the names of suitable gentlemen, I thought it best to consult with you," he added.

Tessa gulped. "I . . . I . . ." For some unfathomable reason, she felt stung to the quick. Today he had finally seemed to warm toward her. That he should suddenly inform her he meant to marry her off to . . . to . . . She knew Lady Penwyck thought she ought to marry. It was just that she thought she had made it clear to Lord Penwyck she had no intention of doing so.

Without thinking what she was about, she brought the snifter to her lips and drained it in a single gulp. Then, because her throat felt set afire, she coughed.

And coughed.

And coughed again.

"I-If . . . if I might . . . *cough!* . . . have a glass of water, sir."

Penwyck leapt to his feet.

An instant later, he knelt on the settee beside Tessa, a glass of cool water in his hand.

Tessa gratefully drank it straight down. She had ceased to cough, but she had not yet sufficiently recovered from the shock of his pronouncement to speak calmly. She absently handed the empty glass back to the earl, who was sitting quite close to her, a look of genuine solicitude on his face.

Tessa raised a hurt, but shuttered, blue gaze to meet his, and was at once perplexed by the raw hunger she beheld in the earl's dark brown eyes. Why, if she didn't know better, she'd think the gentleman wished to . . . to kiss her!

She had never been *this* close to him before. She had been alone with him several times for the few private interviews he'd conducted with her soon after her arrival in Town, and once in the Chalmers's library when he'd burst in upon her and Lord Dickerson.

But, this . . . this was somehow vastly different.

She could not think what it meant or why he would be gazing at her in such a lustful fashion.

Because she'd never before been in such a situation, she did the only thing she could think to do. She sprang to her feet and all but ran from him. Reaching the chair where Lord Penwyck had been seated, she turned to face him.

"A-as I have said before, sir, I have no intention of marrying. I am perfectly content . . . as I am. I apprised you of the true reason I came to London. I have not abandoned my Cause, sir. I still have every intention of doing what I can to forward it, despite your disapproval," she added staunchly.

Penwyck had risen to his feet and they stood facing one another. "I did not mean to overset you, Miss Darby," he began, not wishing to do further damage to the fragile footing he had managed to gain with her, "but if we do not make some sort of show of finding you a husband, there is no saying to what lengths Mother will go to forward *her* cause."

He ran a hand through his dark locks. "Mother can be every bit as tenacious as you when she sets her mind to something, Miss Darby. I rather expect I may have also inherited that trait, but that is neither here nor there, is it?" He grinned disarmingly. "Perhaps you might give me some indication of the sort of gentleman you might favour—that is, if you were to favour one."

He watched Miss Darby chew on her lower lip as if she were

considering his request, but he noted her blue eyes were still clouded with uncertainty. That she did not trust him or perhaps *any* man was becoming quite clear to him. She had seemed to open up a bit with him this morning in the carriage, but he wondered now if he had pushed his luck by remaining alone with her tonight.

He halted that line of thought when she said, "V-very well, if I must. However," she added hesitantly, "m-most gentlemen I have met thus far in London seem . . . far too frivolous for my taste. I do not care for dandies or foppish men."

Penwyck suppressed a grin. He'd never before asked such a question of a lady. Of a sudden, he realized her answer could prove quite enlightening, as well as entertaining.

"In America," she went on, her voice gaining a bit of strength, "men are more rugged than they are here. Many are accustomed to working out of doors. Even gentlemen like my stepfather take to the fields at times. Did you know Thomas Jefferson plants his own garden?"

She seemed to forget her fear for an instant, her blue eyes regaining some of their former animation.

"No," Penwyck murmured. "I did not know that."

"Mr. Jefferson even at his advanced age has one of the largest gardens in the country. He is quite knowledgeable about plants and trees and all manner of herbs."

She stopped suddenly, apparently realizing she'd gone off on a tangent.

"Are you saying you admire gentlemen farmers?" Penwyck asked with interest.

Her lips tightened again. "I do not object to them. But I would not consider marrying one unless he was a principled man, one who is honest and trustworthy."

"Ah." Penwyck continued to gaze at her. "If you will forgive me for saying so, Miss Darby, you appear to have a bit of trouble trusting men. I cannot help but wonder what has caused you to think so ill of us."

Again, a shuttered gaze obscured the lively sparkle in her shining blue eyes and she clamped her lips tightly shut again.

Penwyck drew in a deep breath. "Very well, then. You do not favour fops and dandies. But, you do admire a"—he directed a bemused look at her—"a virile man." His lips began to twitch. "Perhaps I should be jotting this down."

He was pleased to note a slight upturn of her pink lips.

"Are you making sport of me, sir?" She tilted her auburn head. "Because I do not like that quality in a gentleman, either." She seemed to regain a bit of her former sauciness as she thrust her chin up. "I do not understand why men think they are the superior creatures. God gave all of us brains, you know. There are a good many things about the American Constitution, sirrah, that foreign countries would do well to emulate. We are all of us created equal. I take that to mean men and women alike. Whilst women in America do not yet have all the freedom they deserve, I daresay that day is coming. Mark my words, sir!"

Penwyck listened as if transfixed. Once again, he was beholding the fiery passion he'd witnessed in Miss Darby when she spoke that afternoon in William Cobbett's office. Dashed if she wasn't the most arresting female he had ever met. How he longed to delve deeply into her thoughts and uncover everything about her! He'd never felt this way about a woman before.

Cocking her auburn head she suddenly said, "I've an idea."

"I am breathless to hear it," Penwyck murmured. It was all he could do not to gather her into his arms and kiss her senseless.

"If I spot the sort of gentlemen I would like to meet, I will alert you, and you can present me to him straightaway."

"Ah. And, in the meantime . . ." He paused. "What are we to do until you spot this paragon?"

Tessa shrugged. "I don't know. Perhaps I shall simply go about on your arm."

Without considering the effect his words might have, Penwyck blithely replied, "I see only one problem with that plan." He reached into his waistcoat pocket and jerked out a cream-coloured sheet of paper. "I have already drawn up a list."

"Of gentlemen?" Tessa cried. "But I thought—"

"For myself. It is also time I married. If I am seen too much in your company, that will rather spoil my chances with other ladies, wouldn't you agree?"

When she suddenly blanched, he realized he had inadvertently ruined it between them yet again. Her offer to go about on his arm was her way of reaching out to him, of trusting him. His thoughtless remark must have felt like one more slap in the face.

He watched her blue eyes become veiled again. "I see." She made a move to brush past him. "Well, I shouldn't wish to impose, of course. As I said before, I have no intention of marrying, so it makes no difference to me if I meet a suitable man or not."

Penwyck wasn't about to let this day end on an ill note between them. As she sailed past him, he reached to grasp her wrist, but missed and suddenly found his arm encircling her trim waist. With a swift move, he pressed her lithe body against his own.

"Miss Darby," he murmured, his lips mere inches from hers, his dark eyes smoldering with pent-up passion, "we have made such a good start today, first in the carriage, and . . . well, the truth is, you little minx, I wish only to be your friend."

He could feel her quick intake of breath. Fascinated, he watched her pretty nostrils flare. The press of her ample bosom against his hard chest sent a jolt of white-hot desire blazing through him. He tried to ignore the sensation, but when his gaze dropped to the pink bow of her mouth, he could not resist lowering his head and brushing those tantalizing lips with his own.

It was the merest of kisses. He didn't dare give in to the flaming passion he felt. The girl did not trust him as it was. But because she was not resisting his amorous advance, he held her close for what seemed an excruciating time, his fiery dark eyes blazing into her icy blue ones.

Finally, he said, "Truce?"

Her eyes hardened once more, but not before Penwyck caught the glimmer of an answering fire within their depths. "Or what?" she whispered. "You will take me against my will?"

Penwyck released her at once, his eyes narrowing in anger. "I have done nothing to cause you to think ill of me, Miss Darby," he spat out.

Without a word, he watched her stalk to the door and disappear into the corridor.

Penwyck stood staring after her. Indeed, he had never met a woman like Miss Darby before. She was a complex web of mystery and intrigue.

And, he finally admitted, her mystery and intrigue had totally captivated him.

Fifteen

Deirdre Montgomery's wedding took place early one morning the following week. The simple ceremony was conducted before a private altar in a corner of the magnificent nave in St. Mark's Cathedral with only a handful of family members and intimate friends present.

Tessa stood between Lord Penwyck and his mother. She thought Deirdre looked radiant in her ivory satin gown, its bodice and sleeves embellished with blond lace and seed pearls. The long, lace-edged train, attached to a pearl-encrusted tiara, extended a good five feet behind the bride. In one gloved hand Deirdre carried a sweet-smelling bouquet of ivory rosebuds and lacy greenery tied with a pink satin ribbon.

Watching the simple ceremony, a wave of nostalgia and longing overtook Tessa. In a few moments, the one true friend she'd made in London would no longer be a green girl with no direction to her life. By repeating a few words before a man of God in this sanctuary, Deirdre's life would take on new meaning. She would be a married woman, the wife of Mr. Jeffrey Randall. Tessa had yet to meet the gentleman, but because of the loving way he was gazing at Deirdre, she already liked him.

Something pulled her eyes up to Lord Penwyck, standing quietly beside her as the reverend led the couple through their vows. The esteemed earl was as handsomely turned out this morning as the groom, both gentlemen wearing blue superfine coats with brass buttons and dark trousers. Lord Penwyck, however, had elected to wear a jonquil-yellow waistcoat, the whimsy of which brought an amused grin to Tessa's lips.

Since their few moments alone together that night in the sitting room, she'd seen precious little of the earl. He'd been obliged to travel to the family's country estate to settle a dispute involving a pair of feuding tenants. He had just returned to London the previous evening.

During his absence, Tessa and Lady Penwyck had stayed busy executing an endless round of calls every day. Every night, they attended one or another important Society function. Although Lady Penwyck seemed thrilled with the manner in which Tessa's career was progressing, Tessa was already sick to death of attending lavish parties, smiling till her cheeks ached, and dancing till her toes grew numb.

To top it off, she'd been endlessly plagued every day by a nagging worry about Lord Penwyck. Truth to tell, of the scores of gentlemen she'd been presented to these past weeks, she thought him far and away the most attractive, the most intelligent, the most principled, and, Tessa realized with a sinking feeling in the pit of her stomach, the most *desirable* of every last one of them. But when he'd asked her last week what sort of gentleman she preferred, she could not have told him—partly because she hadn't yet known.

But it was firmly implanted in her mind now, as was the fact Deirdre and Jeffrey owed their future happiness to him. Without Lord Penwyck's intervention on their behalf, today's grand occasion would have remained only a dream in Deirdre's mind.

Tessa felt nothing but the utmost admiration for Lord Penwyck now. Everyone in London spoke of him in the most glowing terms. He was quite highly regarded. But, she reminded herself, he had already set down his list of prospective marriage partners and made it abundantly clear Tessa was not amongst them. A sharp pang of disappointment stabbed her, as it did every time she allowed her thoughts to run on in this vein.

"To love and honour for as long as ye both shall live . . ."

Quite against her will, an involuntary sob rose in Tessa's

throat. She hadn't realized her cry was audible until she felt Lady Penwyck's gloved hand squeeze hers.

"We are all very happy for Deirdre," the older woman whispered.

The slight commotion caught Lord Penwyck's notice, and Tessa felt his gaze shift toward her. She blinked away the moisture that suddenly welled in her eyes. She mustn't let him see her cry. What was the matter with her?

Drawing in several deep breaths, she managed to gulp down the painful emotion building within her. And to prove to Lord Penwyck she was quite all right, she cast what she hoped was a bright smile up at him.

A small answering one flickered across his face.

"Let us pray."

Tessa's eyes squeezed shut. *Dear God in Heaven, please . . .*

"We shall be planning *your* wedding next, Tessa dear. You may be certain of that!" exclaimed Lady Penwyck as they all streamed from the church into the glorious sunlight that broke through the early morning haze to cast a glow upon the small wedding party gathered in the courtyard.

Following a sumptuous wedding breakfast held at the fashionable Grillon Hotel in London, Deirdre and her new husband planned to leave for a short wedding trip to the seaside village of Sidmouth.

"You must come for dinner as soon as we return to Town," the flushed bride told Tessa as she warmly embraced her friend. "Jeffrey and I are as happy as can be, and we owe it all to you!"

"Not to me," Tessa demurred. "To Lord Penwyck." She directed another sincere smile up at the handsome gentleman.

Penwyck reached to pump Mr. Randall's hand. "My best wishes to you both, Randall," he said. "And thank you again for your excellent help with the committee's investigation some weeks back."

The gentlemen fell into a short conversation centered around the Parliamentary committee's findings regarding the unlawful practices of several land agents in London.

Tessa's chest swelled with pride as she listened to the eminent earl. She greatly admired him!

That evening, Lord Penwyck accompanied his mother and Miss Darby to a rout at Lord and Lady Wintertons'. During the past week, whilst he'd been away, he had convinced himself his boyish infatuation with Miss Darby was quite foolish. Clearly she had no interest in forming an attachment with him or, for that matter, with any man. She disliked all members of the male sex and was quite content to spend her life on the shelf. Although he had never met a young lady who openly aspired to such a life, he knew several older women who'd had no desire to marry or bear children and were quite content now.

It would, indeed, be a waste of time for Penwyck to attempt to change Miss Darby's mind in that regard. Therefore, he vowed to cease thinking about her altogether. Instead, he renewed his determination to find a proper young lady to become his bride. His younger brother, Stephen, looking after the family's country estate, was quite happily wed. He and his pretty young bride would soon become parents.

Thinking further on the matter, Penwyck was able to come up with several more eligible misses whose names he promptly added to his list. Tonight he meant to conduct preliminary interviews with each young lady. That his mother and Miss Darby had attended a number of soirees last week on their own, apparently without mishap, told him close supervision of Miss Darby was no longer necessary.

Moreover, his mother had happily informed him that her protégée had received numerous calls last week from a variety of gentlemen, a few even taking her for drives in the park. Despite Miss Darby's lack of interest in any of them, Penwyck reasoned she was, indeed, quite well-equipped to go about on her own now and required no further instruction or advice from him.

When the Penwyck party entered the Wintertons' crowded

ballroom, the earl hastily excused himself and set off in search of Miss Maryellen Mortimer, a pretty little blond Penwyck considered especially even-tempered. That Miss Mortimer spoke with a slight lisp was but a minor fault, he told himself, and over time would be hardly noticeable.

Tessa was a bit surprised when Lord Penwyck so hastily abandoned her and his mother so soon after they'd entered the ballroom. She followed his progress through the crowded room until he was swallowed up by the crush of elegantly attired guests milling about. He'd hardly spoken two words to her since his return to London, and she hadn't the least notion why.

Apparently Lady Penwyck also thought her son's hasty departure a bit unusual. "Oh, dear, I was hoping Penny would—well, I expect he has business to—no doubt he will seek us out when he . . ." her voice trailed off.

Quite accustomed now to Lady Penwyck's disjointed manner of thinking and speaking, Tessa merely smiled and nodded. "I am certain he will," she murmured. To herself she added: *I hope.* She had not danced with the handsome earl since her debut and she desperately wished to stand up with him tonight.

Something else was also niggling at the back of her mind—namely the memory of Lord Penwyck lightly brushing her lips as he held her in his arms that night in the family's sitting room.

Try as she might, Tessa simply could not thrust that vivid memory from mind. She had never been kissed before, and although she did not truly believe the feather touch of his lips to hers could be considered a real kiss, the effect it had upon her was unforgettable. Tessa longed to know if . . . perhaps if they danced or took a stroll on the veranda, or even if . . . oh, dear. She drew herself up. She was beginning to think as disjointedly as Lady Penwyck!

She shook herself and, willing a bright smile to her lips, glanced with feigned interest about the room.

"I see a number of your suitors are in attendance tonight, dear," Lady Penwyck remarked brightly.

Indeed, during the next hour, Tessa danced with Lord Chesterton, whom she did rather like. He was a serious young man who had a special fondness for Lord Byron's poetry. He had presented Tessa with a slim volume of it only last week.

Whilst moving through the patterns of a lively quadrille with Lord Hargrove, a muscular gentleman who years ago had risen to the rank of major in the British army, Tessa caught sight of Lord Penwyck dancing with pretty little Miss Mortimer. When Lord Hargrove returned Tessa to the sidelines, she noted Lord Penwyck doing the same with Miss Mortimer only a few feet away.

But her heart sank when Lord Penwyck commenced to promenade about the room, quite alone. After two turns, he stopped beside a plumpish but attractive girl whom Tessa had once met, Lady Amelia Roundtree. Tessa clearly recalled the girl's surname. At the time she'd thought it quite apropos, considering Lady Amelia's girth.

"Tessa dear!"

Tessa turned to find Lady Penwyck and three or four of her friends, all elegantly bejewelled and beturbaned, approaching her.

"Lady Jamison insists on presenting you to her son, Robert, just home from a tour of the continent."

Tessa willed a fresh smile to her lips and allowed herself to be swept along.

"Robert is the sole heir to a dukedom," Lady Penwyck whispered as the entire party marched toward their unsuspecting quarry. "The Jamisons' family estate is second to none."

After Tessa had danced with the prime catch, Lord Robert, and then Lords Marchmont, Cleary, and Hamilton, she begged exhaustion and retired to the sidelines. She'd no sooner been presented with a glass of punch by one of her more ardent admirers when the dandified Frenchman Monsieur de la Rouchet appeared at her elbow.

"*Bon soir, mon amie.*" The gentleman bowed low over Tessa's white-gloved hand.

Tessa cringed, fearful he meant to kiss her fingertips as he had done the night of her debut when she'd first been presented to him, and a smudge of the brilliant fuchsia rouge he wore on his lips had soiled her gloves.

"How per-fect-ly love-ly you look, *ma petite fleur!*" the flamboyant man announced in broken English and, with a flourish, kissed his own fingertips.

"Merci." Tessa smiled. Had de la Rouchet looked less like a painted doll, she might have returned the compliment. As it was, the pungent cloud of French perfume enveloping the gentleman very nearly gagged her. In addition, it was all she could do not to jerk out her handkerchief and rub out the pink rouge staining the gentleman's cheeks.

Instead, she managed to carry on a credible conversation with the harmless man in both French and English. At length, he said, *"Voulez-vous danser?"*

Because Tessa did not wish to dance with him, she was most gratified just then to spot the agreeable Mr. Ashburn strolling toward them.

Monsieur de la Rouchet's sharp eyes had followed hers. "Ah, I see a friend approaches."

"Oui," Tessa said. Before she could stop herself, she added, "I have promised the next dance to him."

"Ah."

"Mr. Ashburn," Tessa greeted the pleasant-faced young man.

When she extended her hand, Ashburn took it and, to her surprise, wrapped it over his arm. "You look lovely tonight, my dear. Blue becomes you," he added, referring to the rich colour of the exquisite low-cut sarsenet gown she wore.

He nodded at de la Rouchet, who politely greeted him in his native tongue.

Ashburn looked a question at Tessa.

"He asked if you are well, sir." she translated, with a smile. "Tell him: *'Je ne parle pas Francais.'* "

Ashburn grinned crookedly. "Why don't you tell him that?"

Tessa protested with a laugh, "But I *do* speak French!"

"Parlez plus lentement, s'il vous plaît!" the Frenchman intoned.

"Pardon," Tessa replied, and said to Mr. Ashburn, "He asked us to speak a bit slower."

Mr. Ashburn tapped his chin. "Now that I think on it, I do recall a French phrase I learned as a schoolboy." Puffing out his chest, he declared, *"Le bébé est petit."*

The Frenchman turned round eyes on Tessa, who had already dissolved into giggles.

"What did I say?" Mr. Ashburn demanded. "I meant to tell him my French is small, like a baby."

Both Tessa and the Frenchman were still laughing.

"I'm afraid you told him the baby is little."

Not a one of the laughing threesome saw the tall, elegantly clad Lord Penwyck approaching.

"Pray tell, what is so very amusing?" he asked, stepping up to join them.

"I just made a cake of myself," Mr. Ashburn replied good-naturedly.

"A not uncommon occurrence," Penwyck remarked dryly, though his lips were twitching. A dark gaze settled on Tessa. "I see you are not dancing, Miss Darby. Would you do me the honour, please?"

"Non!" the Frenchman cried, waving a beringed finger beneath the earl's nose. He reached for Tessa's hand and that of Mr. Ashburn, and with an elaborate gesture brought the two together. "She *danse avec him!"*

"Delighted!" Mr. Ashburn exclaimed at once.

Tessa coloured. Casting an apologetic glance at Penwyck, she murmured, "Perhaps a bit later, sir."

As Mr. Ashburn led her away, she heard a remnant of the remark the Frenchman was making to the earl. Something about his *'cherchez les jeunes filles.'* Did everyone know about Lord Penwyck's list, his *search for young ladies?*

Halfway through her dance with Mr. Ashburn, the mystery was cleared up.

"Penwyck has added five new names to his list of prospective marriage partners," Mr. Ashburn announced lightly.

"Five?" Tessa said. Her anxious gaze sought out the elegant

earl. He was engaged in what appeared to be an intense conversation with a voluptuous brunette Tessa had never met.

"Lady Elizabeth Hubenot," Mr. Ashburn told her as the steps of the dance brought them together again. "Her father is a Belgian duke. Lost an eye at Waterloo, but it ain't hurt his game any."

"His game?"

"Whist. The man can spot a winning card at twenty paces."

They parted for a few turns, an intricate pattern to the left, another to the right, and four steps forward.

When they were again standing toe to toe, Tessa said, "I daresay I am a bit surprised Lord Penwyck has made public the fact that he has drawn up a list of prospective brides."

"He hasn't."

"But Monsieur de la—"

"Word leaks out, you know." Mr. Ashburn shrugged as he stepped away again. A few seconds later, he added with a grin, "I rather expect he will accuse me of being the culprit."

"Are you?" Tessa queried, a grin on her lips.

"Indeed not!" Mr. Ashburn feigned outrage.

"Then why would he accuse you?"

"Penwyck thinks me quite the gossipmonger. Is always accusing me of knowing everyone else's business better than they do and very often *before* they do." Ashburn laughed.

Tessa smiled at the likable fellow. He looked quite handsome in his fashionable evening clothes. "Perhaps that is because you are so very easy to confide in, sir. I expect a good many people take you into their confidence, just as I did when my friend Deirdre required help. She and Jeffrey were married this morning—"

Ashburn was nodding.

"Ah, but you already knew that," Tessa concluded wryly.

Mr. Ashburn winked at her, and lowered his voice somewhat. "I also know that you refused to allow Penwyck to draw up a list of eligible gentlemen for you to consider."

Tessa's blue eyes widened. "Did he tell you that?" she asked incredulously.

Ashburn shook his head as he grasped her hand and turned

her twice about. When she again faced him, he said, "Penwyck said nothing. *Lady* Penwyck told Sally Jersey, who told the Countess Lieven, who told—"

"Enough!" Tessa cried. Her blue eyes rolled skyward.

The music ended then and Mr. Ashburn politely returned a somewhat chagrined Tessa to the sidelines.

"I daresay," Mr. Ashburn started up again, "I was quite disappointed when I heard the news."

"The news?" Tessa glanced at him, part of her mind still mulling over all that he had told her.

"That you had refused Penwyck's offer to draw up a list for you."

Tessa's auburn head tilted to one side. "And why ever would that disappoint *you,* sir?"

Ashburn's blue eyes twinkled merrily. "Because, Miss Darby, I had wished *my* name placed at the top of said list."

"You are incorrigible," she teased.

"On the contrary, my dear." The gentleman's voice grew a trifle raspy. "I am quite serious."

As Tessa cast about for something appropriate to say, she fixed a solemn gaze on the affable gentleman. It was not the first time a man had made a veiled declaration of his feelings toward her. She'd received nearly a dozen offers of marriage this past week alone. She'd even received one scandalous offer of *carte blanche.* She'd shrugged them all off as casually as if the gentlemen had been inquiring if she'd like a glass of punch.

She did regard Mr. Ashburn as a dear friend, however, and did not wish to trample his feelings.

"Thank you, sir," she finally said. "I feel quite flattered. You are one of the few genuine friends I have in London."

Mr. Ashburn's blue eyes were warm. "And I consider you a true friend as well, Miss Darby. I hope you will not hesitate to call on me whenever you need a—"

"I daresay," came a deep male voice behind then, "you two now look as solemn as a funeral procession."

Mr. Ashburn looked over Tessa's auburn head. "Hallo again,

Penwyck." He grinned. "Truth is, I have just declared myself to your Miss Darby, and she has soundly refused me."

Tessa cast a somewhat coy look up at the earl. Again she thought how splendid he looked in his black evening clothes, a froth of white linen gleaming at his throat.

Penwyck's dark brow lifted as his shuttered gaze settled again on Tessa.

"Rumour has it," Mr. Ashburn blithely went on, "Miss Darby has refused two dozen offers of marri—"

"That is absurd!" Tessa cried, with a self-conscious laugh.

His hands clasped behind his back, Lord Penwyck stood solemnly watching her. Though he made no reply, the expression on his face looked as if he thought the claim not unlikely.

"How many offers have you refused?" he finally asked.

"Why, I—I—" Tessa turned palms upward.

Mr. Ashburn laughed aloud. "Now that I think on it, I believe the number was closer to *three* dozen."

"Oh, do be still!" Tessa cried. "Someone is likely to hear you and *voila!* another rumour launched!"

Penwyck rocked back on his heels. "I am beginning to see how you become embroiled in these things, Ash."

"He is only larking!" Tessa laughed again. "I have not received thirty offers of marriage! I have not even received—"

"Ah, zer you are, mademoiselle. Eeet is my dance, now, non?"

For once, Tessa was relieved to see the painted face of the Frenchman. She smiled prettily as she placed her gloved fingers atop the arm he extended.

"Thank you for the lovely dance, Mr. Ashburn," she said sweetly.

Penwyck and Mr. Ashburn watched as Monsieur de la Rouchet led Miss Darby back onto the dance floor.

"You were right," Penwyck murmured.

"About what, old man?"

"Miss Darby does speak French."

Ashburn nodded sagely. "Good thing. I daresay she will soon be obliged to refuse yet another suitor, this time in French."

Sixteen

The following week, Tessa received a morning call from Mrs. Jeffrey Randall. Tessa was thrilled to see her friend again. Deirdre looked radiantly happy as she burst into the cluttered Penwyck drawing room and took a seat beside Tessa on the sofa.

"Do tell me all about your wedding trip," Tessa began. "I have never been to the seacoast in England. I am certain it must be lovely."

"We had a splendid time!" Deirdre gushed. "Jeffrey and I are so very happy. Do tell me you intend to be married one day, Tessa. You really must!" Deirdre's brown eyes sparkled happily.

Tessa looked away. Judging from the tingling sensation she'd experienced when the earl brushed her lips with his, she could imagine how . . . how . . .

Squirming uncomfortably on the sofa, she hastened to thrust the scandalous thought aside. "I confess, I . . . I have considered it," she murmured hesitantly.

"Who?" Deirdre squealed with delight. "Do you have a new beau? Tell me who it is at once!"

Tessa colored. She didn't have a *new* beau. She didn't have a beau at all. She couldn't think what had prompted her to say such a thing. And she could not tell Deirdre Lord Penwyck had kissed her, or that she was harbouring romantical notions about him. Oh, how had everything become so tangled in her mind?

"No, I haven't a new beau," she replied in a small voice. "I just meant . . . well, you looked so beautiful in your wedding finery and you seem so very happy now."

"I *am* happy! Jeffrey and I feel we owe you an enormous debt of gratitude. You and Lord Penwyck and, of course, Mr. Ashburn." She paused, as if to gauge Tessa's reaction to that. "Which is why Jeffrey and I want to invite you and Mr. Ashburn to dinner at our home tomorrow evening. Jeffrey has sent a note to Mr. Ashburn inviting him. He is such an agreeable gentleman, Tessa. Jeffrey and I are certain he fancies you."

"Oh, no." Tessa's auburn head shook. "Mr. Ashburn is very nice, that is true, but . . ."

"But what? I think he would be perfect for you, Tessa."

Suddenly, Tessa popped to her feet. "Would you care for a glass of lemonade, Deirdre? I confess I suddenly feel quite parched."

"I am not the least bit thirsty, thank you." Deirdre eyed her friend suspiciously. "Something is troubling you, Tessa. Do you not wish to tell me what it is?"

Tessa felt her chin begin to tremble, and moisture welled up in her eyes. What was the matter with her? She'd felt dismal since the Wintertons' ball, since Mr. Ashburn told her about . . . about Lord Penwyck stepping up his search for a young lady to marry. But surely that was not oversetting her, was it?

She inhaled an uneven breath.

"Tessa, what is it?" Deirdre's tone was solicitous. "Have you fallen in love and the gentleman does not . . . *do* tell me, Tessa dear. I am a married woman now and I have some experience in these matters, you know."

Tessa worked to calm herself, and presently returned to her place on the sofa beside Deirdre. "It isn't . . ." she began. "I-I have not fallen in love with anyone. I assure you, that is not what is troubling me," she lied. "It's just that I am so very tired of attending balls and breakfasts and routs. I feel I have done *nothing* to forward my Cause. I did not come to London to snag a husband," she rushed on. "I came because I have a mission, because I wish to do something *significant.*"

She sprang to her feet again. "I feel so . . . so frivolous, as if I have lost something—my direction, perhaps. I had a purpose and now I have nothing. I miss *myself,* Deirdre." She paused and leveled an anxious gaze at her friend. "I fear I am making no sense at all."

Deirdre nodded slowly. "Of course you are making sense. I confess I hadn't realized how very serious you were about . . . well, we both became so caught up in the plans for your debut and then my wedding." She smiled. "I do understand how you feel, Tessa, truly I do."

She rose to her feet and grasped both of Tessa's hands in hers. "I recall telling you once Jeffrey and I might be of help to you. Jeffrey mentioned to me only last evening that the Hampden Clubs are to resume meeting again. Mr. Cobbett generally attends and very often speaks. I am not certain when or where the next gathering is to be, but I will ask Jeffrey. Perhaps the three of us might attend a meeting together."

"Oh, Deirdre!" Tessa's eyes widened. "That would be wonderful! But"—she sobered—"I think it best we not discuss the matter tomorrow evening at dinner—in front of Mr. Ashburn, I mean. It would never do for Lord Penwyck to learn of my plans."

Deirdre nodded. "It will be our secret."

The following evening, Tessa, accompanied by a brace of liveried footmen, was delivered up to the Randalls' small but tidy flat just beyond Chelsea.

Mr. Randall himself answered Tessa's light rap at the door, a beaming Deirdre standing behind him in the dim foyer.

"We haven't a butler yet," Deirdre said with an apologetic little laugh. "But we have two housemaids and a cook," she added brightly. "Mama and Papa sent them over."

A grinning Mr. Randall took Tessa's cloak and hung it on a hook beside the front door. "It is lovely to see you again, Miss Darby."

"And you, sir." Tessa smiled.

She and Deirdre embraced. Then a chattering Deirdre, with

Tessa close by her side, followed Mr. Randall down a long, uncarpeted corridor to the drawing room.

On the way, Tessa took in her surroundings. A number of oil paintings hung on the walls of the hallway, one a portrait of Deirdre's parents, which Tessa thought she recalled once seeing in the Montgomerys' spacious picture gallery.

"Mama wanted me to have it," Deirdre explained. "But all the others are Jeffrey's," she added proudly, a hand indicating a small but exquisite Constable and several other lovely landscape paintings by artists Tessa did not recognize.

"Your husband is quite the collector," Tessa murmured appreciatively. She glanced at the tall, attractive gentleman ahead of them. He looked to be about thirty years of age and had wavy black hair and warm brown eyes. Although his dress was not quite the first stare of fashion, he nonetheless looked very nice in a dark coat, trousers, and a gleaming white linen shirt and cravat.

The drawing room was relatively small by *ton* standards, but was tastefully done up with modern furniture, a pretty patterned silk paper covering the walls, and a matching rug on the floor. Mr. Randall said, "I very often take paintings or other art in lieu of payment for my services."

Tessa glanced about this room. Indeed, she spotted several exquisite pieces, a beautiful porcelain vase and a small bronzed sculpture, both of which looked a trifle out of place in these somewhat austere surroundings. Still, they added a certain elegant air to the room, she decided.

"—so sorry that Mr. Ashburn was unable to come tonight," Deirdre was saying, gesturing Tessa to a pretty upholstered chair.

"But it's just as well," Deirdre added as she slid onto one end of a damask-covered sofa whilst her husband saw to pouring the three of them neat glasses of port.

"Thank you." Tessa took a sip of hers while waiting for Mr. Randall to be seated beside his wife.

Once there, he solemnly informed Tessa that a Hampden Club meeting was to be held that very night.

"Tonight?" Tessa intoned with surprise. She cast a wide-eyed look at Deirdre, who smiled.

"Jeffrey said we will have plenty of time to make the meeting after we've had our dinner, if you are certain you would like to go," Deirdre added.

"I have never been more certain of anything in my life!" Tessa exclaimed. One of her gloved hands flew to cover her heart. "How *very* fortunate Mr. Ashburn was unable to come tonight!"

Deirdre and Randall both laughed; then the tall gentleman sobered again. "I must warn you, Miss Darby. Tonight's meeting is to be held in the backroom of an alehouse in a rather unsavory section of London," he said. "Some would argue it is no place for a lady. I do admit to having reservations about taking you and Deirdre along."

"Surely we will not be the only ladies present."

"Women do attend some of the meetings, yes, with their menfolk. It is just . . . well, the atmosphere may not be quite what you are accustomed to."

"I am not easily put off, Mr. Randall." Tessa smiled. "I came to London for the express purpose of becoming involved with the reform movement in this country. I am prepared to do whatever it takes."

"Very well, then."

At that moment, the Randalls' cook stepped to the doorway to announce dinner.

As the unpretentious meal of sliced veal in a seasoned curry sauce with steamed carrots, potatoes, and green peas progressed, Mr. Randall supplied Tessa with a quick history of the Hampden Clubs, the penny-a-week subscription group founded during the war by forward-thinking reform leaders such as William Cobbett, Major John Cartwright, Sir Francis Burdett, and the popular orator Henry Hunt.

"On the whole, it could be said the main object of the reform movement these days is to gain representation in Parliament for the workingman," Randall concluded. "The needs of the industrial class differ greatly from those of the peerage or even the landed gentry."

"Indeed, they do," Tessa heartily agreed.

"Interestingly enough," Randall went on, "there are supporters for reform in both the Whig and Tory camps."

"There does seem to be a blurring amongst the political parties in this country," Tessa remarked candidly.

"That is quite true, quite true," Mr. Randall agreed. "For instance, Lord Liverpool, Mr. Canning, and Mr. Huskisson, all Tory ministers, have declared they are as ready for free trade as are Lords Russell and Grey." He paused to take a sip of the wine before him. "In the opposing camp, Lords Sheridan and Whitbread and even Tierney, as well as some of the younger Whig supporters, purport their readiness for both political and social reform. It is becoming increasingly difficult to draw a clear-cut line between the parties."

"It appears French revolutionary ideals have, at last, reached England," Tessa replied with interest.

"Quite so, as well as some of the new American principles of democracy."

Tessa nodded with enthusiasm. "I recall mentioning that very thing to Lord Penwyck only a few days ago."

"Oh?" Mr. Randall leaned forward. "And what did he say?"

"Ummm . . ." Tessa suddenly grew flustered. Actually, she could not recall what the esteemed earl had said, although what he *did* was quite clear in her mind. But she could hardly tell Mr. Randall Lord Penwyck had pulled her into his arms and kissed her! "I . . . um . . . believe Lord Penwyck would also agree it is time for the English Parliamentary system to become a bit more flexible," she concluded haltingly.

"It must!" Randall declared fervently.

"If it is to survive," Tessa added, proud of the even tone she had managed to muster.

"You are very astute, Miss Darby."

Tessa smiled confidently. "I am merely interested in the betterment of my country, namely in helping the women and children of England."

"They are fortunate, indeed, to have you in their camp."

"We are all pleased you came to England," Deirdre said, with a sincere smile. It was obvious she was enjoying the lively discussion between her husband and their guest.

"Penwyck does seem to be a fair man," Mr. Randall went on. He directed a proud look at his beaming bride. "That he took up our cause tells me a great deal about him."

"Indeed, it does," Tessa agreed. However, she was certain that were Lord Penwyck to know her plans tonight included attending a radical reform meeting, it might be another matter altogether. How very fortuitous that the meeting fell on this particular evening and that Mr. Ashburn was not here. As it stood now, what Lord Penwyck did not know, she decided firmly, he did not *need* to know.

Tessa had never been inside a common alehouse before. The closest she had come was the hurried stop for a quick meal at a roadside inn, or ordinary, as they were called in America, as she and her family traveled short distances from home. In America, such establishments were generally quite civilized. But a ramshackle place known as the Hog's Ear on the fringe of London's notorious Seven Dials area presented Tessa with a picture she could never in her wildest dreams have imagined.

She and Deirdre huddled close to Jeffrey as he ushered them inside the noisy, smoke-filled room. Tessa was at once repelled by the stench of spilled ale combined with the unmistakable odor of dozens of unwashed bodies. The room appeared filled to overflowing with fat, unshaven tradesmen, sallow-skinned women with yellow teeth, and even small boys outfitted in layers of tattered garments straight from the ragpicker's barrel.

She managed to close her mind to the wave of revulsion that swept through her. Closing her ears to the crude remarks aimed at herself and Deirdre was not quite so easy.

"There's a pair of pretty misses! I'll have me some o' what they's servin'!"

Tessa hugged her cloak tighter about her body as the threesome picked their way through the crowd. She had hoped and prayed for the opportunity to be here and nothing, not even the taunts of uncivilized men, would deter her.

"Pay them no mind," she heard Jeffrey tell Deirdre.

"Dunna leave!" cried a bosky man, his leering face moist with perspiration.

"Shud up and drink yer ale!" shouted a nearby serving wench, balancing a tray full of pewter tankards brimming with foam. She slammed one onto the planked wooden table before the raucous man. The amber liquid sloshed over the sides and pooled on the table. "The likes o' them wouldn't look twice at the likes o' you!"

"Then I'll have me some of what *you* got to sell!" The fat man pulled the nearly bare-breasted girl onto his lap.

The wench's loud protests were drowned out by the bawdy laughter from those seated nearby.

Tessa and the Randalls hurried past all of them.

Once safely inside the meeting room, Tessa loosened her cloak and drew in a deep breath, prepared to relax and settle in for a satisfying evening of exchanging ideas with like-minded men and women—intelligent, forward-thinking individuals like herself and the Randalls and William Cobbett, with whom she had high hopes of seeing tonight.

But it was not to be.

In minutes, the windowless room, split down the middle with several rough-hewn, planked wooden tables with backless benches along both sides, had filled up with virtually the same class of people the Randall party had encountered in the common room.

The only difference Tessa could detect was these men and the snaggle-toothed women who'd accompanied them were not yet filled to the gills with ale and port.

That difference was dispelled in the time it took two amply endowed serving girls to slosh foaming tankards of ale on the tables before them. In minutes, the meeting room had grown just as rowdy and smelled just as sour as the common room in front.

Randall ushered his two charges to a small, lone table at the rear of the room. Once the girls were settled, he excused himself and walked to the top of the chamber to speak with a fairly well-dressed gentleman—at least his jacket was less tattered than his counterparts'—whom Tessa assumed to be the chairman, or perhaps tonight's speaker. She craned her neck to see if she could spot Mr. Cobbett amongst them, but it was no use. The room was far too full of people milling about, drinking, laughing, and talking loudly and rapidly to one another. A number of other men leaned against the walls, some speaking quietly with each another, others merely watching the proceedings as they waited for the meeting to begin.

"I don't expect we will stay long," Deirdre leaned toward Tessa. She was also glancing anxiously about. "This doesn't seem quite . . ." her voice trailed off.

Tessa tried to appear unruffled by their surroundings, but the anxiety within her was also building. So far, nothing she'd seen was as she'd expected.

She was glad when Jeffrey returned to their table, although he did not sit down. Tessa noted the serious look on his face, and the way his alert black eyes continually scanned the increasingly rowdy crowd.

Presently, one of the gentlemen climbed onto a chair and began to shout for order. The assembly of revelers—for that is what they seemed to be to Tessa—quieted down somewhat.

"We are here tonight to discuss the bringing of a petition before Parliam—"

"All men should have a vote, not just the rich!" came a shout from somewhere in the room.

"Aye! Not just the landowner!" another called out.

"It's people what ought to be represented not property!"

The chairman stepped to the floor and began to pound the table before him with his empty tankard. "Order! Order! I have good news to report!"

Jeffrey leaned over to speak to Tessa and Deirdre. "He is trying to tell them new union societies have been formed in Oldham and Middleton."

The speaker shouted, "When we get additional support from Lancashire and other industrial areas, we shall have—"

"We don't want no more societies! We want the vote!"

"The vote!" cried another.

Deirdre directed a look of regret at Tessa. "I fear tonight's meeting is getting quite out of hand."

Tessa sighed loudly. "I confess it is not what I expected."

Suddenly, a loud crash caused both ladies to jump with alarm. In an instant, the room exploded into complete chaos, with angry shouts, coarse insults, and doubled-up fists flying in all directions.

Tessa and Deirdre were already on their feet. Jeffrey grabbed his wife's hand, his other reaching for Tessa.

Taking the lead, Randall managed to steer the frightened women along the fringe of the mob as they pushed and shoved their way to the closed door that gave onto the common room.

Fortunately, the noisy commotion in the taproom was such that that from the meeting area had not yet reached their ears.

Tessa's heart raced with fear as she and the Randalls picked their way back through the bawdy crowd in the common room. As they drew near the door to the establishment, it suddenly burst open. Tessa squealed with a mixture of relief and anxiety when she spotted the tall, muscular Lord Penwyck charging inside.

"Thank God, you are safe!" he growled.

At that instant, the angry mob from the meeting room spilled into the common area, their loud shouts and ugly curses mixing with the bawdy talk and laughter in the taproom, all of it quickly becoming a deafening roar.

Tessa had no time to speculate on the degree of the earl's displeasure with her; she was far too pleased to see him.

When he flung a powerful arm about her shoulders and pulled her close to him, she melted with untold relief into his strength.

"My carriage is outside!"

Tessa flung a wild gaze about for Deirdre and Jeffrey, but could not see them. "What about Deir—"

"She is with Randall."

Penwyck half dragged Tessa through the door and onto the flagway in front where she gratefully inhaled a deep breath of fresh cool air.

"Get in the carriage!" Penwyck ordered brusquely.

Again, Tessa flung a wild look about in search of Deirdre and Jeffrey; but, they were nowhere in sight.

"Get in!" Penwyck shouted again.

His strong arms lifted Tessa off the ground even as the sound of raised voices and breaking glass spilled onto the flagway.

"Demmed foolish of Randall to take you and Deirdre to such a place," snapped Penwyck. He climbed in behind Tessa and with a shout, directed the driver to, "Spring 'em!"

As the Penwyck coach sped off into the night, the earl settled himself onto the bench opposite Tessa.

"Mr. Randall is not to blame," she began breathlessly, as the enormity of what had just happened began to sink in. "It was I who wanted to come."

The earl turned a scowling countenance upon her. "Then you are more foolish than I thought."

"How was I to know we would be in danger?"

"Have I not been telling you to leave such matters alone? That women have no business concerning themselves with politics?"

Tessa glared daggers at him.

"Such mass meetings frequently lead to riot," Penwyck spat out. "There is a bill on the floor even now to restrict such public meetings on the grounds they are seditious."

"They cannot *all* be seditious!" Tessa cried. "Many of the working men's grievances have merit. I do agree a more peaceful method of bringing their concerns before Parliament is needed. The gentleman in charge tonight tried to call the meeting to order. The men were too angry to listen. It is obvious they are breaking beneath the weight of oppression."

Penwyck snorted with derision. "They are drunken fools who don't know their own minds!"

Judging from the display she'd seen tonight, Tessa could hardly dispute that, so she didn't even try.

After a lengthy pause, however, in a much calmer tone, she said, "If England is to survive, sir, the industrial class—the workingman, if you will—*must* have a voice in the government."

Because the interior of the carriage was quite dark, Tessa could not see her companion's face. Therefore it was impossible to judge his reaction to her remark.

Presently, he said, "Perhaps. But he will not gain that voice through force or through unruly demonstrations such as you took part in tonight."

"I did not take part in it!" Tessa's chin shot up. She was becoming as angry as the inebriated mob. Moreover, she was not yet ready to let the subject drop. "If reform does not come peacefully," she retorted hotly, "revolution will. It is the way of the world. English politicians who cannot see that, or those who refuse to see it, are not only blind, they are naive."

Again she heard the toplofty earl's snort of derision, but was surprised when he said nothing.

"Do you not believe me?" she demanded angrily.

After a pause, the earl replied, quite calmly, "I believe you, Miss Darby. The thing I find astonishing is that you can see it coming."

"That *I* can see it? Why does that astonish you?" she cried indignantly.

"Because you are a woman, damn it, and women typically do not have the vision to . . . women are not supposed to—"

"I realize you believe I am overstepping the bounds, sirrah," Tessa cut in hotly. "But the truth of the matter is, I cannot help myself. It is just the way I am!"

Her companion was silent for a long moment, then, in quite a steady tone, he said, "I did not say I object to the way you are, Miss Darby." He cleared his throat and Tessa heard him shift his weight on the bench, almost as if he were uncomfortable.

Tessa digested his remark as the carriage wheeled through the darkened city. An occasional glimmer from a streetlamp cast a long shaft of illumination into the coach, but it was not enough to shed any light on what might be going on inside the earl's head. Tessa wondered if he were so angry with her now he would perhaps forbid her to see Deirdre—or send her back to America.

Neither would be fair nor just, she decided.

What punishment would he mete out?

Suddenly, years of unjust treatment at the hands of her stepfather rose to the fore in her mind. Her own pent-up anger and outrage at him made her lash out at this man.

"But you do not like me, do you?" she spat out. "You wish I were like every other young lady in London, sweet-tempered and gentle and malleable to your will!"

There was another long pause. "I did not say that either, Miss Darby."

"But it is what you meant," she taunted, unable to control herself or her anger.

"No. It is not what I meant. What I meant was," he added in an astonishingly even tone, "I have come to the realization that while I occasionally find your actions the outside of enough and at times even vexing, I cannot change the way you are. Therefore, I will no longer try. You are . . . uniquely yourself, Miss Darby. And on the whole . . . I do not object."

Tessa sucked in an uneven breath.

He did not object?

Try as she might, she could find nothing at all to dispute in that.

Tonight had been chock full of surprises, but Lord Penwyck's unexpected admission just now was the biggest surprise of all.

Seventeen

"I have no meetings to attend this afternoon, Miss Darby," Lord Penwyck announced the following morning at breakfast. "I thought perhaps you might enjoy viewing Lord Elgin's antiquities with me. The marbles have been placed on permanent display at the new British Museum."

"Why, what a lovely idea, Penny dear!" the earl's mother declared. A pleased twinkle in her eye, she aimed a keen look at Tessa. "I confess I do not feel up to making a single call today, Tessa. You will not disappoint me by going off with Penny."

Tessa directed a somewhat wary gaze at the handsome earl. He'd never before suggested they go on an outing together. "Thank you for asking me, sir," she murmured. "I would like that very much."

"As would I, Miss Darby."

After agreeing that two of the clock would suit, Lord Penwyck left for a busy morning at the House.

On his way to a committee meeting, he thought over the events of the previous evening. He had decided late last night there was little cause for alarm so far as the *ton* getting wind of Miss Darby's brush with disaster. Neither Randall nor his wife would say anything, nor would Ashburn, who had been the one to inform Penwyck of the possibility that the Randalls might attend the meeting.

Although Penwyck fully expected Miss Darby had been

vastly disappointed by the violence that erupted at the Hog's Ear last night—it wouldn't surprise him to learn someone had been killed or badly injured; tragic consequences often resulted at such mass gatherings—he did not expect her to abandon her Cause. No doubt she would be on the lookout for another such rally to attend, perhaps one held in a less objectionable setting. Which is why Penwyck had concluded this morning if this unfortunate trend toward waywardness on Miss Darby's part was not nipped in the bud, there was no saying what sort of scandal the young lady might fall into next.

He knew he had rather shocked her this morning by suggesting they spend the afternoon together, but in truth the invitation was long overdue. He had intended at the outset to show her the sights in Town, but what with one thing or another—his mother taking her protégée under her wing and the ensuing business of Miss Darby's debut—he simply had not got round to showing her about.

Considering last night's escapade, Penwyck felt it imperative to resume his vigilance over the headstrong young lady and to distract her with agreeable and interesting afternoon outings, outings a young lady of her superior intelligence would find agreeable.

And there was another reason he felt compelled to ask her. He fervently wished to.

In her bedchamber, preparing to dress for the afternoon, Tessa decided not to question Lord Penwyck's sudden change of face in regard to her. That he had chosen not to punish her for her misdeed last evening was reward enough, she thought wryly. That he wished to take her on an pleasure jaunt today was, well, astonishing!

Grinning to herself, she decided to thank her lucky stars for being spared, at the very least, a severe tongue lashing, and simply relax and enjoy the afternoon.

She had, indeed, been disappointed over last night's disastrous turn, but given Lord Penwyck's recent liberal outlook regarding her political interests, she fully expected to be allowed the freedom now to attend other such gatherings. Perhaps not ones convened at alehouses—in truth, she'd rather acquired an aversion to that herself—but Mr. Randall had mentioned in the carriage last evening that at times the Hampden Clubs met in church chapels and other respectable places. She'd ask Deirdre to alert her when and where the next meeting was scheduled to take place.

Deciding it was time to think about what she would wear that afternoon, Tessa had just walked to the pretty cherrywood clothespress and flung the door open when a light rap sounded at her bedchamber door.

Lady Penwyck stepped into the room, carrying a pretty paisley-papered hatbox in one hand. "Forgive the intrusion, dear. I thought perhaps you might need help deciding what to wear this afternoon."

"Oh." Tessa was unable to conceal the wonderment in her tone. She glanced curiously at the hatbox Lady Penwyck was carrying. "I confess I was in a bit of a quandary," she murmured.

Lady Penwyck set the box on a chair and walked to the clothespress. "Let me see." She began to sort through the several pretty gowns hanging inside. "You look especially charming in this lovely blue chintz gown." She pulled out a pencil-slim frock trimmed with black buttons and several rows of narrow black braid, spread the gown across the bed, and turned to Tessa.

"I took the liberty of ordering a little gift for you, Tessa," Lady Penwyck said gaily. "It was just delivered and I wished to bring it up myself."

She opened the box and lifted out a brand new straw bonnet, handsomely decorated with black and blue ribbons and a bunch of bright red cherries.

"Isn't it pretty?"

"It is very pretty," Tessa smilingly agreed, an element of surprise in her tone. Lady Penwyck had never purchased a gift for her before and she could not think what had occasioned this one.

"If you recall," Lady Penwyck went on, still admiring the high-crowned bonnet, "we saw it last week in Mr. Merribone's shop window. I suspect it was designed by that sweet little Miss Grant just before she left to marry Lord Rathbone." She glanced up at Tessa, who was admiring the new bonnet and also listening raptly to Lady Penwyck's explanation regarding it.

"I simply must tell you about the scandal poor little Miss Grant unwittingly fell into!" Lady Penwyck exclaimed. "It began when a girlhood friend of hers, Miss Alayna Marchmont, blackmailed Miss Grant into impersonating her so *she* might run off with an actor fellow. Then, Miss Marchmont's betrothed, Lord Rathbone unexpectedly turned up and, thinking Miss Grant was his intended, he fell in love with her!

"You see," she prattled on, "Miss Marchmont and Lord Rathbone were to have been married by proxy. Lord Rathbone has a mahogany plantation in Honduras, I understand, and was not expected to be on hand for the ceremony, but he learned of some sort of plot afoot to abscond with his inheritance and returned home anyhow. At any rate, it was a horrific scandal. As it turned out, the talented Miss Grant was back at Mr. Merribone's shop for a short while and worked quite diligently, I understand, designing bonnets for him until her beloved turned up and whisked her off to a foreign land. Actually, I think it a rather lovely story, don't you?"

Lady Penwyck reached again for the straw confection and turned it about in her hands. "This design is quite pretty, don't you agree?"

Tessa nodded enthusiastically. "It will look lovely with my blue walking gown. Thank you for helping me decide what to wear and for the thoughtful gift, Lady Penwyck."

"I shall send Martha in to help you dress." The older woman turned to leave. On the threshold, she paused. "I am *very* pleased you and Penny . . ." she faltered, a sincere smile on her lips. "I do hope you have a lovely afternoon, Tessa, dear."

"I am certain I shall, Lady Penwyck."

A half hour later, Tessa was dressed and anxiously awaiting the outing. Drawing on her gloves, she happened to glance up and catch a glimpse of herself in the looking glass . . . and blushed.

Despite the many balls and soirees she'd attended these last weeks, she'd never before felt so anxious or happy all at the same time.

Why, she actually felt like . . . singing!

She felt positively *giddy!*

How very foolish she was being. An embarrassed little laugh escaped her. She pursed her lips primly and tried to calm herself. But, still gazing at her flushed face in the glass, she looked so comical, she burst instead into nervous giggles.

Martha, who was still in the room silently gathering up Tessa's discarded garments and tidying up, glanced quizzically at her. "Is anything wrong, Miss?"

Tessa sobered. "No. Everything is fine, Martha. Thank you."

The maid stood gazing curiously at Tessa. Then, a bit shyly, she said, "You look very nice, Miss. I especially like the new bonnet."

Still trying to collect herself, Tessa cleared her throat. "Thank you, Martha." She sniffed and drew in another sharp breath. "Well then, I shall just . . . be off."

"Yes, Miss."

Tessa nodded. "Well, I am . . . off now."

A sudden rap at the bedchamber door startled both young women. Martha made a move to answer the summons, but, since Tessa stood less than a step away, she reached for the latch and pulled the door open herself.

Lady Penwyck stuck her greying head inside. "Penny is waiting in the foyer for you, dea—oh! Tessa, my dear, you look stunning!" A wide smile split the older woman's face. "I can hardly wait for Penn—for *Harrison* to see you."

She reached for Tessa's gloved hand and the two women exited the room together.

"I expect it is time for me to cease calling my eldest son by that childish nickname." Alice laughed gaily as she and Tessa walked down the corridor arm in arm. "Harrison is nine and twenty . . . or is he still eight and twenty? Well, in any case, I don't expect his age matters a whit." She laughed. "The point is, he is a grown man and he has hated that silly name since he was in leading strings." She gave Tessa's fingertips an affectionate squeeze. "Can't say as I blame him," she added, with a chuckle. "Calling a grown man *Penny* is a bit silly."

Tessa smiled. She rather liked the name. It made the toplofty earl seem a bit more human.

"You look so very lovely this afternoon, Tessa dear. Your pretty red curls are as shiny as copper. I do declare," she prattled on, "I don't think any young lady has received more offers of marriage since her debut than you have! Why, only last evening both Sally and the Countess Lieven were remarking on your extraordinary success . . ."

Tessa ceased listening for a spell. She had received a goodly number of offers, if one could call them that. There were some gentlemen, she suspected, who made a career of offering for every young lady in Town, perhaps in the hope at least one would accept. Several dandies had masked their declarations of love to Tessa in poems or in the words to a popular song, which they solemnly recited in Tessa's ear during a dance or even over tea. Tessa thought it all rather silly.

"I don't mean to pry, dear," Lady Penwyck was saying, "but is there . . . do you . . . has any young man caught your fancy?" She turned an anxious gaze on Tessa, who was walking quietly by her side as they approached the stairwell.

Upon descending one or two steps, Tessa caught a glimpse of the top of Lord Penwyck's dark head as he awaited her in the foyer. The quick intake of breath she experienced at the mere sight of him both surprised and alarmed her.

"No!" Tessa blurted out, perhaps a bit too loudly, for Lord Penwyck, standing in the foyer, glanced up and then back down at the sheet of paper he held in his hand. "I mean," Tessa added, in a more normal tone, "they are all very nice. It's just that I do not favour any one gentleman in particular."

Instead of replying, Lady Penwyck gaily called to her son the second she and Tessa gained the landing. "Penny darling! Oh, silly me." She laughed. "I was just telling Tessa I must remember to address you by your given name instead of that silly diminutive I have used the whole of your life."

One dark brow lifted as Lord Penwyck glanced up to greet the women. "Thank you, Mother. I daresay I would much prefer to be addressed by my given name." His somber gaze flitted from his mother's smiling countenance to Miss Darby's flushed face.

Suddenly, Tessa's blue eyes began to twinkle merrily. "Good afternoon, Harrison," she greeted him boldly.

Penwyck's lips twitched as he nodded. "Miss Darby. Allow me to say you look quite charming this afternoon."

The smile he gave Tessa caused her pulse to race fitfully. Indeed, she admitted honestly to herself, there was *one* gentleman in Town she favoured. It was quite foolish of her, she knew, but the plain truth was Lord Penwyck was far and away the most handsome, the most desirable, the most exciting man she had ever met. Although she knew very well the feeling was not mutual, she couldn't help herself. Suddenly, a wave of sheer nervous tension caused a ripple of laughter to bubble up from her throat.

"You look very handsome yourself, sir," she remarked archly.

Penwyck's sudden bark of laughter joined with Tessa's merry treble and the satisfied trill coming from Lady Penwyck. Tessa suspected her flirtatious reply had surprised the uppity earl. The thought pleased her. How inordinately dull if one always did what was expected of one.

She was still smiling up at him as he offered her his arm.

"Do not wait tea for us, Mother. I've added Gunter's to my list of places Miss Darby and I shall visit this afternoon. We shall take tea there, if we feel so inclined, or perhaps a strawberry ice will suffice. What do you think, Miss Darby?"

As the handsome pair moved across the marble-tiled foyer toward the front door, Lady Penwyck stood gazing after them, a look of supreme satisfaction on her lined face. A strawberry ice sounded perfectly delightful to her.

Eighteen

"I understand the British government recently purchased Lord Elgin's antiquities," Tessa remarked soon after the carriage wheeled away from the Penwyck town house and headed for the British Museum in Bloomsbury.

"That is correct." Lord Penwyck nodded. "A purchase price was agreed upon following the recommendations of a select House committee. Although the offer was quite generous, Elgin maintains it was not adequate to cover all the expenses he incurred in bringing the treasures to England."

"Are you acquainted with Lord Elgin? I do hope he has recovered from his trying ordeal in France. How dreadful for him to have been arrested and imprisoned!" Tessa said with feeling.

Sitting beside her on the comfortable upholstered bench of the tilbury, Penwyck turned a curious gaze upon his companion. "How on earth did you know Elgin had been arrested?"

Tessa smiled smugly. It quite delighted her that she had surprised him again.

"I hardly think it would have been remarked upon in American newspapers," Penwyck added.

Tessa made no immediate response. Truth was she had only just learned of Lord Elgin's unfortunate incarceration. A poem by Lord Byron, *The Curse of Minerva,* loudly decried Elgin's methods of procuring the Grecian marbles. The book of poetry had been given to Tessa by one of her more ardent suitors, who had told Tessa about Lord Elgin's misfortune.

"It is not so very difficult to stay abreast of what goes on in England, sir," Tessa replied quietly.

"Well, I daresay you have succeeded better than most."

"Thank you," Tessa murmured. A moment later, she added, "I am quite looking forward to viewing the treasures."

"As am I," Penwyck replied enthusiastically. "I had wished to be appointed to represent the Lords on the appropriation committee, but unfortunately I was not named. In any event, we shall see the marbles today."

Tessa nodded. "Do you suppose they are called marbles because the ruins are made from marble?" she asked thoughtfully.

"Why, yes, I rather expect that is so. We English have so long referred to the antiquities as Lord Elgin's Marbles that I daresay many of us have quite forgot why."

Giving a small chuckle, he withdrew a crisp sheet of paper from an inside coat pocket. "I have drawn up quite a long list of other places we might visit this week, Miss Darby. I trust you will find these equally as edifying as today's excursion."

Tessa smiled sweetly. "How very thoughtful you are, my lord."

"Yes, well." Penwyck cleared his throat before beginning to read from his list. "The Egyptian Hall in Piccadilly is very often entertaining."

"Oh! That is Mr. Bullock's exhibition building, is it not?" Tessa inquired with interest.

Penwyck again turned an incredulous gaze upon her. "You are aware also of William Bullock's extensive travels? You *do* amaze me, Miss Darby."

Tessa smiled again. "A friend of my mother's, Mrs. Covington, was in London the year the Egyptian Hall opened, and—"

"That would have been in eighteen-twelve," Penwyck remarked, his brows pulling together with consternation.

"Yes. Fortunately," Tessa added with a laugh, "Mrs. Covington is English and was visiting her own family, otherwise she might—"

"Have found herself in enemy territory," Penwyck supplied,

the scowl on his handsome face becoming a wry grin. He was, of course, referring to the fact that in eighteen-twelve England was at war with America. "Have you had occasion to visit your friend's family since you arrived in London?" he asked.

"No." Tessa shook her bonneted curls. "Both Mrs. Covington and her aunt have since passed away. At any rate, she found Mr. Bullock's African curiosities most impressive."

"I understand the collection also includes a number of exotic animals from both North and South America," Penwyck said.

"I look forward to seeing them."

Suddenly, Tessa grew thoughtful. She was enjoying the open-air ride through London and her relaxed conversation with the earl. He looked quite handsome today in a chocolate-brown coat, tan breeches, and forest-green waistcoat. Of all her many suitors, she did, indeed, find him the most enjoyable to be with. However, a moment ago, when the discussion had turned to Mr. Bullock's curiosities, she'd been suddenly reminded of a long-ago incident from her childhood. She had not thought on the painful episode for many years.

It happened long before Mrs. Covington returned to Philadelphia from England to tell the Darby family about seeing Mr. Bullock's exhibit in London. A similar collection of exotics had been put on display in Philadelphia when Tessa had been eight or nine years of age. Tessa had longed to see them and begged her parents to take her. They had agreed but on the day of the proposed trip, her stepfather had flown into a rage at Tessa over some trifling misdeed and refused to allow her to accompany the rest of the family into the city. Instead, he banished her to her room. Tessa had been heartbroken as she tearfully watched the family depart. David had brought her a small toy alligator from the exhibition hall, but not even that had lifted her crushed spirits.

"You have grown exceedingly quiet, Miss Darby." Lord Penwyck remarked in a solicitous tone. "Is something the trouble?"

Tessa had not realized the gentleman was watching her so

closely. She drew in an uneven breath. "It is nothing, really. I had just recalled an incident from . . ." her voice trailed off.

At times, it was all she could do not to tell someone of the harsh treatment she had suffered at the hands of her stepfather. For the most part, she managed to keep the painful memories hidden and the hurtful feelings in check. But for some reason lately, she had not been quite so successful. Deirdre had managed to pry a few of those forgotten images from her, and now with Lord Penwyck being so very kind, so very thoughtful . . . for some reason, she ached to tell him as well. It made no sense, of course, why she would wish him to know what was troubling her. She just did.

"Are you certain nothing is amiss, my dear?" Lord Penwyck's tone was excessively kind. Tessa had never before heard him speak in so gentle a fashion. "If something is troubling you, I would truly like to know what it might be," he added.

Suddenly, Tessa felt hot, stinging tears gather in her eyes. She turned away lest the earl see the unbidden moisture that had welled up and demand she tell him what had overset her.

Apparently she had not turned her face away from him quickly enough. Tessa felt a gentle touch beneath her chin as his gloved finger turned her flushed face forward.

"You are crying, Miss Darby," the earl said simply.

Tessa bit down hard on her lower lip. More than anything she longed to fling her arms about this kind man's neck, to burrow her head in his powerful shoulder and sob out all her secrets.

How silly she was being. She was in no danger now. Her stepfather was not here in London, and since she meant never to return to America, he would never, ever hurt her again. Yet at odd times, like now, it almost felt as if the ill-treatment were still happening, as if she would never escape unless she told someone who would understand how she felt and who would comfort her. Someone stronger than Senator John Hamilton Darby, someone more powerful than he. Someone like . . . Lord Penwyck.

"Miss Darby," the earl moved a bit on the bench, his body

turning toward her a fraction. "I cannot bear to see you so very unhappy. If something has happened, I implore you to tell me at once so I may right the wrong." He paused, his warm brown eyes regarding her with genuine concern. "Has some young man hurt you? Perhaps thrust himself upo—"

"No, no!" Tessa cried. "It is nothing." She jerked her chin from his grasp and sniffed away her tears. "Truly, it . . . it happened a long time ago," she concluded in a small voice. She forced a brave smile to her lips. "I can't imagine why I chanced to think on it just now. Forgive me. I am fine, truly I am."

Lord Penwyck continued to regard her quite intently. "Very well, then. If you are certain there is nothing I can do." He sat back, although the troubled look remained upon his face. Presently, he drew in a long breath and glanced about. "We are very nearly there."

Tessa looked about, as well. The small tilbury had wheeled onto a pretty tree-lined square. The sun peeking through the leafy treetops cast a dappled pattern on the smooth cobbles below. Just ahead, Tessa spotted a handsome wrought-iron sign with gold letters that read *The British Museum.* She determined afresh to relax and enjoy the lovely afternoon.

The new museum in Bloomsbury was chock full of interesting books and treasures—beautiful oil paintings by such noteworthy English artists as Turner and Constable, others by important German and Flemish artists.

Another long chamber contained an impressive collection of ancient Roman utensils and chipped pottery said to have been unearthed from an excavation site near Petworth in England.

"I understand there is a labyrinth of Roman ruins beneath the present city of Bath," Lord Penwyck told Tessa. "An entire Roman bath was recently discovered in a field near Bignor, complete with a tessellated pavement."

"How utterly fascinating," Tessa murmured, as she bent to study a piece of ancient pavement engraved with beautifully wrought figures in dancing attitudes. "Just think." She smiled up at Lord Penwyck. "When young ladies and gentlemen of today take the waters in Bath, they have no idea they are engaging in the selfsame activity that people did in that very spot over a thousand years ago."

Penwyck grinned. "That is quite true, Miss Darby."

Long before they'd reached the chamber that housed Lord Elgin's display, Penwyck was forced to revise yet another of his initial assessments of the enigmatic Miss Darby. He already thought her far more intelligent than most young ladies he'd met. Now he thought her positively brilliant. Her interests in ancient culture and history equalled, and in some cases surpassed, his. Her keen observations on various examples of Medieval and Renaissance art revealed a depth of appreciation and understanding that quite impressed him.

"You seem to know a great deal about artists and their various techniques," he remarked, following an interesting comment she'd made about how Botticelli mixed vegetable pigment in with his egg tempera.

"My stepfather's library was quite extensive," she replied somewhat obliquely as they strolled into another picture gallery.

With a grin, she added, "There are art collectors in America, as well, sir. Mr. Jefferson has a quite impressive collection of Renaissance paintings, as well as a great many books on the subject."

Having exhausted the exhibits on the ground floor, the pair climbed a stairwell and entered a chamber containing a vast array of tools, implements, and weaponry used by British soldiers during the time of William the Conqueror.

Penwyck noted Miss Darby seemed especially intrigued by the ancient suits of armor, most of mail, which consisted of interlinking iron rings.

"It looks so very cumbersome and heavy," she remarked, reaching to touch the once shiny metal.

Penwyck grinned. "I expect it was." In a teasing tone, he said, "Would you like me to rig myself out in a suit of it just to see?"

Tessa cast a sidelong look at him. Once she realized he was larking with her, she laughed. Penwyck quite enjoyed the sight of her twinkling blue eyes. Her loveliness did, indeed, take his breath away. He knew she was wearing a new bonnet today, for his mother had proudly shown it to him before taking it up to Miss Darby's bedchamber. Her blue walking gown looked quite becoming on her lithe form, and set off her charming curves to perfection.

Choosing not to check the warm feelings that were stirring within him, in the same spirit of fun, Penwyck pointed to an exhibit of staff weapons—a lance, spur, pike, and halberd. "Dressed in my suit of armor, I could fend off enemy attackers with these ferocious weapons and thus insure the safety of our fortress."

Tessa laughed again. "And would that make you my knight in shining armour?" she asked coyly.

Penwyck's dark eyes locked with hers. A moment before her vivid blue gaze fluttered away, he replied softly, "I expect it would."

She moved a few steps away from him. "You have already rescued me once," she said firmly. "Forgive me for not thanking you properly, sir. I was quite relieved to see you last night."

Penwyck stepped closer to her. The museum was thin of company this afternoon, and they were the only two people in this particular chamber. A number of times already this afternoon Penwyck's breath had grown short when he and Miss Darby had been leaning over a glass case together or standing shoulder to shoulder gazing at a painting on the wall. In this charged moment of silence, he again felt that same near-overwhelming urge to gather the lovely Miss Darby into his arms and . . .

In an instant, the moment was shattered when a couple and two giggling youngsters bounded into the room.

Miss Darby stepped past Penwyck, and once the pair were in the corridor she said lightly, "I understand there is an impressive collection of British Royal jewellery in the Tower of London."

"Indeed, there is. In fact, an excursion through the Tower is also on my list of proposed outings. The Royal Regalia is quite impressive. With your extensive knowledge of history and artifacts, I expect you will greatly appreciate the royal treasures."

And Tessa did. The following afternoon, she and Lord Penwyck set out again. The day was not quite as fine as the one before, being somewhat cloudy. But she and her eminent escort were hardly aware of the weather as they strolled through the flagstoned chambers visitors were allowed to tour in England's most famous fortress, the turreted Tower of London.

In addition to the fabulous Jewel House that contained priceless crowns, circlets, coronets, scepters, rings, bracelets, and jewelled swords, Tessa counted an array of fifteen gold collars from the reign of James I, each set with sparkling diamonds, rubies, emeralds, and pearls.

"I cannot imagine wearing such costly treasures!" she marveled.

"I thought all women coveted fine jewels," Lord Penwyck replied, his tone somewhat bemused.

Tessa cast a guarded look his way, but said nothing.

"I do not recall seeing you wearing very much in the way of jewellery, Miss Darby. Do you not like precious gems?" he asked.

Tessa's lips tightened. Her lack of rings or pretty earrings was yet another source of pain to her. "I like trinkets and baubles as much as the next young lady," she replied firmly.

"Well, then, we shall have to find something sparkly for you to wear to next week's gala at the Royal Italian Opera House. It's to be quite an occasion, I understand." Penwyck strolled to the next glass case. "Mother has far more jewellery than she can possibly wear. I am certain she will be most happy to see you wear a trinket or two of it."

Once again, Tessa felt suffused with a wave of conflicting emotion. On the one hand, she wished to blurt out the pain in her heart, but something held her back. She managed to swallow the near-suffocating emotion that had risen within her and, instead, force her thoughts another direction. Lord Penwyck had mentioned the gala to be held next week at the Royal Italian Opera House. It was a momentous occasion, indeed. Everyone of consequence, including the Prince Regent, was expected to attend.

"Do you mean, as well, to attend the gala?" She tried for a light tone.

"Indeed, I do," Penwyck replied, with spirit. "I am quite fond of the opera. I find the music rousing and, at the same time . . . restful."

"Restful?" Tessa parroted. Her spirits lifted as she thought ahead to another entertaining evening spent in Lord Penwyck's agreeable company. He had attended precious few routs lately with Tessa and his mother, and Tessa was quite looking forward to this one. "I do not believe I have ever heard anyone refer to operatic arias as *restful*."

Her eyes twinkled merrily as she led the way into the next flagstoned chamber. "Are you saying, sir," she probed in a teasing tone, "that your duties as a statesman are so very fatiguing you must attend the opera in order to rest?"

When she glanced coyly over her shoulder at him, the compulsion Lord Penwyck felt to follow her was so strong that had she been leading him to Tower Green, the site of numerous royal beheadings in Henry VIII's time, he'd have gladly followed without once questioning his fate. Miss Darby, did, indeed, have an unsettling effect upon him.

Because his train of thought had been completely derailed by her undeniable allure, he never answered her question. Instead, they began to talk of other things. At length, both grew weary of dankish towers and decided to take tea at a pretty little tearoom Penwyck knew of located next to the fashionable Clarendon Hotel.

Over the next several days, Tessa and Lord Penwyck did, indeed, visit Mr. Bullock's Egyptian Hall, where Tessa was intrigued to view Napoleon's traveling carriage. It had been confiscated at Waterloo and only just purchased by Mr. Bullock to put on display. They visited the Montague House Museum, toured the newest exhibit at the Royal Art Gallery, and went to Exeter 'Change to see the tigers, which Tessa was quite sorry to see were so poorly cared for.

"They look as unhappy as the bears and lions we saw in the

Royal Menagerie at the Tower of London," she remarked morosely.

"You cannot rescue every mistreated soul on earth, Miss Darby," Lord Penwyck replied. "The animals have plenty to eat and they are in no danger of being mauled or killed."

"But they are caged!" she pointed out. "One can never be happy when one is not allowed to go and come as one pleases."

"Would you prefer them to be released onto the streets of London, then?"

"No, but to be housed outdoors would be a vast improvement, you must agree," she insisted.

Penwyck decided it was time to usher the tenderhearted Miss Darby out of doors. That afternoon, they enjoyed an impromptu picnic on the grass at the Green Park, an event that had definitely *not* been on Penwyck's list of proposed activities for the day. But when Miss Darby insisted the sunny afternoon was far too lovely to spend indoors and she wished to take tea on a rug in the park, Penwyck wisely relented.

Another afternoon, they, along with Mr. Ashburn, went to see a rousing cricket match. Penwyck was surprised once again when Miss Darby cheered as loudly as anyone. She was, indeed, making mice feet of his list of acceptable behaviours for a young lady. By simply being herself, she was all that was agreeable and charming . . . and undeniably alluring.

One evening, accompanied by Lady Penwyck, they took in a concert given by the Philharmonic Society at the Argyll Rooms in Argyll Street. The following afternoon, they all toured Madame Tussaud's waxworks.

Tessa thought their week of outings thoroughly enjoyable. By the end of it, she and Lord Penwyck were talking and laughing with one another like the best of friends.

"This has been the most wonderful week of my life," she enthused as the Penwyck coach wheeled in to Portman Square late one afternoon. "My head is swimming with all we have seen and done."

Penwyck grinned. "I, too, have enjoyed our excursions, Miss Darby. One often becomes so caught up in daily activities one forgets what a wealth of diversions there are to enjoy in London."

It was on the tip of Tessa's tongue to inquire what he planned for them to do next when she caught herself. She knew he had neglected a good deal of his House business this week in order to entertain her. It would be presumptuous of her to expect more from him. Besides, she still had the gala at the Royal Italian Opera House to look forward to.

Lord Penwyck escorted a relaxed and smiling Tessa up the flagway to the house. In the foyer, they were met by a high-spirited Lady Penwyck.

"Tessa darling, you have only just missed Major Lord Spencer. He has been here this age. I am certain he meant to offer for you! He was as nervous and fidgety as the caged lions you saw at the Tower."

"Oh," Tessa murmured. She cast a quick look at Lord Penwyck, but apparently he was not listening.

"The major refused to take tea or eat a bite," Lady Penwyck went on. "He paced before the hearth the entire time. When he was not pacing, he was peering from the window—looking for your carriage, make no mistake."

Tessa didn't know what to say. No doubt the major meant to present his suit. He had been quite attentive on several occasions of late, very often directing long, soulful looks at her.

"So." Lord Penwyck spoke at last. Having handed his black beaver hat to a waiting footman, he was now removing his gloves. "Major Lord Spencer, eh? Do you mean to break his heart, Miss Darby, or will he perchance be the lucky one?"

It surprised Tessa to see a slight twitch of amusement playing at Lady Penwyck's lips. Tessa and the earl's mother both looked at him, but suddenly, he again seemed to lose interest in the conversation and began to sift through a pile of letters and papers sitting on one corner of the sideboard. An odd pang of something stabbed Tessa. The earl truly did not care whom she favoured, did he?

Suddenly, Penwyck said, "Here is a letter for you, Miss Darby. Appears to be from America." He held it up.

"Oh!" Tessa exclaimed, reaching eagerly for the wafer-sealed missive. "I do hope it is from David. I miss my brother fiercely."

Her eyes shining with excitement, Tessa barely glanced at the letter. "Do excuse me, Lady Penwyck. I am most anxious to read my letter!"

"Of course, dear." The older woman smiled.

Tessa hurried up the stairs and into her bedchamber. Flinging her bonnet and reticule onto the bed, she excitedly tore open the seal and unfolded the page.

At once her heart sank.

The letter was not from David.

Nineteen

Tessa's letter was from her stepfather, Senator John Hamilton Darby. After she read the note, Tessa's eyes filled with tears and she fell limply onto the bed.

Later that evening, long after the supper hour—which Tessa elected to spend alone in her bedchamber—she ventured forth from her room in search of Lady Penwyck.

She found the older woman in the sitting room at the rear of the house. Alice looked up when Tessa stepped into the room.

"Are you feeling better, dear? Would you like a nice cup of tea or coffee?"

Though her blue eyes were lifeless, Tessa's lips formed a tight smile. "Coffee would be fine, thank you."

She did not fear meeting the earl this evening. Some time ago, she had heard his footfalls in the corridor outside her bedchamber. A moment later, the heavy front door in the foyer had closed behind him.

Lady Penwyck handed Tessa a cup of piping hot coffee.

"I do hope your letter from home did not contain bad news, dear."

Tessa exhaled a long sigh and stared morosely into the red-gold flames burning low in the hearth. Evenings this summer had been often chilly, and tonight was no exception. The same was probably true in Philadelphia, Tessa thought, except that regardless of the temperature, her stepfather adamantly refused to light a fire beyond the month of May, so if it were cool outdoors, it was also cool inside.

Turning from the fire, Tessa replied in a dejected tone, "My stepfather is demanding I return home at once." She nearly choked on her own words. "To marry George Hancock."

"You are to marry?" Lady Penwyck expressed surprise. "Well, that does explain why you have refused all your other suitors here in—"

"No, Lady Penwyck." Tessa shook her head. "I meant *never* to return to America. I do not wish to marry Mr. Hancock—or anyone."

"There is no one you find agreeable?" Alice asked gently.

Tessa bit her lower lip and turned away. Again, hot tears welled up in her eyes. She hurriedly blinked them away. "I just do not wish to marry Mr. Hancock. And I do not wish to return home to America, either."

"You are welcome to stay here with Penny and me," Lady Penwyck offered, "for as long as you like."

Tessa sniffed. "H-he said he would come to England and take me home if I refused to obey. I shouldn't want that."

"So it is imperative you wed this Mr. Hancock?"

"My stepfather needs his father's vote. There is a bill in the Senate that my stepfather wishes to—I have no choice," Tessa concluded glumly.

It didn't matter, she added to herself. Lord Penwyck did not feel as she did. What's more, she had failed in all her attempts to bring her views in regard to the unfortunate women and children of England before Parliament. It was unlikely she'd ever see Mr. Cobbett again, or attend another meeting of the Hampden Clubs. Deirdre had told her that the next meeting was to be held in some place called Spitalfields.

"Well," Lady Penwyck began sadly, "I will be very sorry to see you go, as will Penny. I am certain he thoroughly enjoyed your outings this past week. It is very unlike him to neglect his House business for pleasure, you know." She paused. "Your stepfather must be a very determined man."

Tessa nodded. "He is *quite* determined."

"Well, then." Lady Penwyck tried for a cheerier note. "Since tomorrow night's gala at the Royal Opera House is to be your last fete in London, we shall have to make the evening extra special. Our costumes were delivered today. Shall we go and look at them?

The following evening, as Tessa was preparing for the masked ball, Lady Penwyck appeared again in her bedchamber, this time carrying several green velvet boxes, which she opened to reveal an assortment of exquisite jewels: diamonds, pearls, rubies, and emeralds.

"Harrison and I have both noticed you rarely wear jewellery, dear." Lady Penwyck gingerly set each opened box onto Tessa's dressing table. "I recall your mother had some lovely pieces; I would have thought they'd have come to you."

Tessa's lips tightened. Once again, she fought to keep a rush of tears at bay. She'd felt sad and weepy all day and had even toyed with the idea of not attending the soiree tonight, for she knew how wretched she'd feel watching Lord Penwyck dance attendance upon every other young lady there.

Lady Penwyck was intently watching Tessa. "Won't you tell me what is troubling you, dear?"

Tessa furiously blinked away her tears. "The jewels are lovely, Lady Penwyck. Thank you for lending them to me."

"I am not lending them to you, dear," the bewigged woman said. She was already rigged out in her costume for the evening, a ruffled pink satin gown draped over a wide hooped skirt. Completing the seventeenth-century ensemble was an elaborate white wig that contained a bird cage festooned with ribbons and assorted wax fruit. "I wish you to choose a necklace and ring you especially like as a gift from Penny and me."

"Oh, I couldn't," Tessa protested.

"I insist."

A small smile wavered over Tessa's rosy lips as she stepped to the dressing table and leaned over the velvet cases to examine the finery. She reached for a sparkling blue sapphire-and-diamond ring and held it under the lamp.

"This ring is very like one of Mama's."

"It is exactly like your mother's," Lady Penwyck said. "We were given identical sapphire rings when we made our debuts. I wonder Helen did not keep hers." She laughed with fond remembrance. "We made a solemn vow to wear them always."

Tessa fell silent again. At length, she said, "Mama did wear hers always. The ring is even now in her jewel case."

Lady Penwyck reached to sympathetically touch Tessa's bare arm.

Again, large droplets of moisture began to glisten on Tessa's long, dark lashes.

"Is there something you have not told me, dear?"

Tessa made a valiant attempt to swallow past the huge lump forming in her throat, but failed miserably. "My . . . my stepfather has forbidden me to touch Mama's things. When she died, he declared all of her jewels and her belongings—her pretty workbasket, her writing table, her lovely books—were to go to David's wife. I was to have"—the lump in Tessa's throat rose up again and nearly choked her—"nothing."

"Oh, my dear child." Lady Penwyck drew a weeping Tessa into her arms and rocked her gently. "There, there."

At length, Tessa drew away. "Forgive me. I should not have said anything." She tried to smile through her tears. "I am just feeling sad that I must leave England. I have had a lovely time here. You and Harrison have been so very kind to me. I shall never forget you, either of you." She snatched up a handkerchief and began to furiously dab at her red-rimmed eyes and nose. "Mama had already given me her diamond tiara," she rushed on, "so it isn't as if I have nothing of hers. I wore the tiara the night of my debut."

"Yes, I recall. It looked quite lovely on you," Lady Penwyck murmured. "But I understand why you would wish to have other mementoes of your mother's, special things that would always remind you of her." She glanced toward her own jewel cases. "I want you to have all of these. This, most especially."

She reached for the glittering ring, and pressed it into Tessa's palm. "Now *you* must wear it always."

"But surely you meant to save these for . . . for Harrison's bride."

"I have plenty more to give to my eldest son's wife. These are for you."

Tessa smiled. "You are too kind, Lady Penwyck. I really shouldn't have said anything." Nonetheless, she slipped the lovely ring onto her finger and smiled quite proudly as she admired it. "Mama was wearing her ring the day she died."

"And you must wear this one always. It will forever commemorate the season of your debut."

On the way to the Royal Italian Opera House that night, Tessa determined afresh to enjoy her last grand fete in London.

She adored her lovely costume. The long flowing gown was of the palest blue silk, as soft as a whisper. Gold braid crisscrossed over her bosom and tied around her waist in the back. Tessa thought it accentuated her figure quite nicely. She had opted to wear her hair in her favourite style, piled atop her head with shiny golden ribbons intertwined amongst the fistful of burnished-copper ringlets that dangled about her bare shoulders.

She felt quite daring with both her arms and hands uncovered. But since the guests were to dress as their favourite character from their favourite opera, Tessa had chosen to be the mythical Diana from the ballad opera *The Olympian Goddess,* and gloves were not part of the costume. Instead, Tessa had donned jewelled armlets from the jewellery Lady Penwyck had given her, the new sapphire-and-diamond ring, and looped an intricately woven golden chain several times about her neck. Her mask was made of a shiny gold fabric, with feathery golden wings jutting from either corner.

As she sat opposite Lord Penwyck in the dim carriage, Tessa cast a shy glance at him. Despite the fact he again seemed distant and aloof, or at least preoccupied, he looked splendid in a ruffled white silk shirt topped by an exquisite maroon brocade coat, jonquil satin knee breeches, white silk stockings, and silver-buckled pumps. Tessa was not entirely certain which operatic persona he was portraying, but certainly there had never been a more handsome one.

He also wore a curled white wig and a large plumed hat. When his sculptured mask was in place, which covered the whole of his face except for his mouth, Tessa realized had she not known Lord Penwyck was sitting opposite her in the carriage, she'd be unable to recognize him.

Apparently his own mother thought the same, for before they alighted from the carriage, she laughingly said, "I do declare, Penny, you don't look a bit like yourself tonight! If everyone wears their costume as well as you do, we shall not a one of us know who we are talking to!"

"That is part of the fun of a masked ball, Mother," the tall gentleman remarked solemnly as he stepped to the ground.

He turned and gallantly helped his mother from the carriage and also assisted Tessa. A shudder rippled through Tessa when she stumbled slightly on the bottom step, and the earl slipped an arm about her trim waist and half lifted her to the ground.

"There you are. You look quite lovely tonight, Miss Darby. I doubt anyone will be unable to pick you out in the crowd with that glorious hair of yours. You were quite wise not to don a wig tonight."

That said, he escorted the ladies into the brilliantly lit theatre. The red-carpeted foyer was already filled to overflowing with masked and costumed patrons. Once inside, Lord Penwyck politely excused himself and, to Tessa's immense chagrin, took himself off.

Behind the concealing cover of her feathered mask, Tessa once again felt unbidden moisture brim up in her eyes. She shouldn't have come tonight. Last week, when she and Lord Penwyck had spent every afternoon together, visiting this museum or touring that gallery, she had blithely thought tonight's gala would be a continuation of their newfound footing, that he'd stay close by her side, anticipating her every wish and whim. A sharp pang of disappointment assailed her. She should have known better.

She couldn't think why he'd taken a week away from his busy schedule to dance attendance upon her, but apparently he'd tired of the diversion and was anxious now to return to his all-important search for a bride.

Tessa's heart was heavy as she tried to force a smile to her lips and greet the elegantly costumed women and gentlemen who thronged about her and Lady Penwyck. Her spirits were genuinely lifted when, sometime later, she heard a familiar feminine voice calling to her.

"Tessa!" Deirdre Randall cried. She lowered her mask, which sat atop a beribboned wand, and happily hugged her friend. "You are the most beautiful Diana here! I daresay, you are the only one not wearing a wig."

"You look lovely, as well," Tessa replied, gazing with admiration on the diaphanous lavender gown her friend was wearing. "Forgive me for not knowing who you are supposed to be. Many of the popular ballad operas being performed in England have not yet made it to the American stage."

"I doubt half the people here can accurately identify the other half." Deirdre laughed. "And many are not dressed as operatic characters. I have seen five or six Grimaldi clowns!"

"Is Jeffrey also here?" Tessa asked.

Deirdre nodded. "Indeed, although we would not have been able to come if my parents had not invited us." She laughed good-naturedly. "At fifty pounds apiece, the tickets were quite beyond our reach."

"It appears all of London is here," Tessa remarked, gazing about with awe.

"Everyone who is anyone," Deirdre agreed. "And a good many who are *not,* if you take my meaning," she added with a grin.

In their splendid costumes of fine silks and satins, with costly jewels sparkling at their throats and ears and exquisite masks covering their faces, Tessa could spot no marked difference between any of the hundreds of patrons squeezed into the glittering red and gold foyer of the theatre.

"I am not entirely certain what you mean," she said.

Her brown eyes twinkling merrily, Deirdre leaned over to whisper in Tessa's ear. "The *Fashionable Impure* are present in full force tonight—actresses, actors, the demimonde. Even my father's mistress is here!" She grinned mischievously.

Behind the shiny gold mask she wore, Tessa's blue eyes became large and round.

"The most fun will be the ball at midnight, after the performances and supper are over. One never knows with whom one is dancing!"

"But, Deirdre, you are a married woman," Tessa pointed out.

"True. But a harmless flirtation is . . . well, harmless! For instance, I have no idea where Jeffrey is now. Of course, I do not doubt his loyalty to me. We are very much in love, but . . . you will understand what I mean one day," she added wisely.

They decided to stroll up the grand staircase to the first tiered landing.

Halfway up, Deirdre asked, "Is that not Mr. Ashburn? Just there between the pillars, conversing with . . ." She laughed. "I am not certain with whom he is conversing."

Tessa looked the direction her friend had indicated. Recognizing the maroon coat and jonquil satin knee breeches, she said, "I believe that to be Lord Penwyck."

"Is not Lord Penwyck taller than Mr. Ashburn?" Deirdre asked as they drew nearer. "Jeffrey and I spoke to Sir Reginald Tremayne a bit earlier and he was dressed in the exact same costume. I believe that to be Sir Reginald."

Tessa hoped Deirdre was right, for she did not wish to encounter the earl again.

Mr. Ashburn warmly greeted the girls, told each she looked lovely, and introduced them to the gentleman he'd been conversing with, who turned out to be neither Lord Penwyck nor Sir Reginald, but Michael Kelly, the current musical director at the Royal Italian Opera House.

"I am very pleased to meet you, sir," Tessa said, her tone

genuinely sincere. "I am quite looking forward to tonight's performances."

The gentleman smiled his pleasure. "I have prepared a sampling from a number of classical operas and popular musicals."

"Are you to perform?" Tessa inquired with interest.

"No, not I. I shall be on hand merely to oversee the musical numbers."

"But you are dressed as Picatti," Deirdre remarked.

"I and three other gentlemen who are present here tonight," Mr. Kelly replied, with a laugh.

"You are the second Picatti I have encountered thus far," Deirdre said. "Miss Darby tells me Lord Penwyck is also wearing the same costume."

"Indeed, he is," Mr. Kelly agreed. "I met up with him a bit ago. I fear I haven't a clue as to the identity of the fourth Picatti."

A few moments later Mr. Kelly strolled away, and Mr. Ashburn turned to Tessa.

"Allow me to extend my congratulations upon your forthcoming marriage, Miss Darby."

"You are to be married?" Deirdre cried. "Why, you little slyboots, you haven't said a word to me about it!"

Tessa forced a tight smile to her lips. "Forgive me, Deirdre," she murmured. "And thank you for your well wishes, sir."

"Whom are you to marry?" Deirdre demanded. "And when?"

Tessa ignored her friend's persistent questions. "I am wondering how you knew of my betrothal, Mr. Ashburn."

The grinning fellow shrugged. "Your sponsor, Lady Penwyck, is the culprit. She informed both Lord Penwyck and myself of the happy news not above half an hour ago. I confess I was crushed, as I am certain a great many other gentlemen will be when they learn of it."

"You flatter me, sir," Tessa murmured. She longed to ask what Lord Penwyck's reaction to the announcement had been but didn't dare. That he had not sought her out to exclaim upon it himself almost certainly meant he didn't care a whit what she did or who she married. Of a sudden, she decided to pretend she was greatly looking forward to the return trip to America and to her future life as the wife of a brilliant young congressman, for that was certainly what George Hancock would become. Both he and Tessa's brother, David, had been destined from birth to follow in their fathers' footsteps. Both young men would one day become United States senators. Tessa was certain of it.

"I am quite looking forward to my new life," Tessa said with what she hoped sounded like genuine enthusiasm.

Deirdre was staring at her friend as if stunned.

"I am certain you will be very happy, Miss Darby." Mr. Ashburn reached to kiss Tessa's bare fingertips. "Perhaps we shall meet again one day."

"I do hope so, sir."

"You will save a dance for me tonight, will you not?"

Trying to ignore the fact that Deirdre was tugging impatiently at her arm, Tessa smiled sweetly at the agreeable gentleman. "Indeed, I shall. Until then, sir?"

Tessa allowed Deirdre to drag her away.

"I demand that you tell me everything at once!" Deirdre cried.

"There is nothing to tell," Tessa replied a bit snappishly. "My stepfather sent for me and I have no choice but to do as he says."

Deirdre's eyes narrowed suspiciously. "You do not truly wish to go, do you?" She studied her friend as carefully as she could, given the feathery mask that all but shielded Tessa's eyes from view. "I do not believe you are truly in love. You have fallen in love with someone here in England, haven't you?" Deirdre declared insightfully.

Tessa's gaze fell and her chin began to tremble. "H-he does not feel as I do," she said, fighting back a sob.

Deirdre said nothing for a moment. Suddenly she cried, "You have fallen in love with Lord Penwyck!"

Tessa's head jerked up. "H-how did you know?"

"Jeffrey and I saw the two of you together last week. You

were headed into the quaint little tearoom next to the Clarendon Hotel. Jeffrey suggested we join you, but there was something about the way you seemed so very caught up in one another. Your arm was linked through his and he was gazing down into your eyes as if he . . . are you *certain* he does not feel as you do, Tessa?"

Tessa nodded drearily. "I am quite certain. He does not love me. He could never love me. I am not proper enough or accomplished enough. He would not wish me to become his countess."

"I am *so* sorry, Tessa. I know how it feels to love someone you cannot have. I suffered for many, many months before Jeffrey and I were allowed to marry. Perhaps it will all work out in the end."

Tessa bravely lifted her chin. "Yes, it will work out. I will return to America and marry Senator Hancock's son and there'll be an end to it."

Twenty

Following the splendid performances and lavish supper, Tessa was abandoned by Deirdre, who went off on her husband's arm to dance. Tessa was not alone for long, however, before she was asked to dance by none other than Lord Penwyck. She was certain it was he, for he had removed his mask during the supper hour and only after speaking with her did he resume wearing it.

They climbed the stairs to the fourth-level landing, which had been designated as the ballroom for tonight's gala. Already the area, as brilliantly lit as the tiers below it, was crowded with noisy revelers who had grown considerably more festive as the evening progressed and their consumption of strong spirits increased.

Tessa and Lord Penwyck took their places as the set formed for a quadrille. When the steps of the lively dance brought them together the first time, the earl said, "Mother informed me you have decided to return to America and that you are soon to be married. Allow me to say how delighted I am for you, Miss Darby."

Although Tessa longed for him to say something that would prevent her from going, she nonetheless thrust her chin up and willed a bright smile to her lips. "Thank you for your well wishes, sir. I am quite looking forward to returning home and to becoming the wife of a United States senator."

"Your betrothed is a politician?" the earl asked with some interest.

"Well, he is not yet a congressman, but make no mistake, he shall be one day."

The earl nodded. "Your confidence in the gentleman is commendable. I am certain he must be a brilliant young man."

"Oh, he is that, indeed!" Tessa enthused. "Quite brilliant. And handsome," she added for good measure.

She thought she noted something akin to a scowl cross the earl's face, but could not say for certain. The steps of the dance soon separated them, and her view of his face was lost for the nonce. They exchanged no further words during the overlong quadrille, and when, at last, the trying ordeal—trying for Tessa, that is—drew to a close, Lord Penwyck silently returned his still-smiling partner to the sidelines.

He stood stiffly by Tessa's side for what seemed an interminable length, then abruptly announced, "As it happens, I, too, am planning to be married."

"Oh?" Tessa again feigned enthusiasm. "And which young lady have you selected to become your bride, sir?" She smiled sweetly. "I fear Mr. Ashburn was unable to keep to himself the fact you have been diligently searching for a mate."

Penwyck cocked a dark brow. "Which hardly surprises me." He glanced about, as if looking for someone.

His intended, Tessa wondered?

"I managed to narrow the field to two," the earl told her in a matter-of-fact tone, "but, as it turned out, one young lady has recently become affianced, so it appears my mind has been made up for me."

"I see," Tessa murmured, still wondering who the lucky young lady was, although it was beginning to appear the earl did not mean to tell her. "Well then, I wish you every happiness, sir." She worked to keep her own agitated feelings tamped down and her tone light and airy.

Penwyck nodded stiffly. "Thank you, Miss Darby."

Tessa thought the gentleman seemed oddly discomfited, but she couldn't think why he should, so she did not remark upon it or question him further about his plans.

Presently, he said, "If you will please excuse me."

"Of course," Tessa murmured.

She watched the tall, handsome earl stroll deliberately away, and continued to watch until his strong back disappeared into the noisy throng. Suddenly, all the pent-up anguish and grief that had plagued her for days came to the fore and it was all she could do not to run after him and tell him that she did not wish to leave England, that she loved him more than life itself and that she wished to become *his* bride!

Instead, shaken to the very core by the unruly thoughts swirling inside her, she flung a wild gaze about for a quiet corner where she might regain herself. Spotting no such place, she hurriedly retraced her steps back down the sweeping staircase and ducked out a side door exit on the ground floor.

Inhaling a deep breath of the fresh night air, Tessa ripped the feathery mask from her face so she might breathe more freely. Unable to halt the hot stinging tears that had gathered in her eyes, she at last gave vent to the agony that had built up within her.

How was she to live the rest of her life without her beloved by her side? How was she to return to America and marry another so soon after her heart had been shattered into a million pieces?

Wrapped in a private cocoon of grief, Tessa stumbled down a narrow pathway. At length, she emerged into a tidy, moonlit courtyard situated at the rear of the immense theatre.

With tears streaming down her flaming cheeks, Tessa sank onto a cool stone bench and wept bitterly, her hands covering her face.

Some moments later, her unruly tears having subsided somewhat, she lifted her flushed face to gaze about. She was quite alone in the secluded garden and she felt a bit chilly. Just as she was hugging her bare arms about herself in a futile attempt to ward off the cool night air, she suddenly felt a blanket of warmth descend upon her.

Jerking about in alarm, Tessa spotted the tall figure of a man half hidden in the shadows behind her. Springing to her feet, she backed away from him as he stepped forward into a dappled pool of moonlight. Because he was wearing a mask, Tessa was unable to ascertain the gentleman's identity.

"Forgive my intrusion," the powerfully built man quickly said, "but you appeared to have caught a chill." A gloved hand indicated his own coat, which he'd gallantly draped about her bare shoulders. His white silk shirt now gleamed like a beacon in the moonlight.

Her eyes round with fright, Tessa said, "I was not aware I was being observed, sir."

With a start, Lord Penwyck realized Miss Darby did not know that it was he, that with his mask again in place he was quite unrecognizable to her. In his own troubled state, it did not occur to him she would wonder for long.

"I mean you no harm, Miss Darby," he said in his normal tone of voice.

But his words did nothing to dispel her alarm.

"How is it you know my name?" she cried. She took another step back from him, her alert blue eyes regarding him suspiciously.

Penwyck swept off his plumed hat and was about to remove his mask when something stopped him. A moment ago when he'd left Miss Darby on the dance floor, he'd felt there was a great deal left unsaid between them. Until his mother had told him of Miss Darby's impending marriage, he had thought—nay, *believed*—she might be coming to care a little for him.

True, he'd come to the soiree tonight determined that before the evening drew to a close, he would settle on one of the young ladies whose names remained on his list. Tonight, in his customary methodical fashion, he had set about conducting the final interviews with each young lady.

But he'd only got halfway through his business when his mother delivered the unsettling news about Miss Darby. It had come as quite a blow to Penwyck. He had thoroughly enjoyed every afternoon in her delightful company the previous week. In fact, their time together had elevated her considerably—perhaps even more considerably than he had realized—in his mind.

He wasn't certain why he'd followed her here just now, or what he wished to say to her. He had not had sufficient time to assemble his thoughts, much less draw up a list. Without that necessary crutch in hand, he felt quite lost, even befuddled, much like a little boy who'd had his favourite toy snatched from him and had no idea how to retrieve it.

He hadn't expected to feel such wrenching jealousy a moment ago when Miss Darby had not only confirmed the stunning news of her marriage, but declared she was quite looking forward to it, and that her future husband was brilliant and handsome.

The news had so overset Penwyck that after wandering away from her, he'd found himself in no frame to approach another young lady to talk or to dance. He'd snapped at both Ashburn and his mother before he'd chanced to spy Miss Darby hurrying down the staircase. On impulse, he had run after her.

But because he rarely did anything on impulse, he hadn't a clue what to do now that he had successfully cornered her.

She was still staring at him in alarm.

"I mean you no harm," he said again. "I wondered if we might sit and talk a bit?"

"We have not been properly introduced, sir," she pointed out.

Remembering she did not yet know it was he behind the mask, Penwyck determined anew to keep his identity to himself a bit longer. Perhaps the subterfuge would buy him time while he properly collected his thoughts. "A gentleman known to both of us told me your name," he said, this time attempting to lower his voice in order to disguise it. "Please look on me as a friend, Miss Darby."

Because she was not wearing her mask, it was child's play for Penwyck to determine what she was thinking. He watched her lower her guard a bit. For the first time, she glanced down at the maroon brocade coat that engulfed her shapely form, then at the lemon-coloured breeches he was wearing.

"Are you Mr. Kelly?" she asked. "Or perhaps Mr. Randall's friend Sir Reginald?"

"No, I am neither of those gentlemen." In a perverse way, he was rather enjoying the little intrigue. Perhaps if he played his cards right, he might extract a bit more knowledge from her before his perfidy came to light. "Will you sit with me for a spell?" He indicated the empty stone bench that stretched like a chasm between them.

Miss Darby tilted her chin up. "I do not think I should, sir. We are unknown to one another," she primly reminded him.

"Spoken like a proper young lady," Penwyck declared, his lips twitching behind his mask.

Hers formed a straight line of disgust. "Not everyone thinks I am proper."

"Whatever can you mean by that? What could anyone possibly find to fault about you, Miss Darby? I confess I find you . . . exquisite." Suddenly, Penwyck realized his concealed identity had the odd effect of loosening his tongue. Suddenly, the words he longed to say to her flowed like honey from his lips. "You are the most beautiful woman I have ever met." Even to his own ears, his tone sounded a trifle raspy.

Indeed, she did look like the very mythical goddess she was portraying in her long flowing gown, with sparkles of moonlight glancing off her copper-colored curls and the golden ribbons intertwined through them. Miss Darby's loveliness tonight quite took his breath away.

But his candor seemed to fluster her.

"You do not know me, sir," she declared, her long lashes fluttering self-consciously against her silken cheeks.

"I know enough to know that I—" Penwyck caught himself before he candidly blurted out *I love you.*

"I really must be going, sir," Miss Darby said firmly.

No! Penwyck cried to himself. "You have nothing to fear, I assure you. Please." He again indicated the bench. "I promise to mind my manners and shan't tell a single soul you agreed to sit here with me. Most especially I shall not tell Mr. Ashburn."

Her vivid blue eyes narrowed suspiciously. "So it was he who told you my name?"

"I did not say that. What I meant was no secret is safe with Mr. Ashburn."

Although she still eyed him warily, Penwyck was pleased when she edged onto a corner of the bench. He parked his large frame at a respectable distance beside her.

Because the shocking news of her impending marriage was still uppermost in his mind, he began with, "I understand you are soon to be married, Miss Darby."

Her auburn head jerked up. "You have, indeed, been speaking to Mr. Ashburn, or perhaps"—her tone lowered—"Lord Penwyck."

Penwyck said nothing.

"They neither one know the whole truth," she added softly.

Penwyck leaned forward. "The whole truth?"

Her auburn curls shook. "I cannot imagine why I am being so very candid with you, sir. I do not know you."

He shifted a bit on the bench, turning his body toward her. "Let us make a pact, Miss Darby. Since it is unlikely we shall ever see one another again after tonight, let us both agree to speak openly and honestly with each another. You may tell me anything you like, and I shall do the same."

He was gratified when the look on her face told him the idea intrigued her. A charming smile appeared on her lips as she looked straight into the dark slits of the mask he was hiding behind.

"Very well, sir." She looked away. Then, in a small voice she admitted, "I've not been able to tell anyone the whole truth since I arrived in England, and I have quite longed to do so."

"Are you saying that you have been forwarding an untruth?" he probed, quite pleased with the way his little impromptu charade was working.

"No." She shook her head. "There are just things that . . ." She glanced up again, a pained look on her face. "I confess it is difficult even for me, at times, to acknowledge the truth."

"Shall I begin, then?" he offered. Without waiting for her to reply, he said, "The whole truth, Miss Darby, is when I watched you alight from your carriage tonight in the company of your sponsor, Lady Penwyck, and the earl, I was quite enchanted by you. Your rich auburn hair and sapphire blue eyes quite charmed me. I wished to follow you then, but felt it unwise to do so. Instead, I kept a distance. At one point, I thought to approach Lord Penwyck to learn your name, but as he can be somewhat of a prig—" He paused, wondering how she might react to that candid observation.

He studied her from the corner of his eye and grinned inwardly when he noted a slight upturning of her pink lips.

"Lord Penwyck is not a prig," she said. "He merely attempts to be all that is proper. He is a gentleman, and I do not fault him for that."

"What do you find about the gentleman to fault?" Penwyck boldly inquired.

Suddenly, Miss Darby startled him by springing again to her feet and darting into the shadows. Alarmed, Penwyck leapt to follow her.

"It was not my intent to overset you, Miss Darby," he said hastily.

Hearing her soft whimpers told him she was sobbing. He felt wretched. Coming up behind her, he could not resist encircling her lovely body with his arms and drawing her close against him in a warm embrace. When he felt the distraught young lady melt into his strength, he fought the urge to tilt her chin upward and kiss away her pain and sorrow. Instead, he tightened his arms about her. "Why are you crying, my dearest?" he asked hoarsely.

"Because I . . . love him," she confessed in a fitful whisper. "I love him, and he does not love me. He thinks I am . . . improper."

Penwyck's eyes squeezed shut behind his mask. He had never meant to hurt her when he offered to show her how to go on. At the outset, he thought she needed . . . but what did it matter now? He had hurt her, and he felt like an abominable cad for his thoughtless words and deeds. "Surely you are mistaken," he said softly. "You are a perfectly lovely girl."

With a disdainful huff, Miss Darby pulled away. Of her own accord, she flounced to the stone bench and sat down.

"No. I am not. I do not know how to simper and fawn, and I do scandalous things, like read newspapers and attend reform meetings. Lord Penwyck was livid the night he rescued me from a meeting that got quite out of hand. But it was none of my doing!"

"Indeed, it was not," Penwyck said, having regained his place beside her.

"I cannot remain silent when I find things about the British government that need improving." She sniffed with outrage. "Did you know, sir, that hundreds of defenseless women and children have been put to work in England's mills and factories? Mr. Cobbett says England's industrial supremacy depends entirely on the efforts of thirty thousand little girls! I find that appalling!"

"You are quite right, Miss Darby. It is appalling."

"I did so wish to write an essay for Mr. Cobbett's newspaper, The *Political Register.* Now I never shall. Instead, I must return to America and marry a man I do not love."

Suddenly, she covered her face with her hands and burst again into tears.

Penwyck did not know what to do. That she'd confessed she did not love the man she was set to marry, but did love *him,* lifted his spirits considerably. That she was crying again and he could not comfort her as he'd have liked without revealing he had shamelessly tricked her into the confession left him quite perplexed. He did not know what to do or say next.

Because he could not bear to see her so unhappy and ached to comfort her, he draped an arm over the back of the bench and sympathetically patted her shoulder with one hand. With the other, he handed her a crisp white linen handkerchief he'd extracted from his pocket. "Do dry your tears, Miss Darby," he said gently. "Everything will turn out—"

"No, it will not!" she cried. "To return to America feels to me like . . . like returning to *prison.*"

"To prison?" Behind his mask, Penwyck's brows pulled together with concern. "Whatever do you mean by that, Miss Darby?"

Her glistening lashes fluttered as she dabbed at her nose with the handkerchief. "My stepfather is a . . . an evil man."

Penwyck longed to draw her into his arms again. Instead, he probed gently, "Are you saying your stepfather . . . hurts you?"

His jaws ground together angrily as the beautiful young girl beside him slowly nodded her head.

His nostrils flared. "How?" he ground out. "How has he hurt you, Miss Darby?"

He waited an interminable length as she silently dabbed at the moisture lingering on her lashes. Finally, in a constricted voice, she said, "He . . . imprisoned me in my bedchamber, and . . . and he flogged me, like one of his slaves, with a leather strap. There were times when I was younger when he tried to force me to do things that cannot be thought proper for a man to do with a very young girl."

White-hot rage twisted Penwyck's insides, but he managed to remain silent as yet another sob escaped her.

"I was able to deter him from inflicting further harm of *that* nature on me by threatening to tell my mother. I was only thirteen, but I knew my stepfather's career was very important to him, and it would be ruined if my mother left him—which she would have, I am certain!"

She glanced up. "I can be quite pigheaded. The truth is I never would have told her, for she truly loved him. My mother was not as strong as I am, and she needed him. But she is gone now and there is no longer anyone for me to hide behind," she concluded sadly.

Penwyck shuddered. Were Senator Darby in England today, he would kill the wretch! He had been prepared another time in his life to kill in order to protect a loved one, despite the fact his brother Joel did not deserve the consideration. Miss Darby did. Yet all he could do now was tell her how very sorry he was for all she had suffered at the hands of her stepfather.

"Is it imperative you return to America?" he gently probed.

She nodded firmly. "I cannot stay here."

Oh, but she could! It was perfectly clear to Penwyck now that he wanted, more than anything, for her to stay right here in England and to become his wife. "So you are determined to return to America and marry a man you do not love."

Without looking at him, she nodded again. "I have no choice. The man I wish to marry does not love me." Her sobs had ceased altogether and she now seemed resigned to her fate. She turned a soulful look on Penwyck. "Thank you for being so kind to me, sir. I have wished for so very long to confide in someone, but I felt as if I had no one to talk to, especially after my friend Deirdre was married. You would like Deirdre. She is a great deal like me. We are both a bit . . . out of the common way."

His eyes behind his mask locked with hers for a long moment. Then he said, "I think you are perfect, Miss Darby."

Smiling shakily, she stood and, after tucking the crumpled handkerchief he'd given her into one of the pockets of his maroon coat, she removed the wrap from her shoulders. "I must go in now."

Penwyck had risen to his feet and stood watching her. He longed with all his heart to tell her more, to say he loved her dearly, that he had not realized how deeply he cared until he thought he might lose her. Yet he held back. "I have enjoyed our talk immensely, Miss Darby. We have each told the other a secret, and now we must go our separate ways."

The smile Miss Darby directed at Penwyck both melted his heart and made it ache. She was not smiling at him, but at an unknown stranger she believed to be far kinder than he.

"I will never forget you, sir. Thank you for listening and for lending me your coat."

She handed the garment to him. When Penwyck reached to take it, he managed also to grasp her bare hand in his and brought it all the way to his lips. With only a few days remaining for him to find a way to gain her trust, all he could do now was gaze deeply into her eyes and will her to know how very, very much he loved her.

"We will meet again one day, Miss Darby," he said firmly. "You may be certain of that."

Twenty-one

Penwyck did not sleep that night. Half a dozen hours after he, his mother, and Miss Darby had returned home from the Royal Italian Opera House, he was still sitting alone in his study. He'd stared for hours into the sputtering embers of the low-burning fire. Then, as dawn streaked long fingers of pink and gold across the dusky sky, he wandered to a window to absently watch the early morning spectacle.

Because he was now privy to the whole of Miss Darby's grievous past, her mystifying attitude and odd behaviour of the past few months made perfect sense to him.

Her passionate obsession with the inequities meted out to the innocent victims of greedy manufacturers in England was a veiled outcry against the heinous wrongs done to her.

The empathy she felt for the caged lions and tigers they'd seen at the Tower was a heartfelt cry against her own unjust imprisonment.

Her initial resistance to his trying to tell her how to conduct herself properly Penwyck now saw as an obstinate reaction to the rigid rules her stepfather had imposed upon her.

Her inability to dance may even have been because the opportunity to learn had been harshly denied her.

Penwyck additionally suspected her consuming desire to do something politically significant in England might also be a sad attempt to gain the approval of the unfeeling tyrant who, even if he recognized his stepdaughter's brilliance, would never acknowledge or praise it.

Penwyck's heart ached for the lovely Miss Darby, for all the hurt and suffering she'd endured at the hands of her heartless stepfather.

That the young lady had seemed uninterested in forming an attachment to any of the gentlemen who had flocked about her since her debut also made sense to him now. Miss Darby did not trust men. Even Penwyck had unwittingly betrayed the thin thread of trust that had sprung up between them when he'd tricked her into confiding her deepest secrets to him.

As the long hours of the night dragged by, Penwyck turned the puzzle over and over in his mind. There had to be some way to show Miss Darby he revered her, that he respected her, held her views in high regard, and . . . that he loved her.

Staring pensively from the window, a solution dawned on the perplexed earl mere seconds after London threw off the heavy blanket of fog it had curled up to sleep beneath the previous night.

Energized by the idea swirling like a crisp morning breeze through his mind, Penwyck crossed the room to the bellpull and gave it a swift tug.

Moments later, a somewhat bleary-eyed Jenkins appeared in the doorway to Penwyck's study. "You rang, sir?"

"I am parched, Jenkins. Have a pot of strong coffee and a plate of buttered scones sent to my bedchamber at once."

"Very well, sir. If you insist, sir."

The butler's tone clearly told Penwyck the sleepy-eyed retainer did not appreciate by half being awakened at such an ungodly hour and that, as everyone knew, no self-respecting gentleman of the *ton* broke his fast before ten of the clock each morning, especially if said gentleman had attended a huge gala the night before, which under normal circumstances would mean the household servants would not be bothered by special requests from their betters till long after noon.

Penwyck noted the butler's unspoken rebuttal to his request with a cocked brow. "I do, indeed, insist, Jenkins."

A moment after the stiff-necked butler had vacated the room, Penwyck snatched up the coat he'd been wearing the night before, which still smelled faintly of the rose-scented sweetwater worn by Miss Darby, and began to rummage through the pockets.

Locating the item he'd gone in search of, he strode purposefully toward the hearth and set to ripping the sheet of cream-coloured linen paper into small squares.

Just as he opened his palm to shower the shreds into the flames, the door to his study creaked open once again.

Penwyck turned about.

"I thought I heard a movement within," his mother whispered. "Whatever are you doing up at this hour, Penny dear?" Clutching a loose-fitting wrapper about her body, her grey hair tucked beneath a lacy nightcap, she silently moved into the book-lined room. Catching sight of the bits of paper drifting from her son's hand into the fire, she asked, "What are you disposing of, sweetheart?"

"Nothing, Mother."

"Well, it must have been something," Lady Penwyck protested. She gazed curiously into the sputtering flames as she drew nearer.

"Very well. If you must know, Mother, it was a list," her son said, his lips pursed in much the same fashion as Jenkins's had been earlier.

"What sort of list, dear?" Lady Penwyck asked with motherly interest.

Penwyck gazed at the persistent woman, who was again peering curiously at the scraps of paper lying atop the red-hot coals, the edges darkening and curling as the flames slowly devoured them.

"It was a list of names I have been carrying with me these many weeks. I have no use for it now, as I have, at last, settled on the young lady whom I intend to marry."

Lady Penwyck's face became a broad smile of delight. "That is wonderful, sweetheart! Tell me at once who she is!"

Penwyck reached to grasp the smallish woman's thin shoulders and, with an affectionate smile on his face, turned her toward him. "That, my very dear Mother, I am not yet prepared to do."

He bent to kiss the delighted woman's wrinkled cheek. Then, snatching up his coat again, he proceeded to the door. Before disappearing into the corridor, however, he mischievously added, "There is no use trying to determine who the young lady might be from those names that have not yet been obliterated by the fire. My future bride's name was never on my list."

Tessa awoke that morning in a considerably better frame than she'd expected. She attributed her uplifted spirits to her secret rendezvous last evening with the masked stranger. The gentleman had listened with a sympathetic ear as she'd tearfully unburdened her soul. Although she was still obliged to return to America, she felt oddly liberated from her disturbing past.

Now and again during the night, as she'd stirred in her sleep and her thoughts turned to the strange occurrence—and again that morning as she absently dressed for the day—she pretended the masked stranger was not a stranger at all, that he had, in fact, been Lord Penwyck. It was not an outrageous leap. She'd never seen the masked man's face and he was dressed identically to the earl.

She knew, of course, it had not been he, for why would he wish to conceal his identity from her? Besides, they had just shared a dance. He would have had no reason to follow her into the garden. Yet it was somehow comforting to pretend it was he who had listened with genuine sympathy to her tale of woe, and that *his* arms had held her tightly.

Before leaving her bedchamber, Tessa sat down before the pretty little writing desk in her room and reached for a clean sheet of linen paper. There were a number of things she needed to do before she left London for good—purchase nice gifts of gratitude for Lady Penwyck and Mrs. Montgomery, make one last call on Deirdre Randall, and write thank-you notes to several *ton* patronesses who had been especially kind to her. To insure that she did not forget a single item, she wished to jot them all down on a list.

She smiled to herself as she wrote. How Lord Penwyck would laugh if he knew she'd borrowed a leaf from his book and was now drawing up a list of her own.

Reading over the items, she bent to add another: Ask Lord Penwyck to secure return passage for her on the next available ship bound for America.

Expecting to encounter the gentleman at luncheon that day, Tessa changed into one of her pretty new morning gowns, this one a becoming green dimity trimmed with blond lace. Securing her long hair back with a pearl comb, she tucked her list in her pocket and headed downstairs.

She found Lord Penwyck in the foyer at the bottom of the stairs, ticking off a list of household instructions to Jenkins, which, no doubt, Lady Penwyck had previously muddled. Tessa waited until the butler had been dismissed before she approached the earl.

"Ah, Miss Darby," Lord Penwyck greeted her pleasantly. Quite pleasantly, actually.

Tessa was a bit taken aback by the genuine warmth in the earl's tone. He looked quite attractive this morning in a navy blue superfine coat, his claret trousers tucked into black leather top boots.

"You look very lovely this morning," Lord Penwyck continued, an agreeable smile on his well-shaped lips.

"Thank you, sir," Tessa replied, a trifle coolly. The earl's friendliness surely meant he was pleased she was leaving England. "I wonder if I might trouble you for something, sir."

He moved a few steps toward her, a look of congenial expectancy on his handsome face. "Anything, my dear, anything at all."

Tessa winced. My, he was doing it up a bit, wasn't he? "I wonder if you would please see to booking passage for me on the next ship bound for America."

Tessa noted a flicker of something cross his face, but chose not to bother herself about whatever was bothering him. He had made his position regarding her departure perfectly clear.

"So your mind is made up then, is it?" he asked softly. After a pause, his mood seemed to alter a whit. "Actually, there is something I have been meaning to ask of you, Miss Darby."

Her chin elevated smartly, Tessa waited. She noted the earl seemed to suddenly grow a trifle uneasy.

"I realize, Miss Darby," he began, "that one of the reasons you came to London was to, ahem, express your . . . views regarding certain political matters to Mr. Cobbett or other influential reform leaders."

Tessa regarded the gentleman curiously. "That is correct, sir. I did wish to, but I realize now that—"

He held up a silencing hand. "I wonder, Miss Darby, if you would please compose the essay and allow me to deliver it to Mr. Cobbett on your behalf. I have no doubt he will wish to publish it once he reads it." As he spoke, he seemed to grow quite pleased with himself. "Write whatever you like, Miss Darby, on whatever subject you choose. I've no doubt it will be brilliant."

Brilliant? Tessa cocked a brow. He was doing it up *quite* brown. "Well, I . . . I have a great many things to do, sir." Digging a hand into her pocket, she fingered the list she'd just drawn up. "In fact, I"—she laughed a trifle nervously—"I have just jotted everything down on a list so I would be sure to remember it all."

She withdrew the folded sheet of paper for him to see.

The grin on Lord Penwyck's face became quite broad. "A list, eh?" He puffed out his chest. "Well, I am quite looking forward to reading your essay, Miss Darby," he enthused. "Good day."

Tessa watched the elegantly attired gentleman saunter to the door and jauntily tip his hat to her before he disappeared through it.

The request Lord Penwyck had just made of her was quite unexpected. In fact, it was quite possibly the last thing in the world she'd ever expected to hear from him.

Nonetheless, that afternoon Tessa again settled herself before the little writing desk in her room. She had no idea why Lord Penwyck had suddenly asked her to write the piece, but because making her views on reform known to Mr. Cobbett was something she fervently wished to do whilst in London and because she hadn't been able to accomplish the feat on her own, she felt compelled to seize this one last opportunity to do so. Maybe, just maybe, her words would reach the ears of someone who could effect change.

She wrote at length about the deplorable conditions under which helpless women and children were forced to toil in the nation's textile factories, about the long hours, poor food, lack of ventilation, and overwork. She wrote about children as young as five and six being sent to work as "trappers" in underground coal pits, how the children spent as many as twelve hours a day in complete darkness and silence. Because women and children were less costly to keep than donkeys, they were harnessed to the coal carts like animals and forced to crawl through the mine shafts on their hands and knees.

She wrote also about the pitiful plight of England's hundreds of climbing boys and girls. These innocent children, many as young as four and five, were forced up burning chimneys by cruel pinpricks to their bare legs and feet. Tessa told how the blackened children, who were very often sent into the cramped spaces unclothed, gasped for air, their eyes and lungs stinging from the thick black smoke they were forced to breathe, their elbows and knees scraped raw and bleeding as they struggled to escape from tunnels so narrow it was impossible to go forward or backward.

She pleaded for the hundreds of dead and dying babies tossed into the streets of London every year, many the illegitimate offspring of the wealthy who thought additional youngsters to raise an inconvenience. Other such babies, who were frequently laid to die in the streets, were born to destitute teenage mothers who had no way to provide for them.

She begged for relief for helpless babies born to poor women in the workhouse, those born underground as their mothers toiled in the coal mines, and for the hundreds of homeless children who were rounded up and sent by the cartload to work sixteen and twenty hours a day in the industrial factories of the north.

Tessa pleaded for other children, as well, for those living in the streets of London dressed in ragged clothing, shivering with the cold, ofttimes ill- and mistreated as they attempted on their own to eke out an existence the best way they could. Many of these boys and girls were lured into the criminal life, gangs of them stealing from the rich, pilfering from merchants throughout the city. Tessa had once watched a small boy steal oats from a horse's feed bag when the driver wasn't looking, then hungrily stuff the grain into his own mouth.

When, at last, she finished with the impassioned plea, she recopied it onto crisp, clean sheets of paper. She did not want Mr. Cobbett to miss even a single word she might have crossed out or smudged in her haste to get it all down.

Tonight at dinner, she told herself with a long sigh of relief, she would give the report to Lord Penwyck.

Twenty-two

Although Lord Penwyck seemed pleased Tessa had complied with his request, he did not immediately read her essay or say a great deal.

The next morning at breakfast, however, after again greeting Tessa quite cordially, he asked if she would like to accompany him to a special House session to be held that afternoon.

Attend a session of the House of Lords? Tessa could hardly believe her ears. "Y-you wish me to accompany you to Parliament?" she repeated numbly.

Penwyck grinned. "Visitors are allowed in the gallery. It is not uncommon for certain interested parties—students of the law and the like—to observe the proceedings on the floor.

"Ohh." Tessa was unable to conceal her excitement and her enthusiasm.

Across from her at the breakfast table, Lady Penwyck was also beaming with pleasure. "I attended a session once," she proudly told Tessa. "Penny's father William was to propose a bill. It was quite a thrill for me as a new bride to hear my handsome young husband speechify. I am certain Penny is every bit as eloquent as his father was."

"Thank you, Mother."

"I would love to accompany you, sir," Tessa intoned with awe. "Thank you for asking me."

"My pleasure, Miss Darby. I have some business to attend

to this morning. I shall call for you at half past two this afternoon."

"I will be ready and waiting," Tessa replied excitedly.

And she was. She had a bit of trouble deciding what to wear to observe a session of the famed British House of Lords, but she finally settled on a pretty, lightweight grey merino gown trimmed at the neck and hem with black braid. She topped it off with a form-fitting forest-green Spencer jacket trimmed at the wrists with the same black braid. With green kid gloves and a black velvet reticule, Tessa felt quite stylish and elegant.

Lord Penwyck thought Miss Darby looked especially attractive when he arrived to collect her, and smilingly told her so.

He had been equally impressed with her essay last night when he read it, but for the nonce said nothing. The report did not sound as if it had been written by a hysterical female. Instead, it was a concise, factual look at a subject far too many upper-class Brits simply did not wish to acknowledge.

Penwyck heartily agreed with the stand Miss Darby had taken. The plight of the nation's neglected children was outrageous, and drastic measures were needed to remedy the unfortunate situation. Penwyck had further decided that Miss Darby's excellent report was far too brilliant to be wasted on Cobbett's twopenny trash. Penwyck had loftier plans for the well-written essay.

Overlooking the floor where some of the world's most famous lawmakers gathered each and every year to propose, debate, and decide upon legislation, Tessa leaned forward in her chair so as not to miss a single thing.

Although large, the dark-paneled, high-ceilinged room seemed close, even stuffy. High up in the gallery, where only a few visitors were seated today, the air reeked of stale cigar smoke mixed with an occasional whiff of pungent tobacco. As Tessa's sharp eyes scanned the august body of elegantly clad gentlemen milling about on the floor, there was no doubt in her mind she was trespassing in a man's world.

The gentlemen on the floor seemed unconcerned that they were being closely watched, some leaning casually against their desks, others openly lounging in their chairs, their long legs crossed, their feet propped up on the desks before them.

As the session had not yet begun, gentlemen were still filing into the room, shuffling papers, talking animatedly to one another and occasionally laughing aloud. Tessa was able to pick out the few faces she recognized: Sally's husband Lord Jersey, Lords Chesterfield and Hamilton and even old Lord Dickerson, who had gallantly offered for her after Lord Penwyck had caught them alone together in Lord Chalmers's library. Lord Chalmers was conversing with Lord Penwyck, as were several other gentlemen with whom Tessa was not acquainted.

Presently, a bewigged gentleman dressed in a flowing robe of black silk rose from his position atop an elevated platform and ceremoniously banged a gavel on the podium before him. Tessa settled back as another gentleman called the roll. It astonished her that even as the statesmen called out *aye* or *here* the general hubbub on the floor did not subside.

The noise, however, died quickly away when the first statesman of the afternoon approached the leader for permission to speak. When permission was granted, the gentleman faced the assembly to report the findings from a committee that had apparently been appointed to look into the high-crime areas of Seven Dials and Covent Garden. The committee was proposing a new tax be levied on shopkeepers in these neighborhoods to pay for gas lines to feed additional streetlamps in the hope of deterring criminal activity.

Tessa thought the proposal sounded quite reasonable. Had she been allowed to, she would have cast her vote in favour of the measure.

Following a number of questions and some debate on the subject, votes were taken and the measure passed.

Then, to Tessa's immense surprise, Lord Penwyck himself stepped to the platform and requested permission to speak.

Tessa leaned as far forward as she could in her seat without risking a tumble over the railing.

"Gentlemen," the eminent earl began, "I mean to address an issue that has too long been swept under the rug in this country. There has recently been a good deal of public outcry on the subject of the abuse of our nation's labouring force, most especially in regard to the needs of the workingman. Today I mean to address the forgotten issue of women and children—"

Tessa very nearly did topple from her chair! Lord Penwyck was speaking on the very subject he had asked her to write about? She could scarcely believe it!

Was that why he had invited her to come today?

But, wait! Her eyes widened with disbelief as she carefully listened to each and every word the earl was saying.

He was not speaking extemporaneously now.

He was reading her report! Her words!

Tessa sprang to her feet.

And sat down.

She jumped to her feet again.

And fell back again.

How dare he? How dare he trick her into pouring out her heart so he might pass off her words in Parliament as his own?

But wait, a small voice in the back of her head cautioned her. Had he not prefaced his speech with the remark that the bulk of his report had been presented to him by another? A *concerned* citizen, one who had made an intensive study of England's labour force and its harsh practices?

Yes, Tessa admitted to herself irritably, she vaguely recalled hearing him say something to that effect, but . . . *how dare he?*

Tessa grew so livid listening to the earl's deep baritone reading her words that she could scarcely breathe. At length, before he'd reached the end of the impassioned plea, which she knew by heart since she'd written every word of it herself, she rose indignantly to her feet and flounced into the corridor to wait until he was done.

In the hallway outside the galley, she paced.

And paced.

A good bit later, the tall gentleman finally appeared at the top of the steps to collect her.

Tessa's lips pursed with annoyance at the loathsome sight of his handsome face looking as pleased with himself as the proverbial cat who'd swallowed the canary.

"Well, Miss Darby," he began magnanimously, as he politely reached to take her arm, "did you enjoy the—"

"How dare you?" she spat out. Her sapphire blue eyes glared daggers at him as she jerked from his grasp. Her chin elevated to an imperial height, she sailed past him toward the stairwell.

Penwyck gasped.

On the flagway, he attempted to hand her into the carriage, but she'd have none of that, either.

She flounced into the coach and plopped onto the bench, her pink lips pressed into a tight line of suppressed rage.

Penwyck hastily directed the driver to be off and climbed in beside his seething companion.

As the closed carriage lumbered down the street, he said, "I thought you'd be pleased, Miss Darby. I—"

"Pleased?" she exclaimed in a shrill voice. "*Pleased*? You never meant to deliver my essay to Mr. Cobbett. You *tricked* me into writing that report for you! You are loathsome and despicable. I hate you and all that you stand for. You are—"

"Wait just a minute, young lady." The now angry earl silenced her tirade with a superior bellow. "Thanks to my *trickery,* the plight of those helpless victims who are being abused in this country has now been dropped into the lap of English lawmakers. Before I left the podium, a select committee was formed to investigate the conditions under which these women and children labour. Is that not the primary reason you wrote that report, madam?"

Tessa sniffed. "I suppose so."

"Well then, at the risk of sounding quite boorish," Penwyck continued, "may I further remind you, Miss Darby, that as a woman you have not been able to accomplish that on your own."

A good bit of the self-righteous anger Tessa was feeling melted away. He was quite right. She had reacted in haste and perceived an injury where none was intended. "I expect I owe you an apology, sir," she said in a small voice.

"No apology is necessary, Miss Darby."

Tessa bit her lip contritely and looked away. What a perfect wretch he must think her.

She glanced up a moment later when Lord Penwyck tapped the small window above his head with the tip of his walking stick and requested the driver take them to Hyde Park.

"We are going to Hyde Park?" Tessa asked tentatively.

"Indeed. I thought it appropriate to end this thing where it all began," Penwyck replied crisply.

Tessa had no idea what the toplofty earl meant by that remark, but as he had so recently reminded her, she was a woman. That, of course, meant it was not her place to question, but to follow.

She directed a long gaze from the coach window. Hyde Park was, indeed, where her adventure in London had begun. A few short weeks ago, she had arrived in Town filled with enthusiasm and awe, atremor with excitement about her new life and all that stretched before her.

Then she had high hopes of bringing her ideas for reform before Parliament. She had handed out her thoughtfully worded leaflets to young ladies promenading in Hyde Park, fully believing they'd take the literature home and eagerly show it to their fathers and brothers.

But her calculated efforts had come to naught, as had her visit with the newspaperman William Cobbett and the ill-fated evening at the Hampden Club meeting.

She'd managed to accomplish nothing until Lord Penwyck took up her Cause. In one short hour on the floor of the House, he had single-handedly brought her dream a giant step closer to reality.

And she had shown her gratitude with harsh words and anger. Tessa's eyes squeezed shut with remorse. How she longed to tell Lord Penwyck how very sorry she was . . . and how deeply she loved him.

The stately Penwyck carriage had already wheeled beneath the magnificent arch that marked the entrance to Hyde Park.

Tessa worked to regain her composure and focus on the lush scene rolling past them. The sight of this beautiful green park, thick with chestnut trees and beds of crimson and yellow flowers, always filled her with joy. Hyde Park was one of the prettiest places in London.

Again she wondered why Lord Penwyck had suggested a drive through the park, since it was not yet the fashionable hour. She cast a surreptitious gaze at his stern features.

Suddenly, he again tapped the small window above his head. "Stop here, John."

The carriage instantly shuddered to a standstill.

Tessa wore a quizzical look on her face as the handsome earl addressed her.

"Would you like to take a stroll with me, Miss Darby?"

A liveried footman had already stepped down from the running board at the rear of the coach and flung open the door.

Penwyck reached to grasp Tessa's gloved fingertips.

"Thank you, sir," she murmured politely.

They walked a few steps in silence before Lord Penwyck said, "You were quite right about one thing, Miss Darby. I did trick you."

Tessa no longer wished to quarrel with the brilliant earl. The realization that her time in London was fast drawing to a close and she would never see Lord Penwyck or his mother again filled her with such sadness she feared her heart might break.

She attempted to draw in a deep breath of the cool, crisp afternoon air. Casting a glance about, she suddenly realized Lord Penwyck had halted the carriage at the same intersection where she had stood and handed out leaflets from the side of a hansom cab the day she'd arrived in London.

"I have been here before, sir," she marveled, her blue eyes wide as she gazed about.

"Indeed, you have, Miss Darby. Mr. Ashburn and I were riding in the park that day. I admit I was quite astonished to see a young lady making a spectacle of herself by handing out radical literature to passersby in the park."

Tessa gazed up at the earl. Lord Penwyck's gloved hand was

curled protectively over her fingertips as they rested in the crook of his strong arm. From the affectionate tone he'd adopted with her, she knew he was not chastising her actions now.

"How did you know my leaflets were radical?" she asked saucily. "They might have been tracts penned by Hannah More."

Penwyck's lips twitched as he cast a sidelong look at her. "You did not have the look of a Hannah More advocate, my dear. You were far too pretty," he teased.

Tessa laughed, although a bit sadly.

"Mr. Ashburn was quite taken with you."

"And what did you think of me?" she probed.

"I dubbed you the Hyde Park Spectacle."

Tessa laughed again.

The lighthearted sound was like music to Penwyck's ears. He hoped when he'd confessed the full extent of his shameless perfidy to her, he'd remain in her good graces. "I *did* trick you, Miss Darby," he began again.

"The methods you employed to entice me to pen the essay do not signify, my lord," she replied sincerely. "I cannot thank you enough for what you did today. Inviting me to attend a parliamentary session with you was a dream come true. Our lovely walk in the park just now is the perfect way to end my . . . my stay in London." Tessa's voice nearly broke. "I shall never forget a single moment of this wonderful day, sir."

Penwyck stopped suddenly. "I fervently hope that will prove to be the case, Miss Darby."

Tessa again gazed up at him quizzically.

His tone was somber. "I have something to ask you, my dear, but first I must confess to a . . . er, transgression of my own and humbly beg your forgiveness."

Tessa's head tilted to one side.

"It will be our secret," he began softly. "Let us speak honestly and openly with one another . . . we have each told the other a secret and now we must go our separate ways. I find you exquisite, Miss Darby. I think you are perfect."

As Penwyck watched realization dawn upon her pretty face, he held his breath. Would she lash out again? Or would she . . .

"It was *you* that night in the garden?" she murmured. Suddenly, her blue eyes filled with tears and her cheeks grew pink. "I-I did, indeed, tell you a secret that night," she whispered softly.

"It was a lovely secret," Penwyck replied, knowing full well to what she referred. "I should have told you the same that night. I followed you into the garden because I love you, Tessa Darby," he said sincerely. "I did not know how very deeply I cared for you until you revealed your plans to wed another. Then suddenly I knew the young lady I had been searching for these many weeks was you. *You* are the young lady I wish to become my bride." He paused, his deep brown eyes searching the depths of her vivid blue ones. "Will you marry me and stay by my side, as my wife, forever?"

Tears of joy spilled onto Tessa's flushed cheeks. Her heart pounded in her ears as she impulsively flung her arms about the handsome earl's neck.

"Yes! Yes, I will marry you. I love you dearly!" she cried joyfully.

Then, even as his arms were tightening about her, she drew away. Gazing up at him with round eyes, she said, "I suppose it is not at all proper of me to throw myself at your head like a brazen hoyden, is it?" She grinned self-consciously. "Is that not far more scandalous than handing out literature in the park?"

His arms still encircling her trim waist, Penwyck laughed good-naturedly. "You may throw your arms about my neck anytime you please, my sweet hoyden." His lips twitched merrily as he gazed lovingly into her luminous blue eyes. "I am not the least bit fearful of our causing a scandal. In fact, I predict the *ton* will talk about you and me, Miss Darby, for many years to come."

And they did.

Historical Notes

In 1816, a Parliamentary committee was formed to find out if the employment of children in England's mills and factories was 'detrimental to their health and morals.' In the same year an Act of Parliament called a halt to the practice of sending homeless children to work in the industrial factories of the north.

In 1817, a bill before Parliament to prohibit the use of climbing boys was defeated. In 1818 and again in 1819, the same bill passed the Commons but was defeated in the House of Lords. Although chimney sweep acts were passed in 1840 and 1864, they were largely disregarded by both homeowners and magistrates. Strict measures against the practice of using small children to clean chimneys were not instituted until 1884, when The Society for the Prevention of Cruelty to Children was founded.

Dear Reader,

If you are like me, you also feel an overwhelming longing to experience life as it was in the romantic period known as the Regency when a real man was a gentleman, right down to his polished Hessians, and a proper young lady still blushed when caught staring overlong at milord's broad shoulders—not to mention his thigh-hugging inexpressibles!

For me, the pull was so great I simply had to delve deeper, to learn more about the past I found so intriguing. Not even traveling to London, or visiting Brighton and Bath, was enough to satisfy me. I had to know more! From this longing grew *The Regency Plume,* a bimonthly newsletter dedicated to accurately depicting life as it was in Regency England.

Each issue of *The Regency Plume* is full of fascinating articles penned by your favorite Regency romance authors. If you'd like to join me and the hundreds of other Regency romance fans who experience Prinny's England via *The Regency Plume,* send a stamped, self-addressed envelope to me, Marilyn Clay, c/o *The Regency Plume,* Dept. 711-D-NW, Ardmore, OK 73401. I'll be happy to send you more information and a subscription form.

I hope you enjoyed reading MISS DARBY'S DEBUT and will want to read my next Regency romance novel. In the meantime, I look forward to hearing from each and every one of you!

Sincerely,

Marilyn Clay

P.S. Visit THE REGENCY PLUME Web site at:

www.freetown.com/Picadilly/Hyde Park/1073/ReencyPlume.html